OUTCOME

CARA DEE

Outcome

Copyright © 2014 by Cara Dee

All rights reserved

Edited by Silently Correcting Your Grammar, LLC.
Cover design by Jada D'Lee Designs.
Formatted by Rachel Lawrence.

THANK YOU

Special thanks go out to Lisa, Deb, Rachel, Emma, Tina, Annie, Nance, Jennifer, and Bonnie. I couldn't have done it without your support and help.

ONE

Never in his thirty-nine years on this planet had the simple task of cleaning a bartop felt as gratifying as it did now. A smile kept tugging at the corners of Chase's mouth, but because he was so used to hiding his feelings, he didn't unleash even an ounce of the satisfaction he felt. But inside him, it was a whirlwind of emotions. *I did it*, a voice repeated over and over. *I fuckin' did it.*

Something often threatened to pull him under again, but he wasn't gonna allow anything to ruin this moment. This belonged to *him*. This moment, this goddamn day, and even this bar. He'd named it Joshua's Place, the sign outside dominated by the letters "JP" and a silver Knucklehead—his favorite bike, his favorite engine.

It was bound to attract fellow bikers, and he hadn't been disappointed at the grand opening tonight.

Merely an hour ago, the place had been packed. Once the doors had closed at two in the morning, Chase had sent home his one employee. He then spent some time quietly wiping down the eight tables, straightening the chairs, returning a few misplaced stools to the bar, and preparing for tomorrow.

What had once been a menial job—twenty fucking years of being someone else's bartender—was now his chosen career. Coming from nothing, it mattered a lot to put "bar owner" to his name.

Doing a final sweep with the rag, Chase deemed the

1

wooden bartop clean. He looked out over his place and drew in a deep breath.

I did it.

He was sure it was no big deal to outsiders, but the memories of two parents who'd been buried in debt had scared him away from ever taking a loan. Which meant he'd saved up all on his own, all while helping his little sister with her college tuition.

It was okay to be a little proud, right?

Heading to the fridge, Chase grabbed three beers, and then walked over to his two remaining patrons—or friends, as they had become in the past few months.

Austin Huntley and Cameron Nash.

They ended their private conversation when Chase sat down.

"Thank you." Austin smiled as he opened his beer. "So, how does it feel?"

Chase showed a ghost of a smile, not sure how to answer the question. He wasn't used to having friends, which made things awkward sometimes. Growing up, he'd been too busy working— even as a kid—making friendship new territory. He didn't wanna be obnoxious and overshare, but he didn't wanna be rude, either.

"Feels…good." He nodded slowly, choosing his words. "Kinda overwhelming?" He glanced out over his establishment and could almost hear the laughter, clinking bottles, and rock music from earlier.

"I can imagine." Austin's eyes always showed a sense of warmth that made Chase feel…*welcome* was probably a fitting word. Warmth Chase hoped to see in his own eyes one day. But as it was, when he woke up every morning and looked into the mirror, all he saw in his deep blues was resignation. "Was it overwhelming back when your brother opened his garage, too?" Austin smirked at Cam.

Cam snorted. "Like I attended that spectacle." It was no secret that he stayed away from crowds, so that made Chase appreciate his coming here tonight even more. Cam smiled tightly. "But tonight we're celebrating, right? Freedom and shit."

Another reason for tonight being significant.

OUTCOME

Today marked the three-year anniversary of seven men's escape from the hands of a fucking lunatic named Ben Stahl.

Chase loathed thinking about it, and it almost made him thankful his parents were long dead. Guilt flared up too easily, as did embarrassment. The reason he'd been in the wrong place at the wrong time and had gotten himself kidnapped was nothing he wanted anyone to know about him, least of all his pops.

"You don't wanna associate with those fags, son."

Despite what these three men had in common, the history they shared, the memories that haunted them, they remained private people. The ten guys who had been taken three years and some five months ago had all been paired up in cage-like cells, and even the year of therapy that followed for the survivors hadn't resulted in any friendships for Chase. He hadn't felt close to Victor at all, the man he'd shared a cell with. *No one to share truths with.*

Hell, Chase hadn't heard from any of the men in a couple years—not counting the two in front of him now, and it was a fluke how they'd ended up in each other's lives again.

Once group therapy was over, Chase had focused on restarting his life. Nearly two years had passed. Then, one day this past February, he'd found himself in this corner of Bakersfield scouting a location for his bar.

In a diner, he'd grabbed some lunch, and he remembered the squeak and the thump as a little girl had crashed into him. A girl he'd recognized vaguely as Austin Huntley's daughter.

Chase had bent down and asked if she was okay, to which the girl had apologized profusely. Meanwhile, another man had rushed over to ask the same question. Just as Chase had noticed it was Cameron Nash, the girl had giggled, rolled her eyes, and said, *"I'm fine, Dad. Stop worrying so much."*

Yeah…

It'd taken a while before things had added up.

Now… Chase's mouth quirked up a fraction as he thought about it. Austin and Cam had gone from strangers sharing a small cell to falling in love with each other in the aftermath. They were married and raising thirteen-year-old Riley together in a house nearby. It was the three of them and two dogs.

Chase twisted the cap off his beer and took a swig. Austin and Cam were wrapping up a conversation about Landon, Cam's older brother, and his wife and twin girls. There was supposedly a family trip planned by Landon, and the two men were weighing the pros and cons about letting Riley tag along.

"As long as she calls often." Cam shrugged. "Ten times a day oughta do it."

"Listen to you." Austin let out a laugh. "Ten times."

Chase wasn't really paying attention, but at the same time, he was. While he didn't care much about the topic at hand, he observed and admired the dynamic between Cam and Austin. Both were quiet, straightforward, and laid-back. They weren't overly affectionate in public, but the bond was evident nonetheless. It was present in Austin's eyes as they seemed to take in Cam's every move; Austin registered the littlest things about Cam. It was present in the way Cam's chair was turned slightly in Austin's direction.

Small touches spoke volumes. How Cam brushed away some invisible lint from Austin's Henley, how Austin grinned and bumped their shoulders together when Cam said something funny, how Austin could calm down a usually fidgety Cam with a simple hand on his leg, how Cam sometimes absently reached over and brushed his thumb over the rings on Austin's finger...the list went on.

They were in tune with each other and they were happy. Chase envied that. For more than one reason.

He did his best to come off as content with his life as it was, but he wasn't sure he pulled it off well. He could sit all casual-like in his well-worn and usually holey jeans, vintage T-shirts, and dusty biker boots, but he could never shake the feeling of being out of place.

Waiting to be judged.

Or to be called "disgusting little queer," which had been Ben's favorite.

Chase didn't give a shit about his appearance, often letting his dark scruff grow and never taming his messy hair, but that was different. His exterior was the least of his problems. It was what was on the inside that kept him on edge.

His chiseled jaw clenched with his struggle to keep up his defenses. Especially when he looked at the couple in front of him. Austin and Cam had been tortured half to death, yet they'd returned to the world of the living and were thriving now.

It embarrassed the shit outta Chase to even think about complaining. He hadn't been the one who'd returned to Bakersfield with broken bones, punctured lungs, and gunshot wounds.

Aside from the deep scars that lingered around his wrists after being cuffed for so long, he hadn't shed a single drop of blood.

His old therapist, Gale, had loved to remind him that his pain was as real as anybody else's, but it wasn't about suffering as much as it was about not being able to help. He didn't want to get shot, for fuck's sake. But he did despise the memory of having to sit still, unable to do a fucking thing, while the other men had screamed in despair.

He'd *always* hated feeling helpless. Five months of not being able to do jack shit had only made it worse. If he saw a problem, he wanted to fucking fix it. It was in his blood.

Snap out of it, Gallardo.

Fuck.

Chase's shoulders stiffened and he took a deep pull from his beer. So he was ashamed and lonely. Big deal.

He always had his little sister—Adriana. And he had friends now, too. That was enough.

"Are we supposed to make a toast or something?" Cam's voice broke the silence in the dimly lit bar. "I don't know the protocol for kidnapping anniversaries."

Austin laughed quietly and adjusted his sleek, black-rimmed glasses. "You don't know the protocol for *any* kind of anniversary."

"Fuck you." Cam's mouth slanted into a smirk. "If you're gonna bitch, maybe I should just give you flowers and chocolate next year."

"Beats the blow-job coupons you gave me." Austin grinned wryly, and Chase huffed a small chuckle.

Cam shrugged and scratched his bicep. "Landon told me Jules likes that shit."

"Yes, to *receive*, baby," Austin pointed out. "But don't worry. It's your birthday soon; maybe I'll just give you the honor of blowing me ten times."

"Are you sure you've only been together three years?" Chase was amused. "Sounds more like fifty-three."

"Eh." Cam shrugged again. "I'm gonna grab a smoke." He jerked his thumb over his shoulder and went for the door.

Austin shook his head and smiled, facing Chase. "We should probably head home soon. Riley will be home from soccer camp pretty early tomorrow."

Chase nodded and fiddled with the label on his bottle. Because Cam and Austin lived so close, only a couple minutes away, they had stopped by every now and then—often with one of their dogs—to say hey and offer help.

Well, mostly Austin. Chase was more like Cam when it came to being social. Austin was hardly Mr. Social either, but he took more initiative and was more welcoming. For which Chase was grateful today. Acquaintances, old coworkers, one new employee—that was one thing…but no friends until now.

His pops had always worked two jobs, and from an early age, Chase had accompanied his dad to the second gig. After a long day in the oil fields, Pops was a salesman who went door-to-door, and Chase was the assistant to an exhausted man. All of which meant there was no time for friends or after-school activities.

"It's hard times, son. Everyone has to help out," his father would say. *"It's what makes us family."*

So Chase had been shocked and hurt when he'd moved out from under his parents' roof at eighteen, only to learn that Pops would no longer accept his help. It was then a new line of lecturing had begun.

"If a grown man can't stand on his own two feet without help, he ain't worthy of bein' called a man. I'll be damned if I gotta take help from my grown-up son. There's no pride in that."

Nevertheless, Chase hadn't been able to stand by and watch as the bills piled up on his folks' kitchen table. Instead of hanging out with peers and finding out what this friendship deal was all about and maybe working to pay for college, he'd worked in order to be able to slip his ma money whenever he could. Medical bills, stuff for Ade, food, loans... Having friends hadn't mattered.

"Everything all right?" Austin wondered.

"Yeah..." Chase blew out a breath and tried to relax back in his chair. "It's all good." He nodded with a dip of his chin for good measure. "Pretty hard to believe it's been three years."

Little by little, the agony had faded. He no longer went to therapy, and he wasn't afraid of the dark anymore. Yet...sometimes, something would trigger him. He'd dream vividly about the hell he'd endured and wake up drenched in sweat and ready to pounce.

"Sometimes it feels like time has flown, and sometimes..." Austin trailed off, frowning to himself.

Chase agreed with that. Sometimes it felt like it was only yesterday they ran out of that burning house and back to freedom.

"Where's Adriana tonight, by the way? I thought she'd be here."

Chase checked the clock on the wall behind the bar, noticing it was nearing four AM. "Right now I hope she's in bed." He grinned a little at the thought of the oops baby in the family. "But she's at home—in LA." In the apartment she shared with two girlfriends she went to college with. He was damn proud of her, and at times he felt more like a father than a brother. That wasn't weird, though; Ade was only twenty-one, a whopping eighteen years younger than Chase. After their parents died ten years ago, he had slipped into the role of a parent instead. The fact she had been shipped off to a foster family until she'd turned eighteen because Chase hadn't been able to prove he could support her financially didn't matter. He was the one she turned to first. "She's taking classes over the summer too, and she's got some paper to hand in on Monday." Austin nodded in understanding. "I told her to stay home and study."

He was proud, but that didn't mean he knew what Ade was really doing. She was a business major, which meant whenever she got started on numbers, economics, and fucking variables,

Chase zoned out.

If someone understood Ade, it was Austin. He was some big shot accounting director or whatever who studied tax laws for kicks and ran a big firm's office here in Bakersfield. The handful of times Ade and Austin had seen each other, Cam and Chase had tuned them out and talked about their shared interest in cars and motorcycles.

"I spoke briefly with Donna earlier," Austin mentioned casually, referring to Chase's only employee. "Nice girl." He tilted his head. "She seems to be very...fond of you. She kept blushing when I talked to her."

Chase couldn't help it; he barked out a laugh. The notion was just that ridiculous, and Austin didn't strike Chase as a matchmaker or one for gossip.

"No?" Austin grinned.

Chase chuckled and shook his head. "No."

Never mind that the blond bombshell was half his age, but she didn't have enough dick to capture his attention.

Ade had tried several times to set up Chase with women, but it wasn't gonna happen. Despite being as lonely as he was, the thought of getting to know someone made his skin crawl.

How could he even begin to describe himself?

The name's Chase. I like to tinker with my Harleys, I can't cook to save my life, but I make a mean grilled cheese sandwich. I leave the toilet seat up and the cap for the toothpaste off, there isn't a drink on this planet I can't make, and oh, that's right: after being held captive by an insane madman for five months, my head is fucked. Permanently.

Fuckin' A.

He was also so far into the closet he didn't know which way was out.

That he was gay was something he'd miserably and reluctantly admitted to himself over twenty years ago, and he had "experimented" when he was young, but those days were over.

He'd only caved once in the past decade, and it had gotten him kidnapped, so he chucked away that haunting memory before he'd have to excuse himself to go vomit.

"Ah, well." Austin smiled and shrugged. Then he looked

over his shoulder as Cam returned, smelling of cigarette smoke.

Chase swallowed past his nausea and wondered idly why the *fuck* he'd quit, but then he recalled Ade's incessant lectures about cancer. Which always led to her playing the guilt card: *"We only have each other, Chase. If you die, I will kill you."* It didn't make sense, but the message was received every time—loud and clear. It had been about a year now since Chase had taken his last smoke.

Of course, it had also been an expensive habit, and Chase was far from financially secure.

"So..." Cam stood behind Austin, his hands on the seated man's shoulders. "We gonna head home, or should I kick your ass at another round of pool?" Cam eyed the pool table in the back of the bar. There was also a dart board.

"Why are you making shit up?" Austin chuckled and tilted his chin up to face his husband. "Even Riley beats you. And speaking of her, we should head home. If she's going with Landon and Jules on their camping trip, I want to plan some activities with her tomorrow."

"All right." Cam nodded and ducked to give Austin a kiss. "We'll probably be up at the ass-crack of dawn, anyway." Now he seemed irritated. "Maybe I should sic Nacho on that fucking woman." Nacho was Riley's annoying little Chihuahua. "Bourbon would only cuddle up with the bitch." And Bourbon was Cam's Husky.

"Take it easy." The warning was clear in Austin's voice. "You and your damn temper."

"Whatever," Cam muttered. "It's why you love me."

Austin laughed through his nose. "I love you in spite of it."

"What woman?" Chase asked, his index finger tracing the hole in his jeans over his knee.

Austin reached up and squeezed Cam's hand, most likely to stop him from going off. "The woman who's renting Remy's house is remodeling." He looked at ease while Cam made a face. And Chase...well, he was *trying* to look indifferent. "The past month or so, we've been woken up several times by drilling, hammering, and yesterday it was a wood chipper, I think."

Chase didn't reply. The only reason he'd agreed to open his bar so close to Austin and Cam's was because they'd told him Remy didn't live in his house, which was on their street. He'd apparently rented it out, and they hadn't seen Remy in over a year.

The last thing Chase wanted in his life was reminders of the man who'd kidnapped him. Remy Stahl, the kidnapper's much younger half brother, definitely served as a reminder.

He still had questions about their long-dead case, questions about the Stahl family, but he had convinced himself it wasn't worth it.

For the time being, he was content to let this new chapter of his life—opening his bar—make him feel like he was genuinely living.

TWO

Remy was floating.

The air in the LA nightclub was stifling, and had he not been drunk and high, the crowd of sweaty, moving bodies would've made him nauseated. Instead, he was drowning in a sea of happy laughter and utter fucking joy.

He jumped to the music with his so-called friends, he drank more and more, he was groped at but didn't give a shit, and he laughed so hard that tears streamed down his face.

Suicide Sunday could wait another week.

His phone was constantly vibrating in his back pocket, but he had no desire to talk to Minna, his best friend.

She lived in his house out in Bakersfield, which... *Hell*, no. It was the last place on earth he'd return to.

One year ago, he'd sold his company—an online site for music streaming—and he'd quit Minna's brother's tattoo studio. Drawing and sketching, once a hobby, a passion, now belonged in the past.

In truth, the only things he did these days involved spending money on booze and hotels. And drugs for the weekends when he *really* let go.

He wanted no part of anything that reminded him of...well, himself.

That included his house, his real friends, the town he grew up in, and family. Not that there was any family left.

The name itself, the name Remy bore like a death

sentence, made him want to shoot himself. But he didn't have the guts like his mom had. Evidently. So, he was now blowing the money he had access to, and by the time it was gone, his vices would have hopefully done the job.

His cell phone vibrated again, though it was easy to tune out with the heavy bass of the music pounding through the foundation of the club.

"Remy!" Someone grabbed his arm, and Remy spun around and snapped up his elbow, connecting it with some motherfucker's chin. *Shit.* It was…what the fuck was his name, again? Something like Travis. He had high-quality coke, very pure, so Remy felt a little bad. The dude had even fallen on his ass.

"My bad." He pulled the guy off the floor.

"Goddammit." Travis-something cupped his jaw and glared at Remy. "I was only gonna say that your friend—that chick…? She called me. She's on her way here."

Remy snorted before disappearing into the crowd again. It would take a long time before Minna even got to LA, so whatever. Losing his buzz, he headed for one of the bars and ordered three shots of vodka.

Vodka was his favorite.

"You're cute."

Remy gave the girl next to him a bored stare then downed the first shot. And the second. *Cute.* Fuckin' hell. That's what you got when you were only five nine, apparently. That shit pissed him off. Maybe he wasn't tall, but cute? Fuck that noise.

Remy looked like an edgy skateboarder. He'd lost count of the tattoos that decorated his arms, neck, ribcage, calves—hell, even his knuckles. Four piercings, baggy chinos, a black T-shirt, a ball cap to hide his half-assed fauxhawk, a joint behind his ear, a jaw that could cut glass…nothing cute about it. His mom used to claim Remy had the cutest dimples and pale green eyes known to mankind.

Mom.

He gave a little shake of his head and let out a breath.

No amount of dimples could erase the past three years that were etched on Remy's face.

OUTCOME

He'd gone from a relatively carefree twenty-seven-year-old to a shell of a man who had aged ten years overnight. Anyone who took a look at him today wouldn't guess he'd only recently turned thirty.

"So…what's your name?" The girl beside him had clearly not received the message earlier.

Remy threw back another shot, grimaced at the burn, then faced the chick. "Listen, toots. Unless you're hiding a cock underneath that miniskirt, it's not gonna happen."

Her startled gasp was the only thing he heard before he vanished into the sea of bodies again.

It didn't take long until he was lost to the music, the dancing crowd, and the air of sex. It was getting late; those who hadn't found hookups yet were on the prowl. Remy didn't care. He wanted fun. Even if it was fake fun.

Hands roamed his body, large hands, a man's hands, tracing the defined abs under Remy's T-shirt.

"Bathroom?"

Remy looked over his shoulder and shrugged. The man was decent, average height, blond hair, brown eyes—sure, why not. He followed the man toward the bathrooms and ducked into the ladies' room, the only option if you wanted a stall.

A gaggle of chicks got pissed because they cut in line.

Inside a stall, Remy locked the door.

"I'm Kirk."

Remy raised a pierced brow. "Good for you." He unbuttoned and zipped down his baggy chinos. The coke made him jumpy and excited his body, but he was so depressed that no drug was powerful enough to erase his indifferent state of mind. Facing the wall, he told the dude to double-bag it.

Kirk found that funny. "Are you serious? You want me to use *two* condoms?"

"Did I fucking stutter?" Remy closed his eyes and rested his clammy forehead on the cool surface of the wall. With a hand down his briefs, he jacked his half-hard cock and listened as Kirk ripped the foil of two condoms. A small packet of lube was next, and it surprised Remy a little.

No one had bothered to prepare him lately.

He preferred it that way because it meant no care was involved.

Avoiding concern and offers of help made his shitty life easier. Otherwise, he would only get hopeful, and that never led to anything good.

"You're gorgeous." Kirk kissed his shoulder as he pushed two lubed-up fingers inside his ass. "I watched you out there—how you ignored all the girls. You looked lonely."

Remy gritted his teeth, losing his hard-on with this sappy bullshit. "Just fuck me."

"Take it easy." Kirk was trying to show he was in control. It probably worked for lots of men, but Remy didn't do affectionate lovemaking. This was a hookup at a nightclub in LA. Not a wine-tasting in Napa. "Let me take care of you."

"No—goddammit!" Remy slapped his hand against the wall in frustration. "Fuck me like you hate me." He inhaled deeply through his nose, his teeth clenched. "Or call it quits."

"I…I…" Kirk was at a loss. "I don't hate you. I don't want to treat you like—"

"Get out." Remy's voice was flat.

*

The dry air swept across Remy's face as he stepped outside and lit up a smoke.

He was surrounded by people who were leaving the club.

He wasn't sure if he was going to stay or go.

Most of his nights ended with a party somewhere else, often his hotel room, but now he was alone. Just standing in front of the exit with all those people milling about.

He claimed he hated everyone these days; others made him sick and angry, yet, for some reason, he was still drawn to interaction. But he made sure to stick to the wrong crowd because they'd never get his hopes up. They'd never help and ultimately disappear.

A woman waved a hand in front of her face and faked a

cough as she passed Remy, to which he rolled his eyes. He couldn't *stand* the Oh-you're-smoking-so-I-have-to-pretend-I-can't-breathe-and-give-you-the-evil-eye people.

Or how about those who asked, *"Did you know smoking can kill you?"*

No. Say it ain't so.

Someone else bumped into him.

Tilting his head up, Remy exhaled some smoke and tried to see if there were any stars out, but then he caught himself. Fuckin' LA—the smog deserved its own zip code. The only stars he'd see here were the movie kind.

"Remy, you motherfucker!"

Whereas people around him turned in every direction to see who the screamer was and who she was screaming at, Remy merely sighed and shook his head.

Waldo's been found.

The little imp loved to fuck with him.

He'd grown up with Minna Eriksson. They became best friends in the third grade and had only spent time apart when Minna went to Minnesota every summer. She had been born there and had a big, fat Scandinavian family outside of Duluth.

Later, Remy had also befriended Andreas, Minna's older brother by two years. And it was Andy who'd offered Remy an apprenticeship at his tattoo studio. It had been a place that grounded Remy; he loved the buzz of the tattoo gun, the rock music, the people…

It's in the past.

Only, not so much, since Minna refused to let him go. She crashed into him, grabbed ahold of his arm, shot him a scowl, and began dragging him away from the crowd.

"Nice to see you too, Min," Remy drawled.

"Shut the fuck up." Minna was definitely ticked off. The girl had a sailor's mouth, but two curses within ten seconds of seeing each other for the first time in a month was still a record. "Do you know how many clubs I've been to tonight looking for your sorry ass?" She kept muttering, getting herself riled up, which Remy noticed by the tightening of her grip on his arm. Damn, the girl had some claws. "Thank God I managed to track down that Trent guy's number." Trent! That was his name. Not Travis-something. Trent. "Why you insist on hanging out with low-life dealers is beyond me, though." Minna suddenly stopped and glared up at Remy, her dark hair fanning out for a second. "Can you even hear what I'm saying?"

"*Dogs* can hear you."

The anger in her lavender eyes intensified, and her skin was flushing with fury. She had this perky nose that scrunched up when she was mad, something Remy had always found adorable.

"Christ, you infuriate me!" She threw up her hands. "You don't even realize you have people who're worried about you, do you?" She poked his chest, and her voice rose. "We've been trying to find you for the past two fucking weeks since you're so fucking fond of disappearing on us. And here you are, smirking that fucking smirk, not giving a fucking shit!"

Remy hid his amusement and tugged on a lock of Minna's hair. "You know, for a kindergarten teacher, you sure curse a lot. You might wanna tone down the fucking."

Minna widened her eyes, as if she was incredulous by his nonchalance, and then let out a noise of frustration before she started pulling him with her again.

"Where are we going?" Remy was casually attempting to loosen her fingers from his bicep, but the girl was packing some strength. "Sweetheart, if by some miraculous chance I die tonight, it's probably a bad idea for you to have my DNA under your fingernails."

At that, Minna whirled around and slapped him across the face. "You self-destructive *asshole*!"

Remy was stunned.

Minna was more than a little upset. "How can you—" Her voice broke, though the moment of sadness was soon replaced by even more rage. "There's no getting through to you tonight." Remy didn't know what she meant by that, but it didn't matter. "I'm not giving up, though. And when you feel better, you'll remember this moment with regret—and pain from my boot up your ass."

Remy frowned. "You haven't put your boot up my ass."

Minna snorted. "*Yet.*"

When they reached her truck, she not-so-nicely ordered Remy to get in, and he gave her the directions to his hotel. Minna merely hummed at that, then peeled out of the parking lot.

"You're awfully pissy tonight." He turned in his seat to observe his friend. "Is my fag hag mad or simply on the rag?" He cracked himself up and slapped his thigh. "I'm a poet and I know it!"

"No, you're a crude piece of shit." Minna spat out the words and made a sharp turn. "Who looks like roadkill."

"Ouch." Remy laughed halfheartedly and removed his ball cap to run a hand through his messy hair. Tilting his head, he glanced at his reflection in the side-view mirror, and fuck. He really did look like roadkill. Or a train wreck, whichever was worse. The shadows under his eyes kept getting darker. The depression that suffocated him was visible, so fucking pronounced. On his face, in his posture...

The chemicals in his system were giving him mood swings; the downers made him tired and indifferent, and the uppers caused his mind and body to stay awake. He was fidgeting, unable to relax, and easily got lost in his head. He went from amused by Minna's behavior to depressed about his existence in a heartbeat.

As they stopped at a red light, Minna eyed him with disdain. "Put on your seat belt, idiot."

"Why?" Remy's mouth curved into a smirk. "That's not something you tell a suicidal person."

Minna actually laughed, but it was completely without humor. "You're not suicidal. You're crying for attention—for someone to save you. But guess what." She reached over to whack his arm. "You're gonna have to play a part in your own rescue. Otherwise it won't fucking work."

Remy gritted his teeth, pissed and embarrassed, and faced his window instead. He wasn't crying for attention, was he? That would mean he wanted help, that he wanted to live, and he didn't. He just happened to be too weak and scared to pull the trigger.

*

17

Remy was startled awake by someone jumping on his head. At least it felt like it.

The sun was shining outside the window, which made his eyes hurt and start to water. The headache kept pounding, and someone was banging something…somewhere. Where the fuck was he?

The irony wasn't lost to him. Waking up without knowing where he was had become *familiar*.

Shielding his eyes from the sun, he glanced around the room, pretty sure he'd been here before. But it had looked different, hadn't it? Now the walls were a muted blue color, the furniture was painted white, and there were fluffy pillows, a plush rug, billowy drapes, and decorative blankets scattered around.

It looked lived-in.

It looked like a woman had done the decorating.

It…*fuck*, it looked like the guest room in his old house out in Bakersfield.

Welcome back to the armpit of California.

"Minna!" he shouted hoarsely. Angrily. Then he slumped back down on his pillow again. A groan of pain slipped through his chapped lips. His mouth tasted like death. When he tried to scrub his right hand down his face, he noticed he couldn't. His hand was stuck. *No*, he amended when he looked to see what was wrong; his wrist was fucking *cuffed*. To the bed.

Had Minna brought him back to Bakersfield and cuffed him? What the hell was wrong with her?

He tugged at his restraints, but it was futile. The furry cuffs Minna had used for God-knows-what with her ex-boyfriend were fucking sturdy. Lifting his head, he took in his surroundings once more, this time to find an escape. A key. A goddamn hammer. Anything!

Remy needed to get the hell out of this house, leave Bakersfield, then find the nearest bar in LA.

The door finally burst open, and a beaming Minna appeared. "Good morning, sunshine!" Stupid, annoying singsong voice. "I guess you want some pain-killers, huh? And maybe some clothes."

Frowning, Remy peered down at his body, only to realize he was wearing nothing but a pair of boxer briefs. All his ink was on display, his most personal drawings, and it left him exposed and pissed.

He shot Minna a glare. "Are you out of your damn mind?"

Minna didn't look bothered at all. "I don't think so. And, regardless, you love me."

"*Love* you?" He growled and tugged more at his restraints. "Yeah—as much as I love a prolapsed asshole."

"Eww." Minna pretended to gag. "The images, dude."

He let out a labored breath. "Why am I almost naked?"

"After I'd dragged you in from the truck last night—or this morning—you threw up *all* over yourself." She scrunched her nose and walked over to the window. "What was I supposed to do, let you sleep in your own vomit? No, thank you. I've worked too hard to make this a livable home for you to ruin it." Her eyes flicked to him for a beat, almost hesitantly, before she opened the window to let some air in. "What does the Joshua tree mean?"

There was no way Remy was going to answer that. Once upon a time, Minna had been privy to the symbolism of his ink, but this was one piece he intended to keep private.

It wasn't new by any means, and it was her brother who'd done it, but Remy didn't make a habit of getting undressed in front of Minna.

"Forgive me if I'm not in the mood to chat." His voice dripped with sarcasm. "How about you unlock these instead?" He gave the cuffs a rattling tug.

"How about no?" Minna spun around and gave him a dazzling smile. "Get comfortable, honey. You're gonna get sober in this bed—they call it detox." She winked. "Give it a few days; then we'll talk."

Remy gnashed his teeth together, plotting instead of cursing her out. Because shouting wouldn't help. If Minna decided to do something, she stuck with it. She was as stubborn as the day was long, and her sometimes-unconventional methods could scare the shit out of the toughest motherfucker. So…Remy needed a plan.

And then I'm writing the witch out of my will.

The bathroom closest to the guest room would do him no good, but if he could convince Minna to let him use the master bath…

There was a window there.

THREE

Chase was in his small office when Donna knocked on the door.

"Boss? I don't wanna interrupt, but I really need to talk to you."

Considering the office was also his temporary home while he searched for a new apartment, he didn't want anyone entering, or even looking inside.

The day Donna had inquired about the shower hose attached to the sink in the tiny bathroom next to Chase's office, he had shrugged and said it was there when he'd rented the place.

It took more than blood, sweat, and tears to start a business. It took money too, and Chase had sold his parents' house—the one he'd fought a decade to pay off the debts on—across town as a final deed to afford everything that came with owning a bar.

Sleeping on a couch worked fine for now. As long as he had his bar and his three bikes were safe in the garage he rented a few blocks over, he didn't need much else.

Pushing his newly started inventory records aside, he left his desk and opened the door, revealing a nervous-looking Donna. To the bikers who had already declared Chase's bar their new hangout, the blonde with crystal blue eyes and big knockers was a sexy addition. To Chase, she was simply nice, genuine, and hard-working. She was also usually shameless and straightforward, so the apprehensive expression was new.

"What's up?" He frowned.

He wasn't exactly a stranger to shit hitting the fan, but in this case it couldn't be too bad, could it? Perhaps the problem was with Donna herself.

Nausea?

Chase knew it'd been risky—*and let's be honest here: stupid*—to hire a woman who'd recently learned she was pregnant, but as had already been established…if there was something that needed fixin', Chase stood first in line.

The day Donna had responded to his ad and shown up, already looking like she believed he'd never give her the job, he'd done just that.

"Well…" Donna wrung her hands together and cleared her throat. "I don't know the protocol for having escaped asylum patients in the bar." Chase lifted a brow, to which Donna huffed. "The dude sure *looks* like he's escaped from some kind of mental institution."

"You're gonna have to elaborate, hon," he drawled.

It was too fucking early in the evening for trouble. That shit wasn't supposed to start until the alcohol had flowed for several hours.

"He's just sitting out there in nothing but underwear!" Donna threw an arm in the direction of the bar. "Do I throw him out? I mean—" She released a breath and appeared to be trying to calm herself down. "I mean, he's not exactly *bothering* anyone, but—Christ. No dress code doesn't mean you can show up here *naked*."

Chase killed his smirk and shook his head. "All right. I'll take care of it." He waved a hand for Donna to take the lead, then followed her down the hall. "Did you finally kick out that boyfriend of yours, by the way?"

Donna chuckled shakily. "I wish. He won't budge. But I left him instead. I'm staying at a friend's for now."

That didn't satisfy Chase, but at least Donna wasn't around the prick anymore. As far as he knew, Donna had never been physically abused, but emotionally seemed to be another matter.

"We'll talk more about this later." He turned to give

Donna a look, silently daring her to defy him. Thankfully, she didn't. "It's your name on the lease; he's the one who should get the boot."

She nodded stiffly in agreement. "Yes, Daddy."

Chase snorted and looped an elbow around her neck, much like a father would with his little son, accompanied by a *"That's my boy,"* or *"Well done, slugger."*

"Fuckin' brat," he chuckled instead, then made a move to open the door that led to the bar. Before he could open it fully, though, Donna stopped him and surprised the shit outta him when she squeezed his midsection. Tightly.

"Thank you, Chase." Her whisper nearly closed up Chase's throat. He was being *hugged.* By someone other than his sister. "For everything you've done for me." She peered up at him with gratitude in her eyes. "I know we've only known each other for a couple weeks, but I want you to know I consider you an amazing friend."

Chase nodded dumbly, having no fucking clue what to say. He didn't help out in order to make friends or to look like a hero. It was just the right thing to do.

"I'm making you uncomfortable, aren't I?" She slid him a small, knowing smile.

He blew out a gust of air, a half chuckle. "A bit." Not the hug, though. Only her words. He wasn't used to that kinda talk. "I think I have a hospital patient to check in on."

"*Mental* hospital patient," she corrected him as she released her hold. "And I'm done being sappy, boss. I solemnly swear." She saluted him for good measure.

Relieved that the awkwardness had passed, Chase gave a quick nod in return and then left Donna behind to see who this "patient" was. The bar wasn't by any means packed with people, but it was still early. A few were happy to see Donna back to taking orders.

"Sorry for the delay, boys," she said, getting busy.

Chase walked over to the end of the bar where a young man wearing only boxer briefs sat. Hell, was the punk asleep? Forearms on the bartop, forehead planted on one of those arms.

Messy hair, shorter on the sides, nearly black, with some streaks of red that looked washed out. Chase's sister dyed her hair in odd colors like that sometimes.

"This is a bar, kid. Not a hotel." Chase folded his arms across his chest and leaned back against the counter behind him. He eyed the ink on the man's arms, shoulders, and neck. It was a stark contrast against the pale and unblemished skin. The artwork was intricate and impressive, albeit depressing. Quotes about suffering, about staying true to who you are, a snake slithering toward a big, red apple, and an inked bullet wound. Dark clouds, a grim reaper, lyrics that belonged to songs about death, something that looked like the beginning of a tree on his ribcage, but Chase couldn't see farther down.

The man spoke at last, quietly, and stayed in his position. "If I can just stay for ten minutes, that'd be great." He sounded drained, as if he'd been drinking too much whiskey.

The voice didn't fit what Chase saw, which was youth. Or perhaps the lithe body with sinewy muscles betrayed him and made the kid look younger than he was.

Admit it, man. You like what you see.

Chase silenced that little voice with an internal growl.

Attraction and romance had no business in his closet.

Because of what he'd been doing when Ben had taken him, the mere thought of finding companionship was connected to his time in captivity. That was why he couldn't stand it. Even if he longed for it.

The reminders made him sick. Not to mention angry.

"You mind telling me why you're only in your underwear?" Chase was starting to feel impatient. "I get that it's summer, but there are limits."

The younger man let out a humorless chuckle. "I'm afraid clothes weren't my priority when I finally escaped that witch." Chase stiffened instinctually at *escape*. Bad fucking joke, if that was what it was. "She's supposed to be my best friend..." The man lifted his head a few inches, only to bury it in his hands. "She called it detox. I call it torture. Three goddamn days, dude, just because I happen to like booze. Three days in handcuffs—even when I went to the bathroom!"

Detox? Chase frowned and heaved a sigh 'cause none of this shit really mattered to him. Clearly, the man hadn't been kidnapped, and that was all Chase needed to know. Maybe he had this compulsion to fix problems, but he couldn't shoulder it *all*.

The fact that this stranger was bitching about wearing handcuffs for three days only made Chase wanna laugh. He'd endured cuffs for five months at one point, without a single reprieve.

He was hiding those vicious scars under two folded bandanas.

"I finally escaped when she let me take a shower in the master bathroom." A huff. "Gotta love windows." Rubbing his eyes, he finally let his hands fall away, and he gave Chase a once-over.

Chase's frown deepened, first registering a handsome face that looked aged from grief, piercings in his bottom lip and eyebrow, then light green eyes that he deemed unforgettable, but... Wasn't there something familiar about him?

"Oh, shit." The man's breath left him in a whoosh, those pale green eyes widening. Anguish and fear—fucking *fear*—took over and made his jaw slack. Then he suddenly pushed off the barstool and stumbled a few steps backward. "I-I'm sorry. I'm sorry." He accidentally knocked over the stool and hurried to right it. "I didn't mean to—I didn't know y-you worked here."

With every stuttered word from the man, with every step he took toward the door, and with each patron's attention he got, it slowly dawned on Chase. Brick by brick. The months of research he'd done after getting back to freedom three years ago. The paper clippings. The miniscule profile photo on a website for music streaming. The article about that website being sold a year ago.

Shock and anger unfurled inside Chase. *This is the kind of reminder I don't want.* His hands clenched into fists. His spine went rigid, and his gaze turned furious. His heart began racing, his chest tightening beyond what was painful. Merely *looking* at this man, facing him for the first time, threw Chase back in time. Three years to be exact.

I don't want you here. Don't remind me. Go away.

The only sensation stronger than the anger was the feeling of getting kicked in the gut.

"I'm sorry, Chase." The man who wasn't a stranger—not exactly—pushed the door open and fled.

Remy Stahl.

∗

Remy's only plan had been to get as far away from the house as possible. When he'd seen the bar, it had been like an answer to his prayers. *Alcohol. Yes.* Of course, then he'd remembered he didn't have any money.

The sun was setting as Remy dragged his bare feet along the hot pavement of his driveway. Had it been earlier in the day, his feet would've had blisters from the heat by now.

Would he have noticed, though?

Minna ran out from the house, first looking angry as hell, but then amazed.

"You came back." Her mouth opened and closed, like she wanted to say more but didn't know what. "I called Andreas—he'll be here any minute, but…" A long exhale left her. Relief. "You came back, Remy."

Remy felt nothing. Not a damn thing. He nodded numbly and passed her, entering the house without purpose and direction. All of his strength and every emotion had seeped out of him as he'd escaped from Chase Gallardo and trudged the few blocks back to what he'd once called home.

He was dead inside.

Collapsing on the bed in the guest room, he stared out the window with unseeing eyes, completely lost in the past. He barely registered Minna's fussing over him, asking what had happened; Remy didn't acknowledge her.

And people wonder why I drink?

One of those reasons evidently worked in a bar just a few blocks from here. Which should've strengthened Remy's resolve to get the hell out of Bakersfield, but he couldn't be bothered at the moment. Maybe in a day or two. Who cared?

"You're worrying me." Minna sounded like she was close to tears. "Are you hurt? What happened?"

Remy slid his empty gaze to his friend, thinking briefly about what she'd asked, then frowned and went back to staring out the window.

The single line Chase had written back to Remy—after he had sent Chase four letters full of remorse, guilt, and apologies—went on a loop in his head.

Don't ever contact me again.
Don't ever contact me again.
Don't ever contact me again.

Remy honestly didn't know what he'd expected when he'd sent those letters to Chase nearly three years ago, but he'd never felt so rejected and embarrassed as the day he'd received that little note.

He'd left the first letter with Cameron Nash, who lived down the street, but then he'd managed to find Chase's address thanks to a PI he'd hired. He hadn't wanted to bother Nash again, but he'd needed to make sure the first letter had reached Chase. So, he had written more. Three more.

It should've been Remy who was kidnapped. Not Chase. Chase was innocent. Chase wasn't cursed with the family from hell; Remy was.

His family history was enough to make anyone dizzy with drama overload.

"Remy. Can you please say something?" Minna placed her hand on Remy's clammy forehead. "I'm worried sick here."

"I'm fine." Remy turned away from her touch. "You don't have to cuff me. I'll stay." Until he could shake this numbness and leave. Maybe kill himself for real this time. The drugs worked too slowly.

The rage he'd seen in Chase's eyes had nearly pushed him over the edge. Remy was intimidated by the man, who was tall, broad-shouldered, and sexy in a lethal way, almost menacing-looking. He would crush Remy like a bug, no bones about it.

"Something happened—where did you go?" Minna wiped

at her cheeks, tears having spilled over.

Remy detected guilt in her expression. As if this was her fault. Christ. She needed to realize he was beyond saving.

Once upon a time, he'd tried. He'd reached out for help. His mom, his so-called family, a shrink… One killed herself, two abandoned him, and the latter never told Remy what he needed to hear. One way or another, everyone vanished.

"All I wanted was for you to sober up and start thinking clearly." Minna choked up and sat down on the edge of the bed. "I knew you'd refuse to go to rehab. This was all I could think of."

"I wish you'd let it go." He really did wish that.

He also wished he could forget his past. His fucked-up father, his mom, his two half brothers—one of whom kidnapped ten innocent men—and one cold stepmother who'd always blamed Remy for the shattering of the Stahl family.

Most of all, he desperately wished he could forget the guilt.

Hell, while he was at it, he wished he wasn't guilty in the first place.

Guilty of unconsciously helping a kidnapper.

FOUR

Chase barged into his office, slammed the door shut, and tore through the drawers in his desk. It was those fucking letters he was in search of, and he didn't even know why. Why the hell would he ever wanna lay eyes on them again? Four letters. Four letters that had killed him in every way except for cutting off his airway. Four letters he despised with every fiber of his being, yet he'd never been able to throw them out.

At the bottom of the third drawer, he found them inside a larger envelope. Four smaller envelopes fell out on the desk as he turned the parcel upside down. Three of them with postage and Chase's old address. Then the first one that he'd received through Cam.

Releasing a heavy breath, Chase slumped down in his chair and just stared at the envelopes.

In a very formal way, Remy had started each letter with *Dear Mr. Gallardo*, and having seen Remy in person now…it was weird. In another time and place—hell, in another universe—Chase might've found it endearing. But he settled for fucking weird now.

Nearly three years had passed since he'd read them, but several lines were forever etched into his mind.

"…were contacted by the police shortly after you and the other six men had given your statements…"

The first letter was full of apologies mixed with explanations.

"...*when we found out that Ben was responsible, that he had put all of you through this...*"

Chase and the other survivors had been revolted and angry after learning that Ben Stahl had been counted as a victim at first. Instead of as the kidnapper.

"...*need you to know I don't agree with my stepmother and half brother, Fred...*"

Remy was clearly ashamed of his family, Clarissa and Fred Stahl in particular, because they spoke highly of Ben to the reporters.

"...*and I'm sure I'm the last person you want to hear from, but I wanted to apologize...*"

Remy seemed to be ashamed of himself, too.

The second letter had been slightly repetitive as Remy hadn't been sure the first one had reached Chase.

Then the third letter...? Goddamn. Chase remembered the awkward fumbling that shone through every line.

"...*haven't heard from you, but that's okay. You shouldn't feel guilty for that. Not that I think you do. Feel guilty, I mean. I did tell you I wasn't expecting any response.*"

Words had been crossed out, replaced by others. Some had been filled in more than once and underlined.

"...*only writing to make sure you don't think*—***believe*** *I think you have to respond*—*that you're obligated to write me back.*"

Remy's handwriting was neat and flawless, just a bit cursive. Though, Chase had studied the letter to the point where he'd been able to see where Remy had paused because his hand had been shaking.

"...*once again, I'm very sorry. For reminding you of what must've been a horrible fucking time, and for contacting you again.*"

The kid hadn't been able to apologize enough.

Remy had also divulged that he wasn't close to anyone in his family—not even his real mom, due to her addictions to alcohol and prescription pills. Or "fucking oxys" as Remy had phrased it. This, Chase guessed, had prompted Remy to send a fourth and final letter. Because it had been full of more apologies, this time for unloading family drama onto Chase.

OUTCOME

"...didn't mean to complain. I know you don't care, and you shouldn't. You've suffered enough, all because of me and my family."

It was true—Chase didn't wanna know shit about the Stahls. And what a fucking lie that was. Remy's words had only raised questions that Chase had struggled to push down for the past three years.

Unlike Cam—Austin too, to some degree—Chase wanted to know *why*. He wanted to know why Ben had kidnapped ten innocent men and forced them to play a part in that twisted game of Who Ruffled Ben's Feathers. Each and every man who'd been kidnapped had received a new name in captivity. A name that belonged to someone Ben knew—or had known.

On Chase's piece of paper, it had said Remy. Ben's young half brother.

Additionally, there had been a high school bully, an old boss, a couple cousins, an old friend who had betrayed him, another brother, a father, an uncle... But Ben hadn't kidnapped them. He'd gone after ten strangers instead and played the most vicious game of pretend that included torture and murder.

There were a couple theories as to why. The one Chase believed in was the scenario where Ben was too intimidated by his real nemeses to even go near them. Daddy issues, Cam had guessed with a shrug at one group session. A guess that fit with Ben's behavior while he'd held them all hostage.

Success was everything. College diplomas were vital. Being unemployed meant you were useless. Wearing a suit was good. Driving a nice car was also good. Blue collar was not.

Everyone who'd been taken had had menial jobs—or so Ben had thought. A mailman, a bartender, a couple construction workers and plumbers, a mechanic... One or two had even been without jobs. Considered lowlifes. Kidnapped. One by one. Held in metal cages in a humid basement out in the desert. For five fucking months. All while Ben punished them for what they'd never done.

Three men had died.

In the end, Ben's little bubble had burst when he'd found out Austin and Tim weren't so worthless, after all. Tim was working toward his master's, only delivering mail in order to pay the bills. And Austin…? Austin had it made. Ben's father would call him a great success with the fancy job, the suit, the Mercedes. But, unfortunately, Austin had been wearing sweatpants with his father's construction company's logo the day Ben kidnapped him.

Naturally, Ben had been under the impression Austin was a construction worker.

It was a fluke how it had been revealed. Austin had made a sarcastic remark after Ben had called him…what was it? Chase couldn't remember—simpleton! That was it. Simpleton. Austin had muttered something about how having an MBA from Duke University should've saved him from being called a simpleton.

If the men had thought Ben was unstable before, it was nothing compared to what came next. Aside from furious shouting and interrogating everyone about their college experience, Ben decided to "terminate the project" and set them all on fire.

That had never happened, thanks to Austin and Tim, but no one would ever be able to give back the five months they'd lost, all the broken bones, nightmares, and, of course, the lives of the three men who had died.

Scrubbing his hands down his face, Chase groaned and leaned forward on his knees. His eyes burned as he reread the letters for the first time in so long. Over and over, he studied Remy's words, and a knot of unease started to grow in Chase's stomach.

He didn't feel the same hatred he'd felt last time. The fury that had dominated for so long wasn't as forceful, nor was it directed at Remy, as it had been in the beginning.

Misplaced as it was, Chase had blamed his suffering on Remy for months before he got his shit together and acknowledged there was only one who was guilty. *Ben.* But even as Chase had realized the truth, he'd clung to the anger.

Anger was easy. Anger could be masked as strength. Anger kept the nausea at bay whenever he remembered he'd been with a man right before Ben had found him, which had landed Chase in that cage—

Christ, please stop.

Chase coughed into a closed fist and forced himself to

move on.

He thought back to the look on Remy's face as he'd stumbled outta the bar. It confused Chase, this feeling of immense *hurt*. Bone-crushing and heart-wrenching pain. It had all been there in Remy's features, and Chase had *felt* it.

He couldn't make heads or tails of this. The whole situation left him weary and tenuous.

Chase spat out a curse and balled one of the letters to throw it at a wall.

Frustrated as shit, he stood up and started pacing in the small office. Questions whirled around in his head, cracking down like thunder, each one demanding to be answered. Whether he despised Remy a little or a lot for storming into his life as the biggest reminder of what Chase was desperate to forget wasn't fucking important.

Remy owed him, and the wounds had been reopened now, anyway. Chase could get his answers from that little motherfucker. But to actually seek out the man? Screw that. Chase couldn't; it felt too masochistic.

Though, one other revelation of Remy's refused to be forgotten. Perhaps Remy hadn't meant anything when he wrote it in the second letter—Chase actually doubted it was significant because the police must've investigated it—but *what if?*

What-fucking-if.

"I'm sorry for every dime I ever gave Ben."

Everyone had learned that Ben had been incapable of keeping a job, but holding ten men hostage for five months couldn't have been cheap, regardless of how little they'd been fed.

Where had the money come from?

There was more than that, too. It wasn't only about quenching his curiosity. It was about moving on. It was about accepting his past and beginning to finally look forward. As it was now, Chase's past haunted him too much. It held him hostage much like Ben had.

Some parts would always stay hidden, but if he could move past a big portion of the anger and gain some understanding, maybe it would be enough.

I guess I'm done running...?

Slumping down in his chair again, he sniffled and wiped angrily at his cheeks. The exhaustion was getting to him; he was close to his breaking point. And to think...just last week, he'd woken up with a goddamn smile because he'd finally opened his bar. Joshua's Place—his sanctuary.

That pinch of joy was gone now, and, unable to help it, his mind wandered back to Remy, and he wondered if the kid had felt any joy lately, too. Judging by the brief glance Chase had received, he doubted it. He'd probably never forget the look of Remy's face. The shadows, the fear overtaking... The morbid theme of the kid's tattoos.

Kid. Chase scoffed and scrubbed his hands down his face. He knew Remy was thirty, though he looked older and younger at the same time. Pale, flawless skin, vulnerability, sadness, loss, lifestyle choices...they pulled Remy in one or another direction.

Chase was all over the place. Losing his fucking mind. Thoughts too jumbled.

Maybe I should go back to therapy.

Or not.

FIVE

Austin grinned as his head hit the pillow, and Cam was quick to follow, all while getting rid of the towel that had been wrapped around him for all of two minutes. His hair was still wet from his shower as Austin weaved his fingers through it and pulled Cam down for a deep kiss.

"How quick do we gotta be?" Cam slid a hand between them, finding Austin hard and ready. Hell, he'd been ready all day. First day of his vacation, and he was already going stir-crazy. Meanwhile, Cam didn't start his vacation until next week.

"I told Riley to be home at six." Austin turned his head to the nightstand and saw it was half past five. He'd already prepared the steaks and the grill, so they were good on time. "Did you speak to Jules?"

Cam shook his head as he reached over to grab the lube. "Landon did. Twins're still sick, so Jules is gonna stay home with them." He dipped down and kissed Austin, softer this time. Slower, more passionately, and deeper.

Austin groaned as two slicked-up fingers pushed inside him. The tediousness of today faded with each little thrust, but it was far from enough. "Today I learned that I don't enjoy Spanish soap operas."

Cam smirked against Austin's jaw and withdrew his fingers. "You need it that bad, huh?" Austin nodded, lifting his head to look between them. Cam was so...incredibly sexy, especially in his naked glory. That pale skin and all that ink on display. The prominent V between his hips, his defined torso...

"Don't worry. I'll take care of you."

Gripping the base of his cock, he leaned over Austin and positioned himself before he slowly pressed inside.

"Oh, fuck..." Cam moaned.

Austin sucked in a breath and pushed back, lifting his hips. He also gripped Cam's narrower ones and released a drawn-out groan when his husband was all in. God, this was exactly what he needed today. Perfect transition between an uneventful day and the barbecue in a little while.

"Do that thing with your hips." At Austin's quiet request, Cam drew out, then pushed back in and rolled his hips, grinding deeper. Austin groaned, parted his legs farther, and slid down his hands to squeeze Cam's firm ass. "Jesus, that's it."

"Yeah." Cam blew out a labored breath and rested his forehead to Austin's. "I gotta pause. You feel too good—" He swallowed. "Oh, for chrissakes..."

"What?" Austin kept one hand on Cam's ass, feeling his muscles clenching, as Austin's other hand roamed Cam's back, up his shoulder blades to his neck, into his dark hair again.

"You know how it is." Cam huffed, only to hiss when Austin gave his damp hair a tug. "*Ungh*—quit it, baby." Austin grinned. "Like, you gotta take a leak, and you're compelled to think about waterfalls. I'm tryin' not to bust a fuckin' nut, and I can't stop thinking about things I wanna do to you." Oh, Austin wanted to hear *that*. Nothing made him come harder than when Cam talked dirty. "Not my fault, though." Cam grunted and slid out, pushing in slower next time. "You've been too busy this week to take care of my needs."

Austin laughed into the crook of Cam's neck and nipped at the skin there. "I had to make sure my minions could cope without me for three weeks." He clenched his ass around Cam's cock, earning himself a gasp from the man on top. "And pardon me, but wasn't it you who was too tired last night and the day before?"

"Yeah, well." Cam quit his muttering, having nothing to say. Austin knew. Because Cam had also been busy at work, all but dead on his feet when he'd walked through the door. "Fine. Whatever."

He smirked crookedly and met Austin's gaze for a beat. He could linger longer these days, which Austin loved, but he also loved the uniqueness that came with Cam's disorder. Whenever he averted his eyes, usually to a spot near Austin's shoulder, Austin was brought back to the day they got married.

They'd stood together at the courthouse with their closest family members present, and immediately after Cam had uttered *"I do,"* he'd dropped a *"Motherfuck,"* faced the judge, and said, *"I gotta say it again 'cause I didn't look at him. You got a problem with that?"*

There were few things he loved more than the lack of a verbal filter that came with Cameron Nash. Or didn't come, rather. And now he wanted to hear just how unfiltered Cam could be. Wicked, raw, downright indecent.

"Come on." Austin sucked Cam's bottom lip into his mouth. "I want to know all the dirty things. Go crazy on me."

Cam stiffened and spat out a curse. When his gaze flashed to Austin's, those mercury eyes filled with possessiveness. "All right." He pulled out from Austin and twirled a finger. "Get on all fours for me." Austin complied and stroked his cock that had softened a bit. Anticipation rushed through him as Cam spread his cheeks and dragged the head of his dick to Austin's hole. "You wanna know what I think of when I jack it in the shower?"

"Tell me." Austin's voice dripped with urgency. "You must've done a lot of that this week." He smiled to himself.

"Nah…maybe once or twice." Cam thrust forward an inch or two, teasing. "This is what you do to me." He slammed in.

It stole Austin's breath.

Jesus fucking Christ.

Pain interspersed with the intense pleasure, causing Austin's arms to tremble and his erection to thicken. The skin around his cock felt tight, and when he moved a shaky hand over his shaft, the head was slick with pre-come.

Cam had a firm grip on Austin's hips and pulled them backward. "Fuck yourself on my dick." Sitting back on his heels, he had his hands free when Austin took care of the movements, which he did greedily. He set a fast pace, knowing this was the position Cam could last longer in. "Let go—" Austin's hand was batted away from his cock and replaced by Cam's hand. "I think about *this* in the shower." He gave Austin's erection a solid squeeze that morphed into a downward stroke. "And I have two go-to fantasies."

"Give it to me." Austin grunted and pushed down hard on Cam's cock. Something ignited in him, the sensations zinging and zapping between all his erogenous zones.

"When you fuck me," Cam whispered in his ear, "and fuck me again. When we don't need any lube." Goddamn, Austin loved that, too. His previous release would be enough for him to just slide home, burying his throbbing cock inside Cam's ass. "The noises drive me wild every fuckin' time." Cam's voice was all sex, raspy and close to Austin's ear. "So wet and hard." He fisted Austin's cock tighter and stroked faster.

Austin gasped and squeezed his eyes shut, ecstasy racing in his veins. His balls felt heavy and tight, but before he could beg Cam for more, he was pushed forward again. His hands hit the mattress, and he looked over his shoulder to see Cam ramming his cock into him.

Fuck!

"My other favorite," Cam gritted out. "When you suck me off—" he leaned over Austin's body to kiss the spot between his shoulder blades "—and you don't swallow right away." Austin flushed with heat and even a little embarrassment, which was ridiculous. "When you ask me to come on your tongue." It was that hot whisper again. "You really *taste* me."

"I love it." Austin hung his head and grabbed his cock, stroking it hard. "I love tasting you." He could both see and feel the effect his words had on his husband. Cam sped up behind him. Austin felt each thrust, heard every slapping sound their skin made upon impact, and sensed Cam's loss of control.

Austin's orgasm rolled around inside him, threatening to erupt at any moment.

Just then, Cam stiffened. "Oh fuck—*Austin*!" Rocking deeper into Austin, he found his release, and by the time he pulled out and was able to catch his breath, Austin was ready to burst.

He was also ready to beg. "Make me come." Desperation

laced his tone, probably the reason Cam hurried to comply.

"On your back." Cam leaned over to the nightstand, still breathing heavily, and found their one and only toy—a vibrator for the G-spot. Austin groaned in suspense and rolled over. "I've missed this." Cam settled between Austin's legs, easily inserting the vibrator, its curled tip pressing against Austin's prostate.

"Fucking me with a toy?" Austin chuckled, out of breath, then moaned when the vibrator buzzed alive. "Oh God, yes."

"No. This." Without another word, Cam lowered his mouth and swallowed Austin's cock. He sucked strongly, as if he hadn't done this in years as opposed to a week. But Austin wasn't going to complain. He watched hungrily as Cam pleasured him, all while that toy vibrated against his prostate.

"Almost," he managed to grit out. He was right there, teetering on the edge, and when Cam's dark silver eyes flashed to his, he was done. Ropes of come pulsed out of his cock, and he groaned breathlessly at the feel of Cam's tongue swirling around him. Those firm lips, the hot suction, the wetness... Austin was beside himself, completely lost to his climax.

It was going to be a goddamn amazing vacation once Cam started his. They'd be activity-loving parents to their daughter, but once Riley went camping with Landon's family, all bets were off. Austin was looking forward to lazy mornings in bed and sun-filled days by the pool.

Before it became too much, Cam removed the vibrator from Austin's sensitive ass and then collapsed next to him. "Fuck me, I needed that."

Austin swallowed against the dryness in his throat and nodded. "Just wait 'til next week when you start your vacation."

Cam moved close, shifting Austin's arm away so he could rest his head on Austin's shoulder. "Sounds like you have plans for us."

"Damn right." Austin rolled them over, half on top of Cam. He kissed his man on the lips, chastely at first, then delved deeper. He hummed as he tasted himself in the kiss, something that seemed to excite Cam.

"Motherfuck," Cam cursed. Then he pushed his fingers

into Austin's hair and deepened the kiss further. "I love you."

Austin smiled against Cam's lips. "Love you—"

The sound of the doorbell reminded them of the fact they had Landon and Chase coming over for a barbecue. Probably some poker too, since Jules wouldn't be here.

Cam raised a brow, eyeing the clock on the nightstand. "What the fuck? Someone's early."

"Can't be Riley." Austin was reluctant to leave the bed but did so anyway. "She wouldn't exactly ring the doorbell, nor would she be early." He peered down at his chest and then grimaced.

I need a shower.

Cam seemed to understand without an explanation. "I'll be Mr. Host until you're ready." He leveled Austin with a serious look as he pulled on a pair of khaki shorts. "Don't be long. Can't have people thinking I like being social all of a sudden."

Austin chuckled, retrieving a pair of boxer briefs from a drawer. "You don't." He grabbed jeans and a T-shirt from their closet, too.

"Exactly."

Withholding his smirk, Austin nodded. "All I need is two minutes."

Maybe it took three, but that was still fast. Austin had a towel around his neck, his clothes clinging to his still-damp body, and he was pretty sure he had a few suds from his body wash behind his ear. One swipe with the towel said yep.

"He didn't show up at the garage earlier, either." There was a frown in Cam's voice as Austin got closer to the hallway. "And he's working right now?" It sounded as though he was repeating something someone else had told him, whoever it was at the door probably. "As far as I know, he's supposed to be here in a little bit."

"The way he's been acting, I doubt he remembers," a woman answered.

Her voice was vaguely familiar, and when Austin finally rounded the corner, he saw it was Donna, the young girl who worked for Chase.

Donna ducked her head, a faint blush spreading over her

cheeks as Austin came up behind Cam. At the same time, Cam turned to Austin.

There was that frown. "I forgot to tell you. Chase didn't show up at the garage today."

Austin's brows knitted together. He'd heard something about Chase having an appointment with Landon, who worked with motorcycles while Cam's specialty was vintage cars. But Austin didn't understand what that had to do with Donna being here. Had something happened?

"Is something wrong?" Austin faced Donna.

"I'm not sure, Mr. Huntley." She wouldn't look him in the eye, and the formality made Austin feel ancient. The brief moment he'd spoken to her at Chase's bar's opening, she'd only flushed scarlet when he told her to call him Austin. "Chase has been acting very…strange." Donna wrung her hands awkwardly. "Um, he's spacing out—like, when I say his name, he doesn't react. I haven't seen him eat anything in a while, either. And yesterday, I asked if I could borrow his phone in his office, and he just waved me along." At Austin's raised eyebrow, she rushed to explain. "He usually doesn't let anyone into his office. It's a thing. He's very private about it."

"All right," Austin said slowly. He didn't quite know what to say, because whereas Austin and Cam were low-key people and valued their privacy, Chase Gallardo was Fort Knox. Austin was certainly worried, though. They considered Chase a friend, but he was one they had to take baby steps with.

Well, Cam only demanded to get to the bottom of things when it concerned his immediate family. He was fine with things as they were, but Austin had often wondered about Chase's well-being. The man was constantly on guard, as if he was waiting for someone to jump out of the bushes and attack.

Given their shared past, it was a valid fear.

Austin also doubted Chase was still in therapy. Cam and Austin didn't go often, but they made an appointment with Gale every now and then. Just to be safe. It provided some stability and comfort.

"You're gonna go." Cam smirked wryly at him. Austin's

own amusement was tinged with sheepishness. *He knows me too well.*
"It's cool," Cam chuckled. "Go do your good deed for the day. I'll
entertain my brother until you return. And—" He cut off there, his
gaze catching something outside.

When Austin peered out the door, he saw Riley coming
closer on her bicycle, Nacho peeking up from her little basket in
the front. Automatically, Austin checked his watch, only to realize
he hadn't put it on after his shower.

Cam did it instead. "The baby girl's fifteen minutes late."
He huffed then faced the inside of the house, or more correctly,
the patio. "Bourbon!" That dog was always in the backyard.

Austin grinned at the plan he knew Cam had. Bourbon
had eaten something he shouldn't have, and whatever it had been,
it had caused diarrhea. Austin would bet his life that Riley's
punishment for being late entailed taking Bourbon for a walk.

But that was the deal. Riley was absolutely awful at keeping
track of time; it had gotten to the point where she was late to
school and missed classes after recess. Cam and Austin had been
called to her school twice about the issue, so they were strict about
that now.

Donna stepped aside slightly as Riley reached the
driveway.

Austin and Cam folded their arms across their chests.

"Before you get mad!" Riley exclaimed, jogging over with
Nacho in her arms. "Dad. Dad." She gave Donna a quick glance.
"Stranger." Then back to Austin and Cam. "I have a *really* good
excuse."

"And I wanna hear all about it," Cam drawled as he
snatched up Bourbon's leash. "Later."

Riley's face fell. "Oh, no," she whispered. "Does he still
have the runs?"

Cam grinned. "Oh yes, sweetheart."

Austin chuckled and pocketed his wallet from the hallway
table. The sun still blazed, so he grabbed his Ray-Bans, too. He put
on his shoes next and hung the towel among the jackets. "I'll be
home soon." He leaned in and kissed Cam chastely, but before he
could move away, Cam kissed him again. Hard.

When it ended, Cam whispered in Austin's ear. "If Blondie crosses a line, I'll be pissed."

Austin backed away, puzzled.

Which only seemed to amuse Cam. "You have no clue, baby." He laughed through his nose and shook his head. It sort of ended the conversation—before it could even begin—and he focused on Riley after that.

Since Austin was hungry as hell, he left the house, praying he could return quickly. Hopefully with Chase in tow. "Like I said, I'll be home soon." He dropped a kiss to the top of Riley's head then nodded down the road, and Donna followed.

He slid on his shades.

The two walked in silence for only a few seconds before Austin fired off the first question.

"I take it Chase didn't send you?"

Donna shook her head minutely. "I saw a Post-it with your name and address in his office. I knew you guys're friends, and I'm worried about him, but I don't know him well enough yet."

Austin hummed, frowning to himself. "Perhaps I should give Adriana a call." She'd given him her number with a hopeful smile one day when he'd mentioned he might be able to get her an internship at the main office in LA. "How long has this been going on?"

It couldn't have been that long. The opening of Chase's bar had only been last weekend, and Austin had even spoken to him on the phone a few days ago when they'd made plans for tonight.

"Since that guy showed up." Donna scrunched her nose. "Three days? No, four. Yeah."

"What guy?" It bothered Austin that he knew so little about Chase. Made it more difficult to help. Though, he did know Chase's family was near non-existent. It was really only Chase and his sister, and Austin had never heard him mentioning friends.

Chase was very introverted and circumspect, but Austin didn't believe it came without reason. He'd seen glimpses of a man who wanted more interaction, especially the times Austin and Cam had visited the bar before it opened. It was almost as if Chase forced himself to remain aloof—indifferent.

"I've never seen him before," Donna replied. "At first, I thought he was some psycho 'cause he showed up in only underwear." Austin's brows shot up in surprise and confusion. "Yeah. I didn't catch the entire—whatever it was that happened, and before I knew it, this guy was stumbling and stuttering apologies, and Chase looked... God, I've never seen anyone so mad."

Austin pressed his lips together in a thin line, suspicion creeping down his spine. "Did this guy have a lot of tattoos, by any chance?" At the end of the lane, they waited to cross a larger street, and Austin could see Chase's bar a few buildings into the next neighborhood.

"He did, yeah." Donna glanced up at Austin. "Do you know him? He had, like, dark hair, piercings—kinda short?"

Austin nodded firmly. He was fairly certain now it was Remy Stahl. "A ghost from the past." He smiled faintly, no desire to share more than Chase was comfortable with. Hell, Austin wasn't exactly comfortable with their past, either.

SIX

Chase had just finished serving the group of four bikers at the bar when Donna entered the establishment. *Right. She stepped out for her break.* Chase had almost forgotten.

What surprised him was that Austin trailed in after her.

Walking down to the end of the bar, Chase met Austin there, only the bartop separating them. In the meantime, Donna got back to work right away.

"How you doin', man?" Chase smiled carefully, curious about the visit.

"Can't complain, my friend. Can't complain." Austin looked around himself as he pushed his sunglasses to the top of his head. His hair was damp, as if he'd just walked outta the shower. "How are you?" Austin's eyes slid back to Chase.

"I'm…" A lie was at the tip of his tongue, but he couldn't do it. His mouth suddenly felt dry, his throat thick. "I, uh, I don't know." He looked away and ran a hand through his hair, tugging at the ends. He'd been doing that a lot lately.

If time could be divided into puzzle pieces, he was missing several. How long had Donna been gone? And wasn't Chase just in his office working on the books?

Then he remembered; his office had felt too stale and suffocating. Remy's letters were like a fire, and Chase was drawn to the burn.

He couldn't shake the queasiness.

Or the memory of Remy's face.

"Chase."

Chase whipped around, his gaze settling on Austin again. Who was here. With what looked like concern creasing his forehead.

"Um. Beer?" That was a reasonable question.

"No, thank you." Austin frowned and rested his elbows on the counter. "You don't look very well." Chase stared at him blankly. Austin seemed to debate something with himself. Before he dropped the bomb. "Has Remy been here?"

With that bomb, Chase's stomach dropped, too. His eyes flicked over to Donna, who was suddenly the picture of forced innocence. Glancing back, he met Austin's firm nod. Confirmation. Yes, he had spoken to Donna. Or Donna had spoken to Austin. And they came here together.

"Can we speak in private, Chase?"

Chase kept staring for a moment then nodded numbly.

*

Chase sat in his swivel chair, fidgeting, as Austin occupied the couch and read through Remy's letters.

Having been unable to keep everything bottled up, Chase had used a minimal amount of words and had chosen to reveal the letters instead. He'd managed to tell Austin about Remy's accidental visit, and Austin had made it clear he stopped listening when Chase had started lying, stating that he was okay. It was just a lot to process. He'd be back in shape in no time. A bit under the weather was all.

His embarrassment had caught up to him, hence the easy waterfall of fabricated truth. He had no right to be this distraught over a few fucking letters when Austin had once been stabbed. *And look at Austin now.* He was fine.

Chase's knee bounced. His fingers drummed on the desk. His foot tapped on the floor.

"Jesus Christ, Chase." Austin shook his head slowly, eyeing the letters in his hands. "You haven't opened up to *anybody* about these?"

Bounce, drum, tap.

OUTCOME

Chase forced himself to shrug. *Be casual. Stand on your own two feet without help.* "Nah." But he knew without a doubt that Austin could see through his act this time. "Ade knows they exist, but not what's in them." Maybe if he kept talking, it would get easier. Maybe his breathing would even out. Maybe his eyes would stop stinging.

Look at me.

Fucking pathetic.

Bounce, drum, tap-tap-tap-tap.

The silence stretched on, appearing interminable when it probably only lasted a few seconds.

Austin faced him again, serious. "You have to talk to someone about this, and I'd actually suggest you turn to Remy."

"I know." Chase's answer was automatic, spoken before he'd even registered Austin's words. "Wait, what?" He'd fully expected Austin to tell him to get over it and stop acting weak.

For fuck's sake, he was almost forty years old. That he couldn't keep his shit together only brought him shame. He wasn't looking for understanding or acceptance.

"Are you seeing Gale anymore?" Austin went on patiently, and Chase shook his head no. *God, no.* There was nothing to talk about. "You should," Austin pointed out. "Cam and I still go."

That shocked the hell outta Chase. His expression gave it away, too.

Austin chuckled and looked down at the letters again. "Not often, but yes. It's a nice security blanket, as Cam calls it." He smirked when he faced Chase once more. "And contact Remy. I think you could both benefit from it." He held up a letter. "He was obviously struggling back then, and maybe he still is."

Chase stared down at his lap, internally searching for the anger he'd lived on since he'd received Remy's letters. It simmered when he needed it to boil so badly.

But Remy hadn't been completely real until now. He'd been an idea, a villain in a comic book—easy to hate, easy to blame. Even if Chase hadn't actually blamed Remy for anything in a very long time, it had been hatred by association. Remy was related to Ben; therefore, he was a bad guy.

47

Too bad it didn't work like that in real life. Now that Chase had actually met Remy, heard his voice, seen the pain he was in, things had changed.

Every fiber of him was reluctant to contact Remy and see him again—even more so to ask for help, or demand it—but Chase couldn't exactly go on like this anymore.

"I—" He cleared his throat. "I think I need to get that over with before I regret it." *Or chicken out.* He met Austin's gaze hesitantly, letting out a breath of relief when there was no judgment in his eyes. "Maybe the woman who's renting his house knows where he is…?"

"It's possible." Austin nodded. "And seeing Gale again?"

"I'll think about it." It was the best Chase could offer right now.

A slow smile spread across Austin's lips. "Well…" Folding the letters, he placed them next to himself on the couch. "There's no time like the present. Remy's house happens to be on my street—as you know. Donna seems quite capable of manning the bar for a while, and your only plan for the evening was supposed to be a barbecue at our place."

Chase blinked. *Barbecue.* What was he…oh, goddammit. He'd talked to Austin. Chase remembered. Landon would be there too, with his wife and twin daughters.

"That was tonight?" He tugged at the ends of his hair, feeling like shit.

"Don't worry about it." Austin chuckled as he stood up. "You have a lot on your mind." He paused, offering a small smirk. "I'm guessing that's why you missed your appointment with Landon today, too."

"For the love of—" Chase cursed himself. The reminder was taped to the frame of his computer screen. *Ten o'clock, Nash's Auto Service.* The original plan had been to fix up his '37 Knucklehead this summer, restore it, and give it a paint job, but he couldn't muster up any enthusiasm for it at the moment.

*

OUTCOME

Chase walked the now-familiar way to Austin and Cam's street. Only this time, it wasn't a game night, poker night, or barbecue—not anymore, anyway. This was…Chase didn't know what the fuck it was.

"Remember what I said." Austin gave him a pointed look. "You can talk to us."

Chase nodded, wanting to thank Austin for…everything. But it would have to wait. He couldn't form a single word, though Austin seemed to understand. As usual. So, the two nodded their goodbyes, and Chase continued along the street.

The smell of pool cleaner and barbecue lingered in the dry air.

Some front lawns were greener than others.

The entire street gave Chase a suburban feel he'd never had growing up. Modest and clean, a few notches above working-class. One-story homes of white brick with picket fences and generous-sized driveways to prove it was a neighborhood for families. Households with more than one car, yet nothing ostentatious like gates or perfectly laid stone paths or ponds.

As he reached Remy's old house, he stuck his hands down into the pockets of his dark-wash jeans, his shoulders stiff, and walked up the paved driveway.

I should've put on more deodorant.

The day hadn't cooled enough yet, and his black T-shirt was like an extension of the sun.

Taking a deep breath, he rang the doorbell that looked new. In fact, everything around him looked new. Or cleaned, restored. From flowerbeds with new soil and a low picket fence that had recently been painted in a soft gray shade, to the brass doorbell that shone in the setting sun, and a kitchen window that still smelled of chemicals from cleaning it.

Chase was anxious, jittery, and uncomfortable, and he knew it showed. There was no sign of life as he leaned a few inches to the side to peer inside the kitchen, but there was a vintage car parked in the driveway. Someone had to be home, right? Everyone drove in California. A parked car meant you were home.

A bike in Chase's case. A cage wasn't for him.

49

He rang the bell again and ran a hand through his hair, getting frustrated. All he knew from Cam and Austin was that a woman lived here now. Could it be the woman—the friend—who had "kidnapped" Remy? No sign of children. The small front yard was empty aside from two flowerbeds with tiny white flowers and one young tree in a corner.

Chase was just about to give up when he heard the sound of feet padding closer on the other side of the door, causing him to stiffen up some more. Was he relieved or disappointed? He couldn't tell.

A petite brunette with red-rimmed eyes and wet tracks down her cheeks opened the door and looked up questioningly at him.

"Hi." She sniffled and cleared her throat. "Can I help you?"

SEVEN

Remy absently cupped his aching jaw and eyed the black steel cuff around his left ankle. This one wasn't furry, but it had white fucking polka dots. Yet, it was sturdy as shit.

Minna's got to be a freak in bed.

A three-foot long chain offered a bit of room to move, but not enough. The other end of that chain was attached to another cuff, which was secured to the solid, wooden footboard of the bed.

His plan had been to get back to LA and drink himself into oblivion. Instead, he'd ended up in the middle of nowhere outside Tehachapi, a shitty little town some thirty-plus miles southeast of Bakersfield.

He pulled at the chain, not for the first time, and cursed. No luck. Trapped.

If Minna was a stubborn little imp, her brother was a sadist. A sadist with good intentions, but a sadist nonetheless.

When Minna had gone to bed last night, Remy had waited a couple hours before he'd tried to sneak out of the house. But the minute he'd stepped out into the hallway, the light had been switched on, revealing Andy leaning casually against a wall. He was fairly slim and lanky, but the death glare he'd shot Remy proved he was more than capable of kicking some serious ass.

Andy sort of reminded Remy of a vampire. Unlike Minna's brown waves, kind eyes in that violet color, and the way she scrunched her nose endearingly, Andreas took after their father with alabaster skin, black hair, and steel-gray eyes. Add ink, piercings, and the fact that Andy was fiercely protective of his little sister, and you had one lethal bastard. Sure, he was Remy's friend too—a very close one, or had been—but he was first and foremost Minna's brother.

"That's strike two, Rem," was all Andreas had said last night. Next he'd proceeded to punch Remy in the face, then hauled him out to Minna's truck, leaving his own Cadillac behind. There'd been several grocery bags in the back seat, and when Remy had cocked a brow in question, Andy had only shrugged and backed out of the driveway.

An hour's drive into the black night later, Remy's heart had sunk when Andy stopped the truck. *The fucking cabin.* A small cabin Andy's father owned but hadn't used in years. That's what you got for befriending people from an outdoorsy family.

What had once been a killer place for high-school parties was now Remy's prison.

The grocery bags told Remy that Andreas had been expecting this. He'd known Remy was going to make a run for it.

Everything smelled like wood, the material Remy was surrounded by. Wooden beams, boards—hell, even the furniture. It was rustic and quaint. Only the fireplace was made out of stone.

As soon as Andreas had secured Remy to the one and only bed, he'd switched on the power, the few electrical items buzzing to life with noises that screamed of disuse and age. The small fridge in the corner was made in the '70s, for fuck's sake.

The whole cabin consisted of one room and a sleeping nook. There wasn't even a bathroom inside. There was, however, an outhouse in the back. If you wanted to shower, you had to go to the camping site farther down the hillside. Or you could step outside and shower under the garden hose, which, of-fucking-course, meant ice-cold water.

Lovely.

The fridge that was now packed with food let out another ringing *trrrrr-kadunk* sound, causing Remy to scowl at it. He'd been quiet about this kidnapping so far because he didn't want to meet the end of another fist, but when Andy returned...oh, Remy was going to pitch a goddamn fit.

Who knew where the sadist was now? Probably calling

Minna. There was no reception up here, Remy remembered. But there had to be more to it because Andy had been gone a few hours.

The old clock on the wall showed it was just past noon.

It was hot, high 90s, and Remy had the mother of all headaches. The trees in the mountain park cast a shadow over the cabin, but this was still California. In the summer. That meant heat, the night being the only exception. With the elevation...? The temperature dropped significantly at night, a big contrast to the dry boil of the day.

Leaving the bed, Remy took one step toward the window near the door. He grunted, the wall a few inches out of reach. The chain received a glare, as if that would help. Then he repositioned himself, stretched as far as he could, and finally managed to open the window with a push. Lastly, he got halfway to the round kitchen table in the middle of the room before the cuffs protested, but it was enough for him to snatch up the pack of smokes and a lighter from the table.

Andreas had been *kind* enough to leave a glass of water on the wooden nightstand, so Remy figured it'd be his ashtray.

He lit up the smoke and ran a hand through his messy hair. A gentle breeze hit his naked torso, reminding him he didn't have any clothes here. He was only wearing a pair of basketball shorts, but perhaps his kidnapper was getting him some more?

The irony seeped into him, but instead of finding it funny, dread filled him. More guilt, too. He was complaining about his friends keeping him away from drugs and alcohol; meanwhile, the men who had been kidnapped by his half brother more than three years ago...they knew *real* suffering.

As it often did, the guilt threatened to crush him, which was exactly why he preferred to stay intoxicated.

The sound of wheels crunching on rocky dirt outside made him push away those thoughts for now, and he kept his eyes trained on the door until Andy entered the cabin with two duffel bags and a white table fan.

"I see you haven't chewed off your leg to escape." Andy gave him a mild look on his way over to the corner cabinets by the fridge and the small sink. He stuffed the cupboards with everything from clothes and soap to blankets and water. "If you succeed, you can always walk down to the campsite, sell your ass for a few bucks, and take the bus to LA."

Remy didn't take the bait. Didn't show that it stung because it was well-deserved. "How long are you planning on keeping me here?"

"As long as it takes." Andy shrugged and sat down at the table, twisting the cap off a bottle of Coke. He also followed Remy's lead and sparked up a smoke. *Menthols.* Gross. "I won't be here all the time—I got the studio and my girl, too."

Right. Remy had almost forgotten Andy's fiancée. Last he heard, she was pregnant. "You can always let me go right now."

Andy's mouth quirked up. "'Cause you've been doin' such a bang-up job on your own."

"Depends on what the goal is."

Andy nodded with a dip of his chin. "Well, our goals aren't the same. I don't give a flying fuck if you're stuck out here for months. You're gonna get all the toxins outta your system, get rid of the worst of the itch, and stop putting your friends through hell."

Months? Try, until breathing wasn't a chore.

And Remy was a Stahl, wasn't he? Putting people through hell was evidently what they did. "For the record, I haven't had a fucking drink in over a week now, and—"

"And who can you thank for that?" Andreas shot at him.

Remy gnashed his teeth and continued. "Secondly, I'm not your responsibility."

"We don't want your death on our conscience, either." Andy looked tired, but no less ticked off. "It's one or the other, Rem. Guess which one we're going with." He shook his head and flicked away some ash into a miniature ceramic cup. "I know what you've been through, but what do you think those guys—the men who were taken by Ben—would think if they knew you were throwing away your life?" He leveled Remy with a serious look. "They had no choice. You, on the other hand, are wasting away willingly."

OUTCOME

Remy knew Andy was right, but it didn't erase the fact that Remy believed he was worthless. During his thirty years on this planet, he'd caused more hurt to people than he'd helped. He'd caused more pain than he'd done good.

"Send me to rehab." It was his last attempt to get away for now.

Andy smiled. "Do I look stupid? As far as I know, you haven't committed a crime, so they wouldn't exactly be able to detain you. You'd be free to leave whenever, and we can't have that."

Remy admitted defeat.

*

The whole day passed in silence.

Andy played with his phone, disappeared a few times to call Minna and his fiancée, prepared a few sandwiches for lunch and dinner, and flipped through a couple body-art magazines to pass time.

Remy did nothing, aside from take two bathroom breaks where Andy followed him like a guard dog. Remy dozed off here and there as well, but sleeping without chemicals in his system to knock him out cold didn't work. There were too many nightmares. If he didn't see his mom's body in a pool of blood or *feel* the piercing screams of ten men being burned alive, he heard Ben's scratchy voice asking for more cash.

In the distance, he could hear a vehicle coming closer, and Andy didn't look surprised. Remy guessed it was a shift change and Minna was going to take over.

"That would be my replacement." Andreas stood up and grabbed the keys to Minna's truck. Did that mean Minna was driving Andy's Cadillac? Probably. "I almost wanna stick around to make sure he won't kill you, but Minna's vouching for him."

Remy sat up straighter in bed. "Who's coming?"

Aside from Minna, it was slim pickings. Of course, it could be Dan or Martinez, who worked at Andy's studio, but Remy had never been that close to them. They were friendly, sure, and they'd all gone out together in the past, but he doubted they'd be up for babysitting an alleged addict.

"I think you know him." The sadist's eyes glimmered. "Chase Gallardo?"

"Wh—?" Remy choked on his own saliva. In a heartbeat, his entire posture changed. Fear threatened to cripple him, and he broke out in a cold sweat. It reminded him of the days after Minna had kidnapped him and he'd ached, sweated, and shaken for alcohol. "You're k-kidding." There was *no* way Chase would come here, was there? No. It didn't make any sense whatsoever. Unless…

Unless Chase had tracked Remy down—couldn't have been that difficult—and had charmed his way into Minna's good graces, gotten directions to the cabin, and was now going to beat Remy within an inch of his life.

That made sense.

"No." Andy shouldered his messenger bag and stuffed his magazines into it. "Minna's under the impression you and Chase have unfinished business, and maybe she's right. Maybe you guys need to talk." He shrugged and reached for the door. "Chase has questions—that's all I know."

Remy couldn't answer because he was too busy fighting off a panic attack.

"I'll be back tomorrow." A flicker of concern flashed in Andreas's eyes before his mouth tightened in determination. Whatever he and Minna believed was about to happen, they were clearly on board. "We want the old Remy back, man. Do you understand that?"

No, Remy didn't. He hardly remembered his old self. It was a whole other person—one who had a sharp wit, loved sarcasm, was carefree, worked hard, and helped his friends whenever he could.

The soft, muted click of the door being shut behind Andy echoed in Remy's head, the sound reverberating inside his skull. Left alone. For now. He could hear quiet voices outside, but no words were clear enough.

His heart was racing, and he swallowed convulsively.

OUTCOME

Why did Andreas and Minna insist on this?
His money had funded a kidnapping.
By default, that made him guilty.

EIGHT

Chase could barely believe he was here. A world away and mindfucked, it felt like.

He pulled off his helmet and pushed down the kickstand on his bike. Around him, he saw trees, a small cabin, hillsides, and more trees. The ground was dry and all but empty of leaves, the shimmering sunlight bouncing off the sandy ground. Laughter traveled with the slight breeze—or maybe it was within earshot—from a nearby campsite he'd passed earlier.

Removing one of the black bandanas he kept tied around his wrists, he wiped his forehead with it, then stuck it into the back pocket of his jeans.

With everything happening so quickly, Chase didn't feel entirely present. It was only yesterday he'd spoken to Austin about seeking out Remy, and now Chase was here. In the middle of nowhere.

I have twenty-four hours when I'm not even sure I'd like twenty-four minutes.

The man who exited the cabin introduced himself as Andreas Eriksson. He seemed polite enough but threatened Chase much like Minna had, although their approaches were completely different.

Chase had only needed to give Minna his full name, and then she'd known exactly what was going on. She knew who he was. Maybe she knew about the letters, too. Maybe she didn't. They weren't mentioned. Minna's only concern was to get her best friend back.

"I think—I think it could be good. If you talked, I mean." She'd stuttered over her words, through her tears. *"But don't hurt him. My brother will kill you."*

"Touch one hair on his head..." Andreas let his warning hang there.

Chase was honestly too busy admiring the loyalty and protection Remy had in his life to be scared of Andreas. Chase had a couple inches on the man, was broader too, but he was sure Andreas could inflict some serious pain. But physical pain didn't really touch Chase. He didn't fear it.

"I only wanna talk to him." Chase didn't shy away from Andreas's stare, nor did he fumble or fidget like he'd done yesterday. "Your sister told me she'd be here tomorrow. She'll find Remy in the same condition you left him." He'd made too many arrangements for this to fail now; perhaps that had been enough to let this whole situation settle.

The only time Chase had really hesitated about coming out here was when he realized he couldn't just up and leave his bar. His hands had been shaking when he'd picked up the phone—too chickenshit to just see Austin and Cam in person—and asked for help. To his surprise, though, Austin had been all for it.

"I'm going crazy being home alone anyway. Riley's with friends, and Cam's working late this week before his vacation starts."

Flooded with gratitude, Chase had probably rambled too much, over and over assuring that Donna could fill Austin in. *"She's already agreed to work double shifts."* Hell, he had *friends*, and he owed them. Repeating the fact that he had friends never got old. Making things up to them would feel...good. 'Cause he fucking cherished them, and he wanted to be a good friend in return.

Refocusing on Andreas, who was obviously considering and regarding, Chase realized he had his own Andreas and Minna at home in Bakersfield.

It strengthened his resolve to get through this, and it was almost as if Andreas could see the determination in Chase's eyes 'cause he nodded.

"All right. There's some shit you gotta know." Andreas pulled out—*what the fuck?*—a small key from his pocket. "For the past year, Rem's been drinking too much. He's not a stranger to drugs, either. Hard drugs."

*

Remy nearly jumped out of his skin when the door opened and Chase walked in. He closed the door and stood still, keeping his back to Remy.

It's a nightmare. He's not really here.

Too bad he couldn't lie to himself.

Remy had been too terrified to analyze Chase Gallardo's appearance last time, only registering *handsome* and *sexy*, but he was prepared this time. Forget about how hot Chase was, though. Remy didn't have a one-track mind. All he could see now was a badass biker in his late thirties who'd been born and raised in conservative Bakersfield.

Not only did Remy carry blame for the kidnapping, but he was a *fag*.

Chewing on his lip ring, he recalled Cameron Nash and Austin Huntley; he knew they were married. Could Chase be friends with them?

The silence was deafening, and Remy couldn't be more on edge. He sat on the bed, his bare feet touching the wooden floorboards. He felt…exposed, and not only because he wasn't wearing a shirt. Shirt! *Oh shit, shit, shit.* He quickly pulled up a leg, his arms hugging it to him. *There.* Hopefully, that was enough to hide the Joshua tree he had tattooed on the side of his ribcage.

After what felt like an eternity and a half, Chase turned. His dark gray T-shirt stretched across his chest, and he only gave Remy a quick glance before he closed the distance to the round table in the middle of the room. Remy followed every movement. Chase tossed his leather jacket over a chair. His helmet landed on the table. There was a small gym bag that was dropped to the floor.

Chase sat down in a chair, imposing and large, and lifted a booted foot up to rest it on his knee. He eyed the pack of smokes Andreas had left behind. He ran a hand through his hair, blew out a breath, scratched his scruffy jaw—Mother of Christ, Remy was losing his mind. Was he even breathing? He kept waiting for Chase to pull out a knife or a gun or something. *Chinese throwing stars?* Who knew.

When their eyes met, Remy swallowed against what felt like razors. Chase's stance was composed and casual, but it was forced.

"Are you here to kill me?" Remy finally blurted out. *Shit.*

Chase's brows lifted then dipped into a frown. "Is that what you want?"

"What—" What kind of fucking question was *that*? Remy scowled, impatient now. If Chase was gonna beat him, kill him…*get it over with*. There was no reason to sit around and chitchat about it. "Are you asking me if I want to die?"

Chase offered a one-shouldered shrug. "After what your friends have told me, I'd say it's a legit question."

That worked like a cold shower, and Remy looked away. Had Andy and Minna told Chase about the drugs, too? Fucking obviously. Otherwise, Chase would've asked about Remy's left foot being cuffed to the bed.

He couldn't reply. His words got stuck in his throat. Because it was easier to treat your loved ones like shit. Sad as it was. He never bit his tongue around Andy and Minna, but telling a stranger about his fucked state…no. And definitely not a stranger like Chase.

"Kidnapping seems to be a running theme around here."

Remy flinched at the reminder. "I'm sorry." He stared at the floor, haunting memories assaulting him hard enough to bring tears to his eyes. There was no way he'd look up now. "Why are you even here? I have to be the last person you want to see."

Chase didn't answer right away, and Remy wondered why. He knew the answer, and Chase didn't strike him as a man who sugarcoated things or held back the truth to spare someone's feelings.

Why *was* Chase here?

Remy couldn't exactly forget the fury Chase's glare had unleashed in that bar. He couldn't forget the only response he'd gotten to his letters, either.

Don't ever contact me again.

"You know it wasn't your fault, right?"

At that, Remy's head snapped up. He must've heard that wrong. Right? Chase's statement had been so quiet; maybe Remy was imagining things now, too.

Blinking past the stinging, Remy's vision cleared enough for him to see that Chase was being serious. Which was un-fucking-believable. It wasn't *fair*. For the past year, Remy had walked the path of destruction he was comfortable on. He *belonged* there. There was a sense of gratification in suffering because his conviction that he deserved it was bone-deep.

Hearing Chase, the ultimate man and threat and victim, say it *wasn't* Remy's fault… He didn't know whether to laugh or cry.

He got desperate. He needed clarification. "Wasn't my fault that Hitler killed so many people? True."

Chase's forehead creased. "What?" He sat forward. "Why are you bringing up the Holocaust? Are you high?"

I wish. "No. I just want to know—specifically—what is not my fault."

"Then fucking say so." Chase sat back again and fiddled with the lighter on the table. "It's not your fault that you had a sick brother who—"

"Half brother." Remy would never refer to Fred and Ben as his brothers. There had been a time when he would've claimed otherwise, but no more. The mere thought made him sick. "We don't have the same mother."

"It's not your fault," Chase repeated. "This shit is all on Ben."

You're wrong, Remy wanted to tell him. He wanted to fucking scream it.

Gone was the fear. Replaced with anger. Anger toward Chase for even attempting to put a pothole in Remy's road. He'd continue to walk it until the day he died. No one could erase the guilt—not even the man who was Remy's biggest source of it.

"We all have our opinions," he told Chase instead. Fuck, he'd actually lost respect for the man. He'd relied on Chase's disgust and fury. He still needed Chase's rejection to burn like a goddamn wildfire. "Who are you, and what have you done to the guy who told me to fuck off?" He got pissy.

This was really getting to him.

Chase chuckled humorlessly. "Kid, if you figure me out, be sure to let me know. Hell if I have a clue." He scrubbed his hands down his face. "Up until a few days ago, I was fine trying to ignore the past and live on anger." As he spoke, his gaze never strayed from the lighter.

A muscle in Remy's jaw ticked. The irritation wouldn't budge, but he was curious, too. "What changed?" But even as he asked the question, he suspected the answer. Something or someone had triggered Chase's change of heart, and it infuriated Remy to believe it was himself.

"When you left my bar…" Chase trailed off, frowning. *My* bar, he'd said. Remy filed that away. "I went through your letters again—"

"You kept them?" Remy asked incredulously.

At first, Chase looked at him blankly, as if it wasn't weird he'd saved Remy's letters. Then a flicker of embarrassment— because he realized it *was* weird? *Let's hope so*, Remy thought dryly. It was weird. It was completely fucked-up that Chase had kept such a reminder of his past. But, regardless, a neutral expression took over, and Chase nodded curtly.

"I read them again, and I didn't…react…as strongly." Chase cleared his throat, uncomfortable. Remy could tell a mile away, and his image of Chase was shattering. "I got sorta lost in my head. A friend intervened, read the letters, and told me to contact you. I agreed. I think."

Remy couldn't believe it. The stone-faced bad boy had caved. Just like that? What, his hatred for Remy had simply evaporated?

"You're out of your mind," he said flatly.

That caused a reaction Remy actually wanted.

"Watch it, kid," Chase gritted out. "I'm not that fond of you, and I don't have much to lose. Breaking my promise to your friends about not laying a finger on you wouldn't take much."

Remy stiffened and went from a condescending prick to a

skittish animal looking for an escape. Chase's glare made Remy feel two feet tall and scoot backward on the bed. The chain clinked mutedly against the bed frame as Remy's back hit the wall.

The sound of the chain garnered Chase's attention, and his mouth twisted into a mocking little smirk. "That's cute—with the polka dots. Does it come with matching wrist cuffs?" He lifted his gaze to Remy's face.

Remy bristled. Anxious or not, no one made fun of him. "Did yours?" he shot back and instantly regretted it. *Holy shit, what's wrong with me?* He could feel his face paling.

Chase said nothing. The only indication that he was furious was the tension in the man's jaw. A storm was brewing in his deep blue eyes.

"I'm sorry." Remy gnashed his teeth together, spotting the uneven, white lines around Chase's wrist. He was still fiddling absently with that fucking lighter, and the scars from Ben's torture shone like a beacon. Without consent, Remy's eyes strayed to Chase's other hand, but there was a black bandana tied around that wrist.

"No. Mine didn't have polka dots." Chase's tone had softened, but it was—if possible—even more threatening now. Lethal. Barely restrained.

"I'm sorry," Remy repeated, whispering. He wasn't breathing.

It dawned on him that he wanted to feel Chase's pain. Literally. Remy wanted to hurt—physically. He already had the emotional drama down. Now he wanted to be shaken, pushed, shoved, *fucking punched*. He wanted Chase to inflict it.

A Stahl had hurt Chase. Chase could hurt a Stahl, too.

Scream at me, kick me, make me feel it.

All he had to do was push Chase's buttons…

But before he could even come up with a plan on how to enrage Chase to the point where he exploded, Chase pushed his chair back and left the cabin with Andy's forgotten smokes.

NINE

Chase hadn't given the cigarettes a single thought when he'd stormed out of the cabin to cool off. Yet, they were in his hand. The lighter, too.

Standing near his bike, his hand shook as he lit a smoke and took a deep pull from it. *Too much.* Fuck, he almost choked. Instead, he coughed into a fist and screwed his eyes shut. They were fucking menthols, *and* it had been over a year since he'd smoked his last cigarette.

That's how much that motherfucker pissed me off.

Chase was torn between ripping Remy a new one and just feeling sorry for him. It was hysterical—this whole situation. Chase wanted answers to his questions, but that was about it. He wasn't here to make friends or explain why he didn't blame Remy anymore. He sure as fuck wasn't gonna coddle the little shit.

In the same breath, Chase also understood him, and he did have sympathy for Remy.

The guilt? It was there. Everywhere. It had been one of the first things Chase had seen. Remy was hanging on by a thread.

Looking down at the smoke between his fingers, Chase mulled over the latest events that had turned his life upside down, which wasn't easy. Too much had happened in the last twenty-four hours, and being so used to having nothing happening at all, Chase couldn't think straight. He didn't even know what he was feeling. Each emotion was too fleeting. Nothing stuck, except for the question he couldn't stop asking himself.

What the hell am I doing?

He took another pull from the smoke, this one smaller, and he chuckled humorlessly to himself. Didn't work. He wanted that sweet fill any addiction gave when indulged, but it wasn't there. All he tasted was charcoal, and every intake of air felt like ice.

Fucking menthol.

Chase dropped the smoke on the ground, stubbed it out with the toe of his boot, then trudged back inside.

The view that greeted him inside the cabin was both amusing and goddamn sad. Remy's head snapped up, his eyes wide—*caught ya, bastard*—and he was frozen in place, mid-tug. The little prick had been pulling at his restraint, and it was surprisingly easy to ignore the déjà vu-like moment.

A little over three years ago, Chase had been struggling fruitlessly against his own cuffs, although he hadn't been cuffed at the foot.

His ankle is red.

"Stop that shit." Chase knew he sounded irritated, indicating that maybe he wasn't so unaffected by the sight, after all.

"I thought you were leaving." Remy sat back on the bed, pulling up his knee.

Chase ignored that and returned to his seat, where his helmet and bag still were. Like he'd leave without that? Kid must be dense. "You asked me before why I'm here." He assessed Remy, annoyed by the fact that he was only wearing those basketball shorts. "I, uh…I have questions. About the investigation." He averted his eyes to the table and traced marks in the wood with the lighter, much like he'd done earlier.

Would it be so hard to put on a damn shirt? Or at least cover the barbells in his nipples. Chase didn't wanna admit that he found Remy's body art sexy.

There were a lot of things he didn't wanna admit to where Remy was concerned.

"I know as much as you do." Remy shifted and sat cross-legged instead but folded his arms across his ribcage. "Actually, you should know more. I only know what was in the papers. Sort of."

Sort of. "Let's visit 'sort of,' then," Chase drawled. "We never learned why Ben kidnapped us."

That seemed to hit a nerve with Remy. "Because he was a sick fuck?" He glared. "Are you looking for a damn interview with me? Huh? You wanna learn the ins and outs of the Stahls?"

Chase shrugged. "Sure. Call it whatever the hell you want." He wanted his answers, and he had no doubt Remy was gonna give them to him. The kid had been obnoxious at best, but he could see through that bullshit façade without trouble. When push came to shove, Remy was scared. Any amount of cockiness... Well, Chase didn't understand it, but it didn't faze him, either.

Maybe Remy wanted to pretend he had big balls.

With an internal chuckle, Chase recalled Minna telling him that Remy lived mostly in LA now, and Chase hoped he wasn't there to become an actor. The kid would suck at it.

"Too bad I'm not in the mood." Remy stared at him defiantly. "You could always track down Fred and Clarissa. They live in Milwaukee now." That would be Remy's other half brother and stepmother. Ben's mother. Chase knew they'd left the state. They'd taken Bill Stahl, the demented patriarch of the family, with them. "Maybe they can help."

Chase furrowed his brows, confused by Remy's behavior. "You never hesitated to share your family drama in one of those letters. Now you're saying you're over it?"

"Maybe." Remy scratched his eyebrow, the one that had another barbell through it. "Whatever. Go chase your Lifetime script somewhere else, dude."

What the fuck?

What was he pushing for? Remy had been a basket case in the letters—not to mention extremely apologetic and shameful— and now he was mouthing off like a fucking douchebag? It made no sense.

"Are you comparing my time in captivity to a Lifetime movie?" Chase asked in an eerily calm tone.

There was no way Remy could hide the way his face turned ashen, but he did try. Instead of looking stricken, like he'd done last time he put his foot in his mouth, he shot Chase a quick, dismissive smirk and looked out the window.

Chase had been thrown for a loop, and he actually looked

over his shoulder to see if anyone else was here. Someone who deserved to be mocked. But no…of course it was only Chase and Remy here.

"So…I think I'm gonna go to bed." Remy faked a yawn and grabbed a bundle of linens off the nightstand. Chase narrowed his eyes on the ink adorning Remy's ribcage and wondered why the hell he had a Joshua tree tattooed there. The view was gone the second Remy fanned out the sheet to use as a blanket. There already was a sheet covering the mattress, but it was too hot out here for blankets and covers.

Chase shook his head quickly, dazed. "Are…" *Are you serious? You're brushing me off, you little pissant? And what's with the goddamn tree?* Chase was unfairly possessive of that tree, and it was infuriating to see an image of one on Remy's pale torso. Remy's behavior didn't make shit better.

Chase had to be missing something. Was all that crap in the letters an act?

"Are, what?" Remy was on his back now, the white sheet covering his body up to his collarbone. One knee up, tenting the fabric. One cuffed foot dangling over the edge of the bed. His arm, slim but tightly muscled, folded under his head.

Chase's eyes followed Remy's bicep, the ink there, passing the dark patch of hair under his armpit. There wasn't much of it; was it soft or coarse? Then he stopped at Remy's face. He was a young man of so many contrasts, and Chase loathed the attraction he felt. Once again, it reminded him of the last time he'd caved.

He knew all his contempt was visible in his glare, but it only seemed to amuse Remy.

Was it real, though? Was Remy having fun with this? Did he think this was some kinda joke? The way Remy worried his lip ring with his teeth and tapped his foot rapidly against the bed frame suggested otherwise. It reminded him of a nervous tick, but Chase didn't know this guy.

"Are you a mute now?" Remy grinned.

The tapping of his foot increased.

Chase tilted his head, studying the kid. It would be incredibly easy to shut Remy up with a threat, but Chase had already warned him once. It would seem empty if nothing came of it. Next time Chase threatened Remy, it would be the last chance before he resorted to violence.

I'm not a saint.

He wasn't stupid, either. Something was up.

"I thought you were gonna sleep." Chase decided right then and there not to let Remy get to him.

*

Obviously Remy wasn't falling asleep. Silence overtook the small cabin, but the tension didn't lift.

Keeping his eyes closed, he tried to summon the courage to carry out the plan that had formed in his head, but he wasn't there yet.

Come on, you coward.

He let out a breath as he heard Chase rummaging around in the fridge. A moment later, a soda can was opened with a pop and a fizz, and the chair creaked as the bad-boy biker sat down again.

A bead of sweat trickled down Remy's temple. His hand shaking, he slowly moved it down his body.

"I want to get off." It was a damn struggle to get the words out. "You d-don't mind, do you?"

The soda can—or something else—thumped down on the table, but that was the only sound. Chase said nothing.

Remy swallowed against the dryness in his throat. Torn between hysteria and despair. He was close to his breaking point, but he needed Chase to do the breaking.

"You're hot as fuck," Remy went on, a slight rasp in his voice. His cheeks heated up with the humiliation he was putting himself through. "If it's all right, I'll picture you sucking me off." He grasped his cock underneath the fabric of his shorts, but there was no way he'd get hard. He was too close to having a full-blown panic attack. "Or you fucking my mouth? Shit. I'd love that."

Still no response.

It was now or never, so Remy sucked in a breath and

opened his eyes. He forced himself to sit up and lean back against the wall, facing Chase dead-on.

Chase was…murderous, no doubt. There was barely any blue left in his eyes, taken over by dark fury. Leaning forward, he rested his elbows on his knees and clenched and unclenched his jaw. A heavy sigh.

Remy saw a flicker of pity.

It was the last fucking thing he wanted to see.

Where was the violence? Where were the fists? Why was he still breathing? Instead, he sat there on the bed like the world's biggest failure and jacked his soft dick under the sheet that pooled around his middle.

"Come on, Chase." Remy plastered a grin on his face, his throat closing up and the edges of his vision blurring. "You want a blow job?"

To Remy's surprise, Chase didn't grow angrier. If anything, dim light swept over the darkness in his eyes. More pity, or whatever it was. Replacing the rage Remy was counting on.

Chase shook his head slowly. "What happened to you, Remy?"

"Oh, fuck you." Remy bit off a choked-up laugh. He wasn't going to last much longer. "I'm disappointed." Unable to go on, his hand fell to his side. "You're supposed to…" He couldn't look Chase in the eye anymore. "I don't know, beat the shit out of me? Don't tell me it's not tempting." With a small tilt of his head, he saw Chase's frown in his periphery. "I'm right here, the little fag who had you kidnapped—"

"Ben kidnapped me," Chase corrected impatiently.

If that's how it's gonna be. Remy only had one more card to play, and he smiled as a traitorous tear rolled down his cheek. "But I funded him. If it weren't for my money, he wouldn't have been able to afford it." Nausea grew like a cancer in his gut as he watched all the color drain from Chase's face. "Yeah, I bet that changes everything." He wondered morbidly which bones Chase was going to break. His nose? Ribs? Arms, legs? "See, I was so caught up in my little fantasy. I wanted Ben and Fred to include me in the family, so I did everything they asked. Fred wanted me to pick up his car and have it cleaned? I was there. Ben wanted money? I gave it to him."

*

For one second, Chase had feared the worst—that Remy had actually been involved in the kidnapping. But then as the kid had continued his sudden verbal vomit, Chase understood it wasn't like that at all. Like the scratching sound of a record coming to an abrupt stop, time slowed or maybe even restarted, and everything became clear.

Remy was trembling, sick with the guilt he carried. Chase saw it.

Averting his eyes to the floor, Chase tuned Remy out and tried to come to grips with what he'd heard, but it was close to impossible. Too many what-ifs that could make any man lose his mind. What if Remy hadn't given a shit about Ben? What if he hadn't done everything in his power to earn the approval from the other Stahls? What if Remy hadn't been fucking loaded?

What if Ben hadn't been insane?

"It—" That came out too raspy, so Chase cleared his throat and tried again, but he kept his gaze downcast. "It still wasn't your fault." The words tasted like acid, regardless of how true they were.

He found himself in a downward spiral, the emotions rolling around inside him making him dizzy. Anger came at him from every direction. Injustice was everywhere, and it never did anyone any good to get stuck in that bottomless pit, but it was hard to stop. With the maniac that was Ben Stahl dead and turned into charcoal, there was no one to attack. Instead the fury grew and grew, and it wasn't enough to just say, *"I'm angry at the whole situation."*

Chase didn't know what to do with all his rage.

"Say that one more time and I'll…" Remy's voice, devoid of any emotion, trailed off into nothing.

"You'll what?" Chase lifted his gaze, his head feeling heavier than ever. "I'm just telling you how it is. You wanted his approval, so you gave him money." Even to his own ears, it sounded hollow. He felt the goddamn truth, but he needed to process it before he could stand by his statement fully. And that…that wasn't right, either. He *did* stand by his words, yet…

Maybe he simply wasn't the right man to help Remy.

"If I'd been smart—" Remy gritted his teeth and tapped his temple. "If I'd at least asked him what he was going to do with the money…"

Like Ben would've been honest.

Chase pressed his lips into a grim line. "Thinking about what-ifs never works. Trust me."

"I want you to hit me." Remy wasn't listening to him. "It's too much. In here." He clutched his stomach, his chest heaving with a labored breath. "I need something. Everything or nothing. If you can't be a man and make me suffer, which I deserve, then give me something to numb it all out."

Drugs. Remy wanted drugs.

"That's not gonna happen." Chase watched Remy lying down in a fetal position. "Would suffering make you feel better? If I punched you right now, would it ease your pain?"

"*Yes.*" Remy screwed his eyes shut. A shudder rippled through his body, and Chase saw how his pale skin glistened with sweat. "I can't, Chase. I can't deal with it."

Chase ignored that and continued. "So you wanna feel better? That's what you're saying?" He stared hard, *willing* Remy to open his eyes. "You say you deserve to feel pain, but you also say it'll make you feel better. Do you deserve to feel better?"

That did it. Remy's eyes flashed open. Bleary and teary, he glared at Chase.

Chase merely stood up and walked over to the fridge. The sun had set, so he switched on a couple smaller lamps on the way. "I'm not gonna hit you. When was the last time you ate?"

"Get the fuck out of here." Remy coughed and wiped his forehead on the sheet. "You're useless."

Your brother's told me that before, Chase thought, but he wasn't about to surrender. The part of Chase that always wanted to fix problems had taken over. He couldn't help it. He was involved now, and if he couldn't take care of his own issues, then perhaps he could at least help with Remy's. Whether Chase was ready for it or not. Hell, whether *Remy* was ready for it or not.

Chase made a simple sandwich and grabbed a bottle of water, then headed to the little sleeping nook.

"Don't," Remy warned.

Chase ignored him and set down the food and the water on the nightstand. Only, the second the plate touched the wooden surface, Remy twisted around and kicked the nightstand hard enough for it to fall over.

"I said, don't!" Remy shouted. "Are you fucking deaf, Gallardo?" His outburst stunned Chase into immobility for several seconds. "I don't want your help." Remy started struggling against his restraints. "I'm not looking for a damn savior! Just let me go! Let me out of here!"

The chafing of the cuff around Remy's ankle was enough for Chase to snap outta his frozen state, and he tried to pull away Remy's hands from tugging at it.

"No!" Remy pushed at him, though Chase didn't budge. "You motherfucker, I don't want you here!" When he managed to deliver a knee to Chase's gut, Chase had had it. "Get out!"

"Enough!" Chase growled. In a swift move, he had Remy pinned to the bed, and he glowered lividly as the kid's eyes grew large with fear. Not for the first time. "Jesus Christ, Remy." He gnashed his teeth together at the pain in his stomach. "What the hell is wrong with you?!"

Earlier when Remy had pulled that stupid stunt—about "wanting to get off"—Chase had struggled against his desire for about a second. Until he'd seen through Remy's charade.

This, however, wasn't a game. And there was no lust anywhere. Chase was bewildered and shocked; he couldn't get a grasp on why he had this need to give Remy simple *comfort*. In other words, there was no room for anything else right now.

"Let go of me." Remy thrashed under Chase, the chain to the cuff rattling every time Remy tried to kick himself free. "You're fucking heavy."

Chase grunted and gathered Remy's wrists above them on

73

the pillow, then looked down between them and cursed when he saw blood trickling from Remy's foot. At a loss for what to do, Chase tightened his grip on Remy's hands and planted his knee over the leg that was cuffed to keep it from moving.

"Stop fighting me!" Chase snapped.

"Get off," Remy choked out. He was...fucking lost. Panicking or falling apart, Chase didn't know, but Remy was *gone*. Tears streaked his cheeks. "Please, I can't..." His eyes closed, and his entire body started convulsing.

"Shit." Worry and dread crept up Chase's spine, and he cupped Remy's cheek. "Remy. Look at me."

"Leave me," he whimpered through shallow breaths.

"I can't do that." Chase eased away as Remy stopped struggling. Producing the key Andreas had given him earlier, Chase unlocked the cuff and gently lifted Remy's foot. "Come on. We're getting some air."

Considering how Remy could barely walk on his own, Chase didn't worry about anybody escaping. He hooked Remy's arm around his neck and guided the kid out the door.

It was completely dark by now, and after helping Remy into the one and only lawn chair below the window, Chase hurried back inside and retrieved the water bottle from the floor and a packet of tissues. Then he joined Remy outside again and squatted down on the ground in front of him.

Remy's breathing was coming easier now, but he was still crying silently.

Chase lowered one knee to the ground. "What happened in there?" he asked quietly as he brought Remy's injured foot up to his leg.

Remy shrugged then winced and hissed when Chase poured some water over the redness that circled his ankle. "Sometimes it's too much."

Chase nodded, carefully patting the wound dry. "You break down often?"

"No." Remy raised his gaze. "That's why alcohol is amazing."

Chase sighed and sat back on his heels. "You don't want

any help, do you?"

He already knew Remy's answer, but what he chose to focus on was that Remy hesitated before he actually replied. Vulnerability shone in his pale green eyes until resignation tightened his features and he delivered a steely no.

So stubborn.

He was even worse than Chase.

"I'm done talking." Remy leaned back in the chair and blew out a slow breath. "What a fucking night." He closed his eyes and absently scratched his bare chest.

Chase eyed the Joshua tree on Remy's ribcage, wanting to ask about it, but he refrained. It felt personal—too personal—and Chase wasn't ready to get to know Remy. Talking about the past they shared…it was becoming abundantly clear Chase had suppressed his need to do that for a long time, and he was done running. But more than that…? No.

"We could get through this, you know." Chase squinted due to the faint porch light above Remy. He felt exposed talking about this—especially with Remy Stahl—but the sooner he could defeat his demons, the faster he could move on with his life. One day, he'd like to sit down with his friends and not have to force his smiles. "I got my own guilt to deal with," he admitted to Remy for the first time, "but I'm not even gonna pretend I can do it alone. I've tried and failed these past three years."

One of the countless knots that made up the tight ropework around Chase's chest loosened at his admission. It was a fucking relief, but the feeling of exposure had grown.

Gallardos weren't supposed to show weakness. Or rely on others.

Stand on your own two feet without help.

Gallardos weren't supposed to be gay, either…

Remy frowned and pulled his lip ring between his teeth. "What on earth could you possibly feel guilty about?"

Where do I start? Chase chuckled, a quiet and wry sound, and ran a hand over his head. "I could tell you right now, but…" A plan took shape as the words left Chase's mouth, and he tilted his head at Remy, wondering if this could work. Or would he be giving

75

Remy too much credit? Fuck it. He decided to try. "You know what?" He stood up and crushed the used tissue into a ball. "Let me ask you this. Would you help me work through my shit?"

There. I've asked for help.

Remy nodded slowly, his brow furrowing. "Of course I would help. It's the least I could do."

There was no "of course" about it, in Chase's opinion. He had never taken anybody's offer of help for granted, and he wasn't about to start now. "I'd like to help you, too," he said. "So, whenever you're ready, we can start."

"Wait a minute." Remy sat up straighter and scowled. "Are you saying you won't get help for yourself until I do the same?"

Chase shrugged. "Yeah."

Remy sat back with a scoff. "Minna and Andy have tried for a whole year—even before then, before I shut down. What makes you think I'd magically come crying to you?"

Irritated but up to the challenge, Chase leaned down and planted his hands on the armrests of Remy's chair, towering over him.

"No magic." With their faces only a foot apart, Chase was drawn to the little details in Remy's features that made him even more attractive. "I'm not saying it's gonna happen before I leave tomorrow." His gaze flicked from Remy's faint five o'clock shadow to his eyes. "Your friends have my number. Feel free to use it." Up close like this, Chase detected flecks of silver—or was it blue?—mixing with the green.

Remy held his stare, defiant but not without apprehension. "Don't hold your breath." He feigned confidence and threw Chase a devil-may-care smirk as he reached up and brushed a thumb over Chase's jaw. "There's only one reason I'd call you."

Chase made sure to keep his expression blank, but it was a far cry from what he felt. Remy was clearly doing this to push Chase away, send him running, yet the part of Chase that was lonely and screaming for affection couldn't help but wonder if he held at least a little appeal to Remy.

And wasn't that a kick in the head? Could he be so lonely that even the smallest part of him actually wanted Remy—fucking

Remy Stahl—to…what, find him hot? Christ.

Revulsion mixed with the yearning.

Remember what happened last time.

"You want to know why I'd call you, Chase?" Remy murmured.

Chase's mouth twisted into a dark smile. "No, I'm good." He swallowed as Remy's fingers ghosted down his throat. "Do you try to push away everyone like this? By pretending to wanna fuck them?"

Remy's smirk turned sly, his eyes way too inviting for Chase's liking. "Who said anything about pretending? You're so sexy you make my mouth water." He leaned forward a few inches, and Chase froze. "Disgusted yet?"

Little did Remy know, huh? Chase straightened before his cock could cause an issue, and he took a couple steps back to clear his head.

"My offer stands," he said eventually, clearing his throat. "When you're ready to talk—really talk—call me." Then he motioned to the door. "Time to get back inside."

TEN

Remy shot the body-art magazine splayed on his pillow a death glare.

Minna popped her chewing gum and drummed a bottle of nail polish on the kitchen table.

Triple-digit heat.

Goddamn headache.

A few birds chirped outside, flocking to the makeshift birdbath Andy had set up a couple days ago.

The table fan whirred with life, keeping the hot air in the cabin in motion.

Tap, tap. Tap. Tap, tap, tap. Minna started tapping her foot. *Pop, smatter, pop.* Fucking bubble gum.

Frustrated and bored out of his mind, Remy pushed the magazine aside and sat up in the bed.

He eyed his restraint and huffed.

It was a sturdy leather cuff these days, but a key was still needed to unlock the damn thing. Minna had bought it when she'd seen the effects the other one had on Remy's ankle.

No more polka dots.

He looked at Minna. "You know, when Andy's here, he lets me walk around without the cuff."

Andy had even taken him to a doctor a couple weeks ago, but he'd been in too much pain to even think about escape. *Let's be frank: I feared for my dick.* Feverish, nauseated, and with a burning sensation when he pissed, he'd been resigned to find out he'd contracted a damn STD, but he was lucky. It was only a bladder

78

infection, and he'd had those before, thanks to issues with kidney stones when he was a kid.

Nothing a little antibiotics and a whole lot of water couldn't fix.

"That's because he can outrun you." Minna smiled. "Have you reconsidered my offer?"

Remy pressed his lips together, sick of all the *offers*.

In the weeks that had passed since Chase had been here, Remy had broken down a handful of times, and Minna was taking it the hardest. Her offer involved having a therapist drive out here and get him to talk, but more than that, prescribe him medication for his anxiety.

"I don't need a mind-fucker, but thanks." He shot Minna a sarcastic smile, then let his expression fall back in to one of boredom as he stared out the window.

Weeks. Fucking *weeks*. He didn't know the exact date—nor did he care—but he knew it was August. Yet, even as the days passed, he thought about Chase as much as he had the day after the man had left.

Another offer right there. *"Your friends have my number. Feel free to use it."*

More often than not, Remy found himself wanting to ask Andy or Minna for Chase's number. Remy wanted to know why Chase felt guilty, why he hadn't been able to move on these past three years, and why the *fuck* he thought Remy could help.

He remembered Chase mentioning he had questions, but if that was all there was, he could simply send a note along with Minna or Andreas, and Remy could write back. Then Chase could go on with his life—if the answers mattered so much.

Remy was uncomfortable with the idea of being responsible for another man's well-being; it would only add to the mountain of guilt that threatened to crush him at every hour of the day. But at the same time, he acknowledged the fact that there was something he could do here. He wasn't helpless or clueless. There was a chance of doing something *good*. Remy ached for it, but the asking price was too steep.

He was stuck. He wasn't looking for salvation, but if his

friends asked him now whether or not he wanted to go back to LA, Remy didn't have an answer. Oh, it would be easy to lie and deliver a *fuck yes*, but it would taste bitter.

The thought of seeing the LA crowd he'd partied with for so long now made his stomach churn. Though, he wouldn't say no to a drink. Hell, he'd be all over that shit. Or a few sleeping pills, to allow him one night's sleep where he didn't wake up drenched in sweat from nightmares.

He kept seeing Chase's face, too. Some nights, he was there to offer comfort, which Remy wanted to run toward, but fear held him back. Other nights, Chase shouted at him, cursed him out for being a pussy, and blamed Remy for everything that had happened.

A few nights... Well, it had been a long time since Remy had gotten off, so no wonder he had an active imagination.

"Are you hungry?" Minna asked softly.

Remy shrugged. "I'm sick of sandwiches and chips." It was what Andy offered, and Remy didn't feel like cooking—not that he'd be able to do much in this sad excuse for a kitchen. *Kitchenette*. In another life, he'd enjoyed trying new things every now and then. He'd even taken a couple cooking classes.

He frowned to himself, flickers of his past visualizing in his mind. Laughter, teasing, music, the buzz of a tattoo gun, Minna's beaming smiles, Andreas's good-natured ribbing...

While Remy had fought to be accepted into the Stahl family, he'd had a real family in the Erikssons all along.

"I can bring some Vietnamese food next time I come." Minna looked hopeful. "Remember? We'd get Vietnamese at that place near Andy's studio. Or some El Taco Loco? We used to bring it over to the Bluffs at night."

Remy remembered. *Another life.* "Don't you have a new school year to plan?" Minna's shoulders sagged with defeat, and Remy wanted to kick himself in the gut. "I'm sorry, but...fuck, Minna." He groaned and tugged at his hair. "You have to stop taking trips down memory lane. It won't work." He loathed hurting his friends like this, but what could he say? "I'm never gonna feel better."

OUTCOME

"Not unless you want it." Minna threw a wistful look at the floor. "But I can't give up on you, Rem. I need to believe that we'll look back on this one day as a war you won—"

"Pizza!" Remy blurted out. Minna's brows rose as she looked up at him. He blew out a breath. "I could go for some pizza."

One thing had changed in the past few weeks, and it was related to Minna's fairy-tale ramblings. Used to scoffing and laughing at them, Remy now hurt whenever she got started. The hole in his chest gaped open wider every time she mentioned happiness in the future.

"Nobody delivers up here," Minna reasoned.

"I know." Remy nodded slowly. "But you can go get it."

Minna hesitated, not on board with the idea. "I don't want to leave you here alone. Driving down the hill to get reception and make calls is one thing, but I'd be gone for at least an hour if—"

"So?" Remy didn't get it. "One hour isn't going to kill me."

"My brother can do that—stupid ass." Minna made a face. "But it's not safe to leave you restrained all alone."

Remy smirked. "Hey, you can always unlock the..." The rest of the sentence died with Minna's withering look. "Never mind."

"But you know what?" Minna stood up and walked to the kitchenette in the corner. "We have all the ingredients for my cinnamon toast. Want me to make some?" Remy offered a placating smile and nodded. At least Minna didn't look defeated and hurt anymore. "I've realized something." She opened a cupboard to pull out the one and only skillet for the portable stovetop. "This is the most we've talked in a long time." A pang hit Remy squarely in the chest, but Minna hadn't said it to be mean. Instead, she grinned over her shoulder and said, "That's what I like to call progress."

Remy adored that woman, and he didn't deserve to be included in her positive outlook on life, but he was beginning to feel the need to make things up to her. Long overdue though it was.

He was having a good spell, he knew. With the mood changes he experienced, it was a miracle Andy hadn't beaten him into a pulp yet.

"Maybe you'd like to tell me more about, um…" Minna gave him a sideways glance before refocusing on mixing cinnamon and powdered sugar with butter. "About Chase." Well, that put a damper on things. "You only told us that he knows about the money—that you supported Ben, and he didn't freak out. That's good, right?"

Remy sighed and stared down at his hands, imagining the blood he had on them. Regardless of Chase's reaction to Remy having given Ben money, there was no shaking the guilt.

He didn't want to talk about it with Minna—or Andreas.

In the past, he'd told them pretty much everything about the whole ordeal, but it hadn't been to share his pain or whatever. His shrink had kept telling him he was a victim, and he couldn't agree, so he'd opened up to the Erikssons in an attempt to get them to side with him and say, *"Yeah, you carry some of the blame."*

They hadn't done any of that.

Even the police had dismissed it after they'd asked if he'd known about Ben's intentions.

"Or we don't have to talk about it." Minna smiled tightly.

"I'm sorry." Would Remy ever run out of reasons to apologize? "It's not easy. I barely even know what to say, and…" How could he explain? He didn't want to hurt Minna; he didn't want to expose her anymore to his moods. "I don't want to lash out on you."

"I don't mind," she said quickly. "It's part of it, getting off drugs. I've read up on it, and I'm aware you can be like a ticking time bomb—"

"*I* mind." He pointed at himself, irritated that Minna was okay with being treated like shit. "As fruitless as I think all this is— what you and Andy are doing—I know you guys have good intentions. You want what's best for me, I get it, but I'm kinda done using you as my proverbial punching bag." He slumped back while Minna stared at him. "What?" He scowled.

She snapped out of…whatever that was…and beamed at

him. "I see glimpses of the old you, you know. The Remy who was considerate and selfless."

"Shut up." He gave her a flat stare and ignored the bloom of warmth in his gut. It was fleeting, soon snuffed out by his normal state of depression.

Minna gigglesnorted. "Well, it's true. But anyway, if you don't want to talk to me, that's fine. Andy will be here tomorrow, and you *know* he can handle your bitching. Perhaps you can tell Andreas about the Joshua tree, too?" She raised a brow, teasing. "I'm crazy curious."

"Actually—" Fuck. That word came out of nowhere. Or not nowhere, but it wasn't supposed to be voiced. Nevertheless, it was there now, and Remy felt compelled to finish. "I think I want to talk to Chase."

He had no plans to agree to Chase's terms, but Remy was ready to bargain.

*

It was past ten PM when Chase finally made it to Austin and Cam's house. What with it being Friday and all, he hadn't been able to leave Donna with the bar earlier. Hell, had it not been for the music festival taking place in Bakersfield this weekend, he wouldn't have been able to get away at all. But as it was, only a dozen patrons were at the bar now, and Donna had promised to call if there were any problems.

If Donna didn't call, Tucker would.

Old Tuck was a new addition, and Chase had grown fond of the man. In his late sixties, the merry Santa look-alike could drink an Irishman into oblivion while he remained unaffected himself, he had traveled all over the world on his bike, his glare from his corner of the bar could end any kind of "ruckus," as he called it, and he had taken the position of security detail, only accepting payment in beer.

Chase could definitely live with that.

As he rang the doorbell, he could hear the guys on the other side of the house. *Happy birthday to Cam.* It had been his wish to have a poker night once the parents, in-laws, and nieces had gone home.

It was a sleepy Riley who opened the door, Bourbon and Nacho wagging their tails by her feet. "Hi, Chase." She smiled and opened the door wider.

"How you doin', pip-squeak?" Chase grinned a little and tugged on one of the braids in her hair. "Nice pajamas." Cam's brother Landon had no doubt given them to her, as they had little motorcycles printed all over the shorts and top.

If Chase loved bikes, Landon was obsessed.

"Uncle Landon's promised to teach me to drive one when I'm older." Riley's smile widened before she made a face. "My parents won't like it, but I wasn't born to make things easy for them, right?"

"Right." Chase chuckled, relieved he wasn't in Austin's and Cam's shoes. Chase liked children, but he'd be the kind of father who locked up the kids until they were thirty, unless he wanted a series of heart attacks. "Everyone's in the back, I take it?"

Riley nodded and Chase entered the house, closing and locking the door behind him.

"Dad—I mean Cam," she clarified, "is like the only one who hasn't had one too many. Uncle Derek is the *worst*." She giggled. "He gives me money when he's had too much wine." A sigh full of contentment slipped out. "I love it when he visits."

"Never heard of an Uncle Derek." Chase pushed the sleeves of his Henley past his elbows as they walked through the living room. "Is he on Austin's side?" He'd met everyone in Cam's family as they were all local. But the Huntleys were spread around a bit more.

"Yep, he's Dad's cousin. He lives with his husband in Maryland."

Huh. Nothing much Chase could say about that. But gay men popping up all over Bakersfield was certainly strange. The city where Chase was born and raised wasn't like most places in California. If anything, Bakersfield represented the Lone Star State in all its conservative, cow-tipping, country music-loving glory.

A poker table was set up on the patio, Austin, Cam,

Landon, and this Derek guy already seated and laughing about something Austin was saying. Derek looked to be in his late forties and reminded Chase of the actors from Hollywood's golden age. His mom used to watch *Gone with the Wind* and *Casablanca* until the sun rose.

"Well, fucking finally!" Landon slapped a deck of cards on the table and grinned at Chase as he stepped out on the patio. Riley disappeared back inside. "I've called you four times tonight, man. I need some support among these dicks-over-chicks lovers."

Hate to disappoint, but I'm one of those men.

"The sound's off, sorry." He shook hands with Landon and then moved on to Austin. "Thanks for having me."

"Of course." Austin gave Chase's hand a squeeze. "I'm glad you could make it. This is my cousin—Derek Huntley." He gestured to the man on his right. "Derek, meet Chase Gallardo."

"I've heard a lot about you today. Austin's been bragging about his bartending skills." Derek smiled and greeted Chase with a handshake. "It's nice to meet you."

"You too, Derek." He raised a brow at Austin, amused. "You ever wanna take another shift, you let me know."

Cam groaned. "You shouldn't have fuckin' said that. It was one time several weeks ago, and he's still talking about it."

"Would you prefer if I discussed tax laws with you?" Austin laughed and looped an arm around Cam's neck, bringing him close for a kiss. "Maybe I should consider a career change."

Cam laughed through his nose. "Like you'd ever give up numbers."

Sounded like Ade. Chase's sister loved that crap. Math…of all the damn things.

"I can't argue with that," Austin conceded with a chuckle.

Chase smiled at their exchange, envious but happy for them, and moved closer to Cam. "Happy birthday, man." Knowing that Cam didn't like having his personal space invaded, Chase stuck to a quick squeeze to the man's shoulder before backing off. "Free beer at the bar 'til next birthday sound good?"

Cam seemed to approve of that idea. "Now that's a fucking gift. Thanks, Chase." He jerked his chin at the empty seat between Derek and Landon. "Let's get this game started. I wanna send Landon home poor."

Landon snorted. "Dream on, little brother."

Remembering his missed calls, Chase brought out his phone as he sat down and figured he could quickly check his messages while Cam shuffled the cards.

As Landon had said, he'd called four times. Additionally, there was a text from Ade; she told him she was coming home next week for a break between summer classes and the next semester. Which Chase looked forward to. It had been a while since she'd had the time to let go of her textbooks and visit.

Lastly, there was a text from an unknown number.

Hi, Chase. This is Minna, Remy's friend. He asked me today if you could come to the cabin one day. You can reach me at this number, and if I don't answer, it could be the crappy reception out here. Just try later. Thanks.

The relief Chase felt nearly floored him, but it crashed against conflicting emotions of nervousness, the anger that always flared up at the reminder of three years ago, and a newfound sense of resentment toward Remy.

The latter wasn't Remy's fault; it was all on Chase and the dreams he'd been having lately. If they weren't fighting furiously, they were screwing each other's brains out. In each scenario, Chase woke up with a hard cock and with Remy's name on his lips.

More than that, Remy's reasons for being riddled with guilt made Chase feel like shit. In the days that had followed his visit to the cabin, he'd been depressed and extremely pissed at himself. Once again, he found himself in a situation where others were going through hell much worse than his own, yet Chase could barely function.

It wasn't a competition by any means, but he couldn't help doubting himself at every turn. Combined with how he was raised, he barely knew what was up and what was down anymore, and he craved solid ground.

"Are you all right?" Austin set down a beer and a glass of whiskey in front of Chase.

He nodded hesitantly, debating whether or not to say

anything. When Austin had asked about Remy a couple weeks ago, Chase had actually opened up a bit more. So, both Austin and Cam knew about the trip to the cabin, but Chase had stopped at filling them in on what'd happened. He wasn't ready to air out his damn feelings, mainly 'cause he couldn't make heads or tails outta the crap going on in his head, but also because he didn't wanna be a burden.

Seemed stupid to lean on shoulders that had been shot and stabbed.

He hadn't told his friends just how much he had anticipated this reaching out from Remy. Feared it would come, dreaded it wouldn't.

"A call I've been waiting for." Chase kept it vague, but realization lit up in Austin's eyes anyway.

"Good," he replied firmly. "How about we throw some steaks on the grill tomorrow and talk about it?"

Humbled by the offer, Chase nodded. "Yeah. That sounds good. Thanks." This sharing thing was taking some getting used to, and he was eternally grateful for Austin extending a hand. God knew Chase wouldn't have been able to *ask*. It was a miracle he'd admitted to Remy that he was struggling in the first place.

For the next couple of hours, the ground he was on became even shakier. Having Austin and Cam in his life, a happily married couple, was enough of a struggle for Chase to keep his longing in check. But to add Derek's stories about his husband and the fact that Chase couldn't get Remy off his mind... It was becoming too much for him to fight off.

ELEVEN

The following Monday morning, Chase rode his bike up the mountain park outside Tehachapi. The cabin was closer to the foothills than any peak in the mountains, but the climate still differed significantly from Bakersfield and the rest of the San Joaquin Valley.

Whereas it was another dry, hot-as-fuck day back home, here—merely thirty-five miles away from Bakersfield—a fog bank blanketed the area today, and it was impossible to see where the fog ended and the overcast sky took over.

The closer Chase got, the more the knot in his gut tightened. He wasn't delusional; it was unlikely that Remy was ready to get help, but *something* had made the man reach out to Chase.

The air was clammy and charged, and unwelcome thoughts of sharing one of his favorite things with Remy occupied Chase's mind for the last bit before he reached the cabin. Growing up, he'd borrowed his dad's car and found a spot in the flatlands, usually among the vast oil fields, where he could see thunderstorms rolling in over the mountains.

It'd been years since Chase had done it, and it was something he missed.

Coming to a rumbling stop at the cabin, Chase killed the engine and pushed down the kickstand. As he removed his helmet and hung it on a handlebar, Minna left the little wooden house with a duffel. Her overnight bag, no doubt.

"Hello, Chase." She smiled.

"Hey." He got off the bike and noticed Minna's bag must've been heavy by the way she was struggling with it. "Here, let me help."

"Oh. Thanks." A faint blush spread across her cheeks as he picked up the bag and carried it to her truck. She followed and opened the door on the passenger side. "What's that?"

Chase followed her gaze to the punching bag strapped to his bike. He smiled faintly and then set down Minna's bag in the seat. "A friend advised me to bring a physical outlet."

Austin's exact words had been, *"If he's self-destructive, perhaps he should try taking his anger out on something other than himself."*

It had made so much sense that Chase had asked if Austin had ever studied psychology. In return, Austin had laughed, a little sheepish, and admitted that he'd asked Gale for advice.

"God, that's a brilliant idea." Minna stared at the punching bag in wonder. "I'm the first one to admit I'm in way over my head. I'm a teacher, for chrissakes. Not a psychologist." She sighed. "My only thought was to get him away from the people in LA, and hopefully down the road, get him to see a therapist."

Hey, Chase wasn't gonna judge her. Minna was a good friend, and Remy couldn't really be helped unless he wanted it. But yeah, research didn't hurt, and Chase was lucky he had friends who had opened his eyes.

Chase couldn't deny it anymore; he'd given up therapy way too soon. Even Cam had shared a muttered piece of advice that made perfect sense. *"Don't get hung up on the word therapy. See it as getting a new perspective instead. Gale's good at sorting shit out."* Then he'd whacked Chase in the arm and added, *"You should fucking know, man. You've had sessions with her before."*

A new perspective.

A bartender who didn't only listen, but talked as well…?

Chase had to try.

Ironically, Chase had never hesitated to turn to research before. He'd always had the need to understand everything and everyone around him. Three years ago, it was the Stahl family. He'd been submerged in articles, interviews, and clips from news segments—anything to get a grasp on *why*.

But when it came to himself? Not only did he fail to understand what was going on inside him, but he studiously avoided finding out.

With a shake of his head, he cleared his thoughts and focused on Minna, who was filling him in a little on what had happened since last time. Andy apparently let Remy walk around uncuffed, which was a relief. Chase had to admit that while he understood why Remy was restrained, the whole concept still made him uncomfortable.

"He has mood swings," Minna went on. "And make sure he drinks a lot of water. My brother took him to a doctor a while ago for a bladder infection and Remy's done with his antibiotics, but more water can't hurt." Chase nodded in understanding then sneezed because his nose tickled. "Oh, *gesundheit*. Hmm, what else, what else…" She tapped her chin. "We've brought an inflatable bed up here. I've been fine sharing with Remy, but my brother, not so much." She grinned. "And speaking of Andy, he will be here tomorrow night." She tilted her head and looked up at Chase. "He's off tomorrow, so if you want him to come earlier, just send him a text."

Chase shook his head. "It's all right. A couple friends are covering for me at the bar."

Mondays and Tuesdays were slow, and Austin had volunteered before Chase could even muster the courage to ask— and probably chicken out. Luckily, it was only for a couple hours before closing that Donna would need help, and Landon had invited himself to be Austin's *Cocktail* partner.

In the end, Cam's comment had made Chase fold. *"You've had what, two days off in the past month? Go see that little fucker and let me sit on the sidelines and laugh my ass off while Austin and Landon make fools outta themselves."*

And now Chase was here, ready or not, for approximately thirty-six hours with Remy Stahl.

*

Remy's heart was about to jump out of his chest when

OUTCOME

Chase finally entered the cabin.

He actually came.

Chase nodded hello with a single dip of his chin and then turned to set down his two saddlebags and his helmet on the camping bed across the cabin. It gave Remy privacy to pull up the hem of his black wifebeater and wipe some sweat off his brow.

Chained to Minna's wrist, Remy had showered and shaved down at the camping site less than an hour ago, but with thunder in the air, the heat plastered itself to Remy's skin soon enough.

"How are you?" he asked Chase, feeling stupid. Nervous. Kinda terrified.

He didn't even know why, only that Chase had that effect on him.

"Decent. You?" Chase shrugged out of a dark denim vest, leaving him in well-worn jeans, boots, and another T-shirt that clung to his chest. Two folded bandanas around his wrists to hide the scars.

"Bored," he answered honestly.

It was impossible not to admire the view, but Remy did his best to be discreet. He wasn't going to play games this time and push Chase away. At least, that wasn't the plan.

"Yeah, I bet." A ghost of a smirk appeared on Chase's lips, and he walked forward with a key in his hand. *Thank God.* "You won't escape from me." It was a quiet statement.

Remy stared as Chase bent over to unlock the small padlock attached to the leather cuff. Long, callused fingers occasionally brushed over Remy's skin. The lock seemed to put up a fight, so Chase cupped Remy's heel to hold it steady and tried again.

It had been years since Remy had been touched by a man who pushed all his buttons and made more than his dick react; therefore, he needed a goddamn distraction before he put his foot in his mouth.

Noticing the traces of oil under Chase's blunt fingernails and along his cuticles, Remy found a safe topic.

"Are you a grease monkey?"

Two seconds without an answer, but then the padlock fell

away, landing on the floorboards, and Chase looked up. "Grease monkey?" Remy nodded at Chase's hands. "Oh. A little, I guess." He stood up and tossed the lock and the key onto Remy's nightstand. "I haven't driven my Panhead since last winter, so I needed to change the oil on the way. The one I was using couldn't handle the heat, and my stupid ass had forgotten to change it before."

There were different kinds of oil? Remy probably looked like a question mark. "Panhead?" he asked dumbly.

Chase jerked his chin at the door. "Come on. We're going outside."

Remy stood up and snatched his smokes and lighter from the nightstand, pocketed them in his basketball shorts, then stuck his feet into his checkered Vans. He followed Chase outside like an obedient dog, his eyes immediately catching the motorcycle, or more importantly, the punching bag behind the seat.

What the hell?

"This is a Panhead." Chase tapped something on the side of the bike. "It's a Harley engine." He spoke as he unstrapped the punching bag.

Remy leaned against one of the posts holding up the narrow porch's roof. "Thanks for the lesson." He knew jack shit about bikes, but he had to admit it was sexy as fuck. Even without direct sunlight, the dark green-painted vehicle gleamed as if it was brand new. But it screamed of vintage at the same time.

Chase grunted and hauled up the punching bag to rest on his shoulder, which…yeah, that was hotter than the bike. Remy lit up a smoke and enjoyed the show, content to wait with his questions about whatever Chase had planned. Watching how Chase's arms bulged and how his torso stretched the fabric of his T-shirt was much more fulfilling.

Or perhaps "fulfilling" was the wrong word, as it made Remy want more.

It was like taking a whiff of vodka but not being allowed to taste.

"Get over here and help out, pretty boy." Chase's remark killed the moment.

Remy scowled and stubbed out his cigarette. "Pretty boy? Fuck you." He trudged over to the tree Chase was looking up at. "I'm not a twink."

The only reason he'd bottomed exclusively in the past year was because he'd had issues maintaining a hard-on with all that poison in his system.

Chase gave him a mild look, unimpressed. "Anyway..." He stepped away and took hold of a sturdy branch that hung relatively low, pulling it down a couple feet. Remy's gaze slid to Chase's arms again. *Damn.* "Come here. Hold it like this while I get the bag in place."

Remy heaved a heavy sigh and walked over to where Chase was holding down the branch for him. He grabbed onto the thick branch and sucked in a breath when Chase let go. Okay, so it wasn't as easy as it looked.

It irritated Remy to be bested. He hated looking like the fool. So, in true Remy fashion, he had to make it worse.

He blatantly checked out Chase's ass. "After you're done reenacting *Million Dollar Baby* out here, you wanna head back inside and maybe suck my cock? It'll show you who the pretty boy is."

Much to Remy's frustration, Chase remained unfazed. He slung a rope over the branch and started raising the punching bag in the air.

"You're in that mood again, huh?" Chase side-eyed him before refocusing on the knot he was tying. "I'm afraid shoving your sexuality in my face won't do the trick." He nodded at the branch. "You can let go."

Remy let his arms fall to his side, and he glared at the ground. "I'm stuck with the only man in Bakersfield who won't jump at the chance for some gay-bashing? Just my luck."

Chase snorted. "You're reaching, kid."

Remy knew he was. Ten minutes ago, he'd been relieved to have Chase here, and now he was back to being a prick.

"Hey, Remy?" Chase tilted his head as Remy looked him in the eye. "Three years ago, I spent over five months being called 'disgusting little queer' by Ben." That was a punch in the fucking gut, but Remy kept his face blank. "You being gay didn't come as a surprise, nor do I give a fuck. I'm okay with it, so stop pushing for a reaction."

In order to mask the hurt that Ben had caused, Remy went for sarcasm. "Oh, thank you so much for being okay with someone else's sexual orientation. You're a real liberal." He rolled his eyes, sick of this, and headed back toward the cabin instead.

He didn't hear Chase following him until Remy found himself pinned to the wall of the cabin, a strong forearm pressed to his sternum and Chase's lethal glare searing into him.

Shit.

Remy's eyes widened with shock, and he half expected Chase to give him the beating he deserved now. But Chase said nothing. Did nothing. Second by second, the man's glare grew less murderous until there was no anger left at all.

Chase broke eye contact and looked down but didn't move away. "I wanna tell you to stop pissing me off, but I have a feeling that'd be impossible." Lifting his head again, he got fixed on some point near Remy's shoulder. "You gotta stop with the crude shit, though." When Chase finally met his gaze again, Remy was trapped.

He became hyperalert to every inch of him that Chase was touching, mainly his impressive junk pushing against Remy's lower abdomen. With something dark burning in Chase's eyes, this new awareness would get Remy in trouble if they didn't break apart soon.

"I make no promises." Remy could barely believe he had the balls to say that. But if it got Chase to back off…

The man pressing up against him glared again, something sinister curving the corners of his mouth. Remy watched how Chase licked his bottom lip and inched close enough to speak in his ear. The musky combination of soap, man, and spearmint hit Remy's senses, and he nearly groaned. He could already feel his dick stiffening.

"Then I make no promises of the outcome." Chase's voice was quiet and steely in his ear. A bit rougher and darker than normal.

He finally stepped away, kind of taking Remy's ability to

breathe with him.

*

Chase was losing his *fucking* mind.

Disappearing into the cabin, he located the tape he'd bought and tried fruitlessly to clear his head. He passed Remy on the way out again and clenched his jaw at the frustrating combination of fury and desire unfurling inside of him. The physical outlet Austin had suggested couldn't have arrived at a better time.

"Get over here," he snapped irritably, reaching the punching bag. Raindrops started to hit the ground, and he could hear thunder in the distance. If he got lucky, the incoming storm would cleanse Chase the way it cleansed the air. As it was now, the heavy charge threatened to suffocate him.

He side-eyed Remy, noticing the vulnerability had reappeared in his features. The kid was a walking roller coaster of emotions. With shoulders bunched up tight, arms folded, eyes downcast, and frown knitting together his brows, he was probably working up his internal defenses.

"Here. Tape up your knuckles." Chase tossed the roll of tape to Remy, who picked it up off the ground. "Who're you pissed at?"

Remy's frown morphed into a scowl. "What?"

"Who are you pissed at?" Chase repeated patiently—somewhat, anyway. "We're always mad at someone, Remy." He placed his hands on the bag and looked up at the blackening sky between the branches and leaves. There were no trees in the circular clearing in front of the cabin, but they'd get soaked in no time even here at the edge of the forest. His gaze slid to Remy again. "Whoever it is, pretend this is him. Or her."

Remy snorted. "You're joking. That's the nonsense you see in movies."

"Yeah, because Hollywood invented this kind of therapy," Chase drawled.

That remark seemed to annoy Remy, and he stepped

forward as he angrily taped his knuckles. "You know, I fucking hate it when you make me look like an idiot."

Chase lifted a brow. "A comment that wasn't packed with sarcasm? I'm impressed." He threw in a thumbs-up for effect, which Remy seethed at. Chase chuckled. "Maybe I got it wrong. Are you the only one allowed to speak Sarcasm?"

Remy flipped him off and positioned himself on the other side of the punching bag. "Whatever. Can I pretend this thing is you now?"

"If you're mad at me, sure. Go for it." Chase shrugged and took a couple steps to the side. By now, the rain was coming down heavier, and he felt his T-shirt sticking to his skin. "What have I done to piss you off?"

It was Remy's turn to shrug, and he gave the bag a half-assed fist that barely rattled the chain above them. "You're supposed to hate me." He glared and punched harder, mostly—Chase suspected—to get the bag to move. "Fuck." With a scowl directed at the sky, he wiped raindrops from his forehead and ran a hand through his messy hair. "Can't we go back inside? This blows."

Nah. They hadn't even scratched the surface. "Do you want me to hate you?" Chase began to circle Remy and the punching bag. Measured steps. Eyes trained on Remy's face.

"Fuck what I want." Remy chuckled humorlessly and delivered another punch. This one had a little more force to it, and bitterness seeped into his eyes. "I didn't want to screw up my life, but it happened anyway. I didn't *want* my mom to kill herself, yet…" He pulled the trigger of an imaginary gun to his temple. "So yeah, it's not really about what I want."

Chase narrowed his eyes, remembering what Remy had written in one of those letters. He hadn't been close with his mom…something about an addiction to prescription drugs…but Chase didn't know she'd died.

"She shot herself?" He glanced at Remy carefully, guessing it was a sore subject. Judging by the next blow Remy gave the punching bag, Chase was right. The whole chain trembled above, a few leaves falling to the wet ground.

"Yeah." Remy gritted his teeth, then punched again and again and again. "I was the one who found her. It was last year, in the beginning of one of our 'on' periods." He rolled his eyes, though indifference was the last thing Chase would see there. Plenty of pain instead. "Sometimes we were close, but then she'd meet a new guy... Nothing original." A grunt slipped through his lips with the next punch, and then he paused to catch his breath and lean his forehead against the bag. "She'd recently been ditched, which obviously sucked for her, because she only dated suppliers." His jaw ticked. "It'd been over a year since we'd talked regularly, so I was pretty stoked. I needed her—even though I knew it wasn't going to last. But whatever."

Last year... Minna had told Chase that Remy had tried therapy, but he'd given up and shut down—*about a year ago.* Feeling alone and trapped, maybe even looking for a way out, Remy had sought out his mom, needing her, only to find her dead...?

No wonder Remy had checked out.

"Don't pity me." Remy's warning hung in the air until a hard punch to the bag was accompanied by a loud crack of thunder.

Chase looked up, more rain falling down, and he closed his eyes for a beat to feel the drops spattering over his face. "I'm not." He pushed back his damp hair and nodded at the punching bag. "Keep going. Are you angry at your mother?"

"Not anymore. Now I kind of envy her."

Chase didn't believe that for a second. "You're full of shit, but I'll let it go for now, pretty boy—"

"Cut that shit out!" Remy abandoned the bag and stalked over to Chase, shoving him backward. "Call me that again, I fucking dare you!"

Instantly prepared, Chase flinched forward and glared back at the little shit. "Pick your battle, Remy," he growled. "You can lash out at me all you want, but I'm not your goddamn enemy." Grabbing Remy by the shoulders, Chase forced him to turn around. "You wanna hit something? Hit this, for Christ's sake." Remy cursed at him and tried to turn again, but Chase gripped his neck and leaned close, furious as hell. "Last warning. Hit the punching bag 'cause, unlike me, it won't hit back.''

Remy slowed his movements, and Chase regretted his wording the instant Remy looked back at him, his eyes sparking up with pure satisfaction and challenge.

Before Chase could even take that shit back, Remy shoulder-checked him and sent his fist flying, connecting it with Chase's jaw.

TWELVE

In the pouring rain, Chase found himself dodging punches instead of fighting back. Something stopped him from swinging at Remy. No matter how much his jaw ached from Remy's fist.

"Come on!" Remy's voice was as strained as every muscle in his body. Flushed with anger, soaked from the storm, and livid for shit that had nothing to do with Chase—directly—Remy came at him over and over.

When he planted his hands against Chase's chest and tried to shove him, Chase retaliated by pushing back so Remy ended up on the muddy ground.

"That's all you got, sweetheart?" Chase chuckled, a bit outta breath, and rubbed his scruffy jaw. "You're only humiliating yourself."

"Go fuck yourself." Remy got off the ground, mud and water causing his T-shirt to cling to his lean torso. But lean didn't mean lanky. Remy's abs were cut underneath that shirt, and Chase cursed himself for getting distracted. "You're no different from all the other rednecks in Bakersfield." Remy sneered as he ripped off the tape from his knuckles. "All you need is conservatism and a good fight with a fag, and you'll go yee-haw."

That crap only amused Chase. It wasn't the first time Remy had taken digs at the people from Bakersfield, and like the other occasions, it was without valid reason and definitely the wrong moment.

Did Remy *want* to be hated for being gay?

Idiot.

"Someone needs to get off his high horse." Chase shook his head. "Where are you even from?"

Remy could act all high and mighty, but he didn't strike Chase as a *preppy* guy.

"Oildale," Remy muttered defiantly.

At that, Chase barked out a laugh, and he laughed *hard*. For the first time in a long, long time. 'Cause…Oildale. Remy was a damn 08'er. Christ. The area used to be worse, but it was still a fucking dump. Home of meth labs and reasons to use condoms.

Chase had no room to talk, having grown up near Cottonwood Road, but he wasn't the one talking smack about their hometown, either.

"You crack me up, kid." He snorted and turned to walk back inside. The thunder was almost directly above them now, and the rain was coming down so hard it was difficult to hear anything other than the storm—

Remy's grip on his bicep halted his step, and he looked over his shoulder to see Remy glaring at him.

"We're not done here!" Remy put all his weight into the shove and sent them both to the ground. Chase, caught off guard, hissed at the pain in his tailbone, then grunted when Remy sat on his stomach and dug his fingernails into Chase's chest. "Come on, you fucking coward! Fight back!"

Chase's vision went blurry, his stomach churning as Remy's words triggered a flashback from three years ago.

"It kills you, doesn't it?" Ben smiled gleefully through the hatch in the steel door. "It kills you that you can't fight back. But, you see, queers aren't supposed to fight, Remy. It could mess up your hair or ruin your makeup." His cackle echoed in the cage, making Chase sick with revulsion. "Just sit tight and let me do the work. Because you're fucking useless."

With an internal roar, Chase rammed his knee against the man's spine, then rolled them over and tried to choke the motherfucker who had kidnapped him. In the back of his mind, he registered the feeling of mud and heavy rain, and it went against everything he'd grown used to: the smell of mildew and vomit, the sense of hopelessness and grief, endless suffering and guilt. Dank, humid air.

OUTCOME

Someone yelled his name, but it sounded off—far away and muffled.

*

Remy coughed and spluttered, struggling against Chase's hold on his neck. The sheer terror that gripped Remy was unlike anything he'd ever felt, and it only increased when he saw Chase's gaze. Those deep blue eyes swirled with murderous rage and heart-wrenching despair, but they were unfocused.

He's not seeing me.

"Chase," Remy choked out. Raindrops splattered on his face, in his eyes, and he continued to fight. As his airway was cut off completely, he finally managed to loosen a few of Chase's fingers, and he sucked in a sharp breath before he mustered all his strength and clocked Chase in the jaw. Same side as last time.

Chase froze for several seconds. His eyes remained unseeing, but then they widened in horror, and he wrenched away from Remy.

"Oh, God..." Remy closed his eyes and gasped for breath. He was soaked to the bone, lying there on the muddy ground, but he couldn't give a fuck. Because...Jesus Christ, that had been a close call. While Remy had been busy bitching about his own issues, Chase was clearly in deep shit, too.

This couldn't go on.

Something had to give, and...maybe his future looked bleak as fuck, but he was willing to take one step in the right direction. *Whatever that may be.* Forcing himself to sit up, he looked over to Chase where he was sitting on the ground, forearms resting on his knees, head hanging low. And instead of being angry for the physical pain Chase had caused or feeling guilty for probably having triggered this—whatever it was that had happened—Remy only wanted to help.

He needed Chase to feel better, and he ached to be part of the recovery.

He scooted closer, not having a clue of what to do, and carefully lifted a hand to Chase's shoulder.

In return, Chase stiffened. "Don't."

"I'm sorry." Remy had given so many apologies lately that this one had tumbled out automatically. But he didn't remove his hand. "Was that...I mean...what happened?" Chase shook his head minutely, his lips pressed together in a grim line. He looked like he was about to fall apart, which affected Remy more than he thought was possible. "Does it happen often?" He wondered if it was some kind of panic attack, like the ones he suffered from every now and then.

"No." Chase's reply was barely audible over the thunder. His Adam's apple moved with a hard swallow, and then he tilted his head away from Remy. "Fuckin' flashback," he rasped. "First one in a year. Usually I just have nightmares here and there."

Remy nodded and looked down. "I set it off." A quiet statement. He knew it was true. "What did I say?"

"Doesn't matter, Remy." Chase sounded drained. "Wash off and head back inside. I'll be there in a bit."

Yeah, no. Remy wasn't going anywhere. He had a feeling that if he left him here, it would be a lot longer than a "bit" before Chase got off the ground.

"I'm sorry about..." Chase's apology died out with a roar of thunder, but it didn't matter.

"Come on, man." Remy stood up and nudged his knee against Chase's shoulder. "Let's freeze our asses off under the hose behind the cabin. And let's do it before my mood shifts again."

Chase muttered curses under his breath, but Remy paid no attention. He rounded the first corner of the cabin and pulled his wifebeater over his head. The fabric landed with a splat on the ground as he reached the back. His shoes were next, and then his shorts.

"Hell." Remy eyed the reddening on his legs, tiny cuts and scrapes everywhere. His arms were the same. *That's what I get for rolling around in the mud like a child.* He released a breath and turned the nozzle to the garden hose, and icy water began trickling out.

He could hear Chase a few feet behind him, so he didn't turn around. Shrinkage warning or not, the sounds of clothes landing on the ground told Remy it was safest to stay where he was.

Evidently, Chase had other plans. To Remy's frustration, Chase walked up way too close, and the bastard was only wearing a pair of dark gray boxer briefs that hugged his junk so fucking perfectly.

Chase inched even closer, a frown directed at Remy's throat. "I'm sorry—I was outta control."

"You have a valid excuse." Remy quickly ducked to hose off his legs. "I'm fine." What he wouldn't give for a drink at this moment. He shuddered and clenched his teeth together, standing straight to hold the water above him. The rain was helping, so he didn't have to suffer for many seconds. "Here." He stepped back and let Chase take over. "I'll go in and..." He trailed off, his eyes following the water that sluiced down Chase's body. *Holy shit.* Chase's nipples tightened under the cold spray, and goose bumps appeared over his defined torso. What Remy wouldn't give to touch the dark dusting of chest hair and then kiss his way down to the trail of hair between Chase's navel to his—

"You're staring."

Remy wasn't even embarrassed. He avoided eye contact as he stuck his feet into his wet shoes, but he spoke the truth. "You're sexy as hell. If you don't wanna be eye-fucked, don't shower in front of a gay man." He shrugged slightly and turned toward the outhouse. After a quick trip, he was more than ready to be indoors.

The day was slowly catching up to him, and he wondered if he'd exhausted himself enough to get at least a few hours of sleep tonight. He hadn't even analyzed his earlier confessions about his mom because he feared it would be too much. Between his mood swings and the effect Chase had on him...Remy was weary and spent, yet itching for what else Chase might have in store for them. Remy wanted more, fucking yearned for it.

It felt like progress in a weird way, but had they really accomplished anything?

Kicking off his shoes outside the front door, he stepped inside the cabin and hurried to the stack of towels that lay in a pile on the floor by the bed's footboard. He dropped his underwear and wrapped one towel around his hips, then ran another over his head.

His stomach rumbled with a reminder that he hadn't eaten since this morning, so while he was still toweling himself dry, he walked over to the kitchenette to find something to eat.

After acting like a complete tool ninety-nine percent of the time he'd spent with Chase, Remy now thought about what food he could put together as a peace offering.

I can be nice. I think.

THIRTEEN

Numbness had set in by the time Chase entered the cabin, both from the cold shower and the events of the day. He set his boots to the side of the door to dry then opened his saddlebags for new clothes. Remy stood a few feet away, his back to Chase, busy cooking something in the miniscule kitchen.

Whatever it was on the stove smelled good.

"There're towels by my bed."

Chase muttered a thanks and crossed the small space to grab one. Back by his inflatable bed, he got outta his soaked boxers and into a new pair.

"Nice ass." Remy whistled. "Not gonna lie—I peeked."

I'm not surprised, Chase thought. And he liked it. Pulling on a pair of sweats, he looked at Remy over his shoulder, but the kid had his back to him again.

After everything that had happened today, Chase was sick with loneliness. He was left emotionally drained by the flashback, brief as it had been, but they didn't happen often anymore. Like he'd told Remy, it had to have been at least a year since the last one. So when they did happen, they were all-consuming and exhausting. The fact that he'd hurt Remy filled him with remorse and guilt, too.

If he was honest with himself, he wanted closeness with Remy—at least for the moment—but it freaked him out.

With Remy, it was probably easier to get a blow job than a hug.

Chase should want neither. He'd shut that part of him off,

partly because of how he'd been kidnapped, and partly because of the pity he felt toward his pops. He had his desires and wants, but they hadn't been this demanding in the past ten years.

Six months after his father had died of cancer, his mom got closer and closer to mourning herself to death. First, one heart attack. *"You do your father proud, ciccio. I know you will."* Pat, pat, her frail hand on his. And the second heart attack had finished the job.

Some said hope was the last thing that died. Not Pops, though. No, it was pride. Which, for most of his dad's adult life, was all he'd had.

What kind of bastard would Chase have been to take that away?

Dragging a towel over his upper body, he watched as Remy brought two plates of food over to the nightstand by the bed. Sausage, scrambled eggs, muffins, and toaster waffles. In a second trip, where Chase tried not to get distracted by the gleaming silver barbells in Remy's nipples, Remy put coffee, sodas, chips, and a bowl of grapes on a tray that he set down next to his pillow on the bed.

I want him.

Remy smiled sheepishly. "Once I get under the sheets, I'm not going anywhere until I've defrosted from that shower." Fiddling with the ring in his bottom lip, his gaze flicked between the bed and the round kitchen table. "Um. You can eat at the table if you want—obviously. I just figured this was more comfortable."

Chase ran the towel over his head, hiding his face, and went with a blatant lie. "I don't have a preference. The bed's fine." Okay, the last part was true.

Knowing that it'd be hot soon enough, Chase decided against putting on a shirt.

He hung his towel over the open window by the door, the rain still coming down hard outside, then joined Remy on the bed. One man on each end and a bunch of food between them.

They ate in silence, the first bites of food only fueling Chase's hunger. Aside from a few dinners at Austin and Cam's place, Chase didn't exactly eat well. Microwave dinners and ramen, shitty coffee and snacks from the bar. But this…? Hot damn, this was perfect. Especially the waffles and the coffee.

"This was…goddamn delicious." After they were done, Chase leaned back against the wall and let out a sigh of contentment. "Thanks for the grub." He tilted his head in Remy's direction and found him dozing off with the bowl of grapes in his lap.

The sight was fucking adorable, and it made something snap inside of Chase. The past blurred into nonexistence, effectively silencing any voice that would prevent him from taking the smallest step outta line.

Tired and temporarily stripped of his internal defenses, Chase cleared the bed of food. He put away almost everything in the kitchen then returned for the bowl still in Remy's lap. The guy sat in the corner, his chin nearly touching his chest. Eyes closed.

"Wake up, Remy." Chase spoke quietly as he set the grapes on the nightstand. "That doesn't look very comfortable." Remy raised his head and blinked drowsily. "You should lie down."

Remy blinked again, gaining his bearings, then suddenly jumped up. "Shit!" He spun around on the floor as if expecting something to be missing. Adjusting the towel around his hips, he faced Chase again and squinted. "That was the weirdest fucking dream."

Chase's eyebrows rose, and he chuckled as he sat down on the edge of the bed again. "You were only out for a few minutes."

Remy huffed and sat down beside Chase. "Don't you ever have dreams when you're half awake? Like, you know it's a dream because you're not completely out of it yet."

Chase nodded slowly, not a stranger to any kind of dream. "What was yours about?" Sitting this close to Remy, Chase had to physically restrain himself to keep from reaching out. Instead, as he listened to Remy talking about a dream where a storm washed away the cabin, Chase let himself drink in the sight. He bit his tongue when his gaze fell to the damn Joshua tree on Remy's ribcage, but in the end, the temptation was too much. "Is there a significance to that tree?"

Guess the question didn't feel too personal anymore.

Remy's brows furrowed, most likely 'cause Chase had

interrupted his storytelling about a dream, but the instant he was caught up, the light in his pale green eyes dimmed.

He looked down and brushed a hand over the large tattoo. "I stopped covering it up because I thought maybe you'd forgotten." His voice was barely audible. "Or that it didn't matter. I don't know." So it was connected to Chase? "You really want to know?" He seemed reluctant to share, but yeah, Chase wanted to know.

"Spit it out." He was on edge suddenly.

Remy blew out a breath and shifted, facing Chase a bit more. "You only gave one interview after you guys got back to freedom." Chase wasn't about to forget. "I remember the reporter asked you when it really hit you—that you were free again."

Chase didn't need to hear anymore. It had been a week after they'd left the desert. Chase had been released from the hospital, and he'd given his statements to the police. The only thing he'd wanted was to go home with Ade, who'd been left mostly alone during those five months—only eighteen years old at the time. Those days were still a haze, and when Chase was approached by a reporter, he hadn't been prepared, nor eager, to take part in a damn interview. But he'd dutifully answered a few questions, and when he'd gotten that question... He could give a wry chuckle about it today, though the significance remained.

"When did you realize that the horror was finally over? Was it immediately or did it come later?"

Chase had scratched his head, thinking back, and then blurted out some stupid shit. *"I saw a tree. We were sitting in a rundown barn, and I looked out over the flatlands and saw a Joshua tree. That's...yeah, I think that's when it started to settle."*

The tree had happened to stick out like a sore thumb. A sign of life in the middle of nothing, just sand and rocks.

Somehow, that fucking tree represented freedom to Chase.

Now the symbol was inked on Remy's ribcage. A dark silhouette with ominous shadows hugging the contrasts and a hint of barren landscape in the background.

"Why?" He had to ask, because freedom couldn't possibly be Remy's reason. "Why the tattoo?"

"I wanted a reminder."

Chase sensed there was a lot more to it than that, but he couldn't tear his focus away from the art on Remy's body. And it was without permission that Chase's hand inched closer.

He caught himself and looked tentatively at Remy. His eyes asked the question.

Can I?

Remy nodded hesitantly and lowered his head as Chase ghosted his hand over the ink. Pale skin and all that black and gray. Flawless, beautiful. Smooth aside from some goose bumps appearing. *How will I fucking stop?* Chase applied the barest amount of pressure, his hand warmer than Remy's skin, and brushed the pad of his thumb over the knotted design of the Joshua tree's branches.

The way the tension crackled and thickened made it impossible for Chase to look past it and pretend to be ignorant. Nevertheless, the last thing on his agenda was walking out. He shifted closer instead, more drawn than ever to Remy's body.

In return, Remy released a shaky breath and twisted his upper body more in Chase's direction. By placing his hand on the mattress behind Chase to support himself, Remy also drove Chase mad with lust, because there was no escaping Remy when he was this close. The feel of him, the smell of him, his shallow breaths hitting Chase's neck and shoulder.

"I did the stencil," Remy blurted out. Quick breaths. "I drew it and Andy filled it in."

Chase didn't reply. He was too far gone. The top branch of the tattoo teased the underside of Remy's pec, only a few inches from one of those nipple barbells that had haunted Chase for weeks now. His fingers traced the ink slowly and didn't stop at the end of the tattoo.

"Oh, fuck." Remy panted out a breath as Chase swept a digit over the piercing.

Chase's move had ended all pretense; this wasn't about the tree. Maybe it'd started that way, but… Now, Chase touched him on purpose. *With* purpose. When Remy's forehead landed on top of Chase's shoulder, Chase glanced down to see a prominent bulge under Remy's towel.

Jesus Christ, I need more.

Remy's erection rivaled his own, currently pressing against the fabric of his sweats.

The way this guy could intensify everything for Chase, turn anger into rage, want into need, heat into fire—

"Please stop." Remy's words worked like a cold shower.

Chase sat back in stunned silence, the desire nearly brimming over. Every muscle in his body was taut, and he couldn't clear the haze enveloping him. In the meantime, Remy stood up a few feet away and kept his back to Chase.

"You can't do this." Remy hissed. "Any of it—barge into my life and turn it upside down. *Fuck*." He kicked at a kitchen chair and tightened the towel around his hips. "I can't have you changing things, and that's what you're fucking doing."

Chase swallowed hard and rose from the bed. "Changing things?" He had to force his fists to unclench, but it was no use trying to relax completely. His mind was swimming with images of Remy, and they weren't going anywhere.

"Don't get any closer, asshole," Remy spat out over his shoulder.

But like a man possessed, Chase continued. "What's changing?" As Chase reached the middle of the floor, Remy turned and glared at him.

"*I* am." Remy went on to speak through clenched teeth, taking a step back for every step Chase took forward. "With you…being here, being all—" He cursed and waved a hand at Chase. "It makes me…it makes me…" His back hit the door, to which he shot Chase another withering look. "It makes me want things, goddammit. It makes me hopeful—Stop moving!"

Chase stopped.

Could this be it?

Could Remy be ready to accept help?

"What do you want?" Chase asked, his voice like gravel.

Remy let out a humorless laugh, hollow and pained, then ripped the door open and walked outside and into the pouring rain.

Chase stared after him, an invisible band stretching further and further with every foot of distance Remy put between them. He felt the phantom pain as Remy paced in a circle, muttering to himself—too quiet for Chase to hear—pinching the bridge of his nose, then scrubbing his hands down his face...some cursing, more pacing.

Ignoring his boots, Chase stepped outside and hoped they were near a breakthrough. He'd finished running a while ago, and now it was Remy's turn.

"What do you hope for?" He blinked against the downpour, raindrops trickling down his face and torso.

Remy groaned, and he was the picture of defeat. Shoulders sagging, face buried in his hands. "Don't start."

Start? Chase walked closer and shook his head. "We started this weeks ago."

"Then end it!" Remy exploded. Fury radiated off of him, but it was thin. Breakable. He was holding on to it for all he was worth. "I'm done!"

"Bullshit!" Chase shouted. Remy's anger was evidently contagious, and it caught on quick. "I'm right fucking here, Remy!" He threw out his arms. "You think I'm blind? You think I can't see right through you?" Seething, Chase wiped at the raindrops rolling down his forehead and walked closer. "You don't want this anymore than I do, and you can't even lie about it anymore." Only a couple feet separated them as Chase leveled Remy with a furious stare. "Tell me. Tell me right now you don't wanna get better."

Remy opened his mouth, fire in his gaze, but he had *nothing.*

Another foot vanished between them, and Chase struggled to contain his frustration. "Come on." He lowered his voice. "Tell me you don't want help."

"I—" Remy's chin wrinkled. More than raindrops clung to his eyelashes. "Everyone disappears," he gritted out thickly. "This is easier."

"I'm not going anywhere." Chase slid both his hands up Remy's neck and dipped low to rest their foreheads together. In response, Remy's eyes widened. Uncertainty flashed past. "Trust me."

"Chase, w-what're you—"

Before Remy could get out another word, Chase kissed him.

Remy gasped, his hands flying to Chase's waist. Chase took the opportunity to push his tongue into Remy's mouth, and it triggered Remy to kiss back. He moved his hands up Chase's chest and groaned.

The heat that had simmered beneath the surface erupted at once; the steady acceleration of Chase's heartbeat turned into a furious drumming. His cock throbbed as blood surged south, and his pulse skyrocketed. The kiss was bruising and passionate, tasting of grapes, coffee, and rain.

Chase lost the last ounce of restraint when Remy stood on his toes and threw his arms around Chase's neck.

The impact of their slick torsos colliding sent a shiver down Chase's spine. "Inside," he grunted, sucking lightly on the ring in Remy's bottom lip. They had to get back inside. *Now.* Where it wasn't pouring down, where there was a bed. His hands roamed over Remy's body and turned them around.

"Yeah. God, yeah." Remy deepened the kiss and let Chase guide them toward the cabin. Never breaking contact. The rain, the wet ground, the thunder—none of it was obstacle enough. "I thought it was just me." Remy moaned as he swept the tip of his tongue over Chase's scruffy chin. Then back to his mouth for a deep kiss. "Oh fuck, Chase." At that point, Remy's back hit the wall right next to the door of the cabin, and with the strip of roof overhead shielding them from the storm, Chase's libido decided it was time for a break. "Never—never in a million years did I think…"

Chase let out a gritty groan as he thrust his pelvis against Remy's and felt their cocks sliding together. "Don't think." 'Cause Chase couldn't. He didn't want to. He'd deal with the consequences afterward, but his body buzzed with too much urgency right now to stop and think. There was only one thing he had to say right now. He slowed the kiss and grasped Remy's chin, opening his eyes to find the most incredible sight ever. "It's not just you, though."

OUTCOME

Remy's cheeks were flushed with exertion, his eyes full of desire, and Chase kissed away a couple raindrops along Remy's jaw and neck.

"Yeah, we need a bed," Remy muttered, outta breath.

FOURTEEN

Remy was still shocked by the time they fell down on his bed, but he went with it. The questions he had for Chase grew steadily in the background as they got lost in each other, though with Chase underneath him, they were easy to ignore.

Chase was an intoxicating kisser, passionate and affectionate and aggressive all at once, and he was all hands. They moved over Remy's body with a hint of desperation and a whole lot of greed.

It allowed Remy to unleash every ounce of longing he had inside him. For now, he didn't have to force himself to push everyone away. Instead he could get as close as he wanted and give and take and give and take.

He moaned into Chase's mouth, feeling all that ruggedness beneath him. Chase was a man's man; he had the outlaw biker look down, but there was more, wasn't there? When they kissed, they kissed long and deep. When they touched, it was sensual and purposeful.

When Chase gave Remy's towel a tug, Remy broke the kiss and sat back between Chase's parted legs. The towel was easily taken care of, and then he leaned forward to get rid of Chase's sweats.

Fuck me. Chase was a big man everywhere.

"Come here." Chase shifted to the side to make room for Remy, who complied—maybe a bit too eagerly. "Is this a bad idea?"

"Probably." Remy hitched a leg over Chase's hip and

pulled Chase half on top of him. "I'm not stopping, though." *Please don't stop.*

"Good." Chase kissed him again as more thunder moved over the small cabin. A breeze from the open window stirred the air inside, and Remy drew closer to Chase's warmth. "Christ, Remy." Remy shuddered violently at the desire in Chase's husky voice and exposed his neck as Chase dipped low to kiss his skin. "You're beautiful. A beautiful fucking mess."

Those words wrecked Remy. Not long ago, he would've been pissed off at the smallest compliment, but with Chase…the words were sincere and they *fit*. If Remy had any good qualities left, he felt like he could count on Chase to see them. The good *and* the bad. *A beautiful fucking mess.*

"You want to sort me out?" Remy closed his eyes and groaned, feeling Chase's hand gliding up his thigh. "You're supposed to—" But he couldn't finish that sentence. He couldn't add *"hate me,"* because he was done. One last time, he was going to allow himself to hope. "Touch me."

"I can do that." Chase wrapped his fingers around Remy's cock, and they both tilted their heads together to kiss hungrily. "I have to."

They moved on instinct, urgency taking over. Remy's goal was to get closer and closer and closer, a goal Chase seemed to share. Remy bucked into Chase's hand, moaning in pleasure. But the cravings ran too deep for him to stop at hands.

He nudged Chase back and crawled on top of him, his hands dropping to the pillow above Chase's shoulders. Lining up their cocks, he fisted as much as he could of both of them and leaned down to kiss Chase's chest.

"Jesus fuck." Chase weaved his fingers through Remy's hair and tugged enough for Remy to feel it everywhere. The sensation shot sparks throughout him, awakening him further.

Remy licked and teased Chase's nipples until they were tight little points. He reveled in the heat between them, the closeness, the feel of Chase's hard cock rubbing along his. *Wet.* He wanted them slick and throbbing. Kissing farther down, he made Chase moan with a sharp nip to his hipbone.

"Spread your legs more." Remy settled down on the mattress and nuzzled the base of Chase's cock. He breathed in the musky scent, his mouth watering. Without permission, Remy's mind flashed forward, and he cursed the fact that they didn't have protection nearby, but… "Is it safe?"

He'd never been with anyone he trusted enough to ask that question. Not even before his life was shattered. But Remy was desperate enough to throw caution to the wind with Chase and *trust*.

"I'm cleaner than a fucking virgin." Chase let out a breathy laugh, a little bitter, a lot aroused. "I gotta feel you, Remy."

That was that. Never breaking the gaze, Remy licked the underside of Chase's thick cock before taking as much as he could inside his mouth. And Chase's reaction… God, it turned him on. He watched as Chase tensed up and let his head fall back. His torso became more defined, and the sexiest hissing sound slipped through Chase's lips.

The salty flavor of pure man made Remy zone out and focus on his own pleasure. He traced the ridges of Chase's cock with his tongue, sucking harder and harder until his jaw ached. He finally closed his eyes and allowed his body to take over.

"Christ, Remy." Chase groaned. "Your fucking tongue…"

Remy breathed through his nose and hummed, enjoying himself even more when Chase began to fuck his mouth slowly. Being framed by Chase's muscular thighs, sucking his cock, feeling his body heat…Remy was forced to grab his own dick to relieve some pressure.

"I wanna take care of you." Chase's gritty whisper caused Remy to snap back to the present. The sheer ravenousness Chase's eyes unleashed made Remy's cock painfully hard. "Now. Get up here before I lose it."

Remy complied without a second thought and soon found himself in Chase's strong arms. They circled him possessively and protectively as Chase pressed his cock against Remy's, and with the demanding kiss that followed, Remy was soon stripped bare of his internal armor.

His thoughts came out unfiltered and raw. "Don't stop.

Whatever you do, don't fucking stop." He panted against Chase's neck, tasting the skin there when he licked his lips. "God, you taste so good. Oh, fuck." Pushing his hips forward, he dug his fingernails into Chase's firm ass and pulled them together harder. *More.* "I need you." Chase groaned and sank his teeth into Remy's shoulder. "I might resort to violence if-if—*fuck.*" Remy screwed his eyes shut for one second in an attempt to clear his head. "I know I haven't earned your trust, but I swear I'm clean—"

Chase grabbed Remy's jaw and cut him off with a hard kiss. "You don't gotta twist my arm. What do you want?"

Remy blew out a breath and dropped his forehead to Chase's collarbone. "You." Slipping a hand between them, he palmed the heads of their cocks and smeared pre-come along the shafts. "I'm vers, so it doesn't matter to me right now, as long as we fuck."

Chase cursed, his lips brushing over Remy's temple. "I'm guessing vers stands for versatile?"

"Oh. Uh, yeah." Remy was used to guys who could be found on Grindr, and they knew the terminology. The fact that Chase was probably the last man to have an app on his phone for hookups only made Remy want him more. Remy was so fucking done with all that. "What about you?" He kissed his way up to Chase's mouth. "Top...?"

Chase kissed him back slowly, so deeply, and shook his head no. "I've enjoyed both."

To Remy, it sounded like Chase was speaking more in past tense than present. A couple more questions were added to his list, but now certainly wasn't the time to ask. Instead, he shifted on top of Chase and shivered in anticipation, his body having decided what he wanted.

"I want you to fuck me." He sucked lightly on Chase's bottom lip. "I need it." The more he thought about it, the stronger his desire became.

Chase swallowed audibly and nodded minutely. "But I don't have anything—"

"I do." Remy jumped off the bed and aimed for the kitchen. "I have a best friend with dry hands, thanks to spending the last six years with kindergartners and glitter glue." Therefore, Minna always had a small bottle of baby oil with aloe lying around. Remy found it in a cupboard under the sink and returned to the bed.

Chase halted him by sitting up and gripping Remy's hips. "I would've figured it was a tattoo aftercare thing."

Remy hauled in a breath as Chase leaned forward and pressed his mouth to where thigh met groin. *Please suck me.* "Baby oil? Oh, no." He threaded his fingers in Chase's hair, keeping him in place. Though, it didn't look as if Chase had plans to back away. He kissed and nuzzled closer to Remy's cock. "That—that would be one awful tattoo artist." Why the hell was he still talking? "*Fuck*, Chase."

Chase sucked him down, not stopping until Remy's cock hit the back of his throat. Two large, warm hands palmed Remy's ass, and he shuddered at the hot, wet suction.

Too good. Unless they wanted it to be over soon, it was time to ease off.

*

Few things could stop Chase once he'd gotten the taste of Remy's cock, but Remy begging to be fucked was one of them. He pulled Remy down with him on the bed and covered his lithe body with his own. He was insatiable, eager to lick and kiss every inch of Remy's skin.

Remy gasped when Chase flicked those tantalizing nipple piercings with his tongue. "Shit—do it again."

Chase settled next to Remy and grabbed the oil from the nightstand. While drizzling some into his hand, he lowered his mouth to Remy's piercings, then returned the bottle. "Spread." He nudged Remy's legs farther apart and began rubbing in the slick oil. In slow, firm strokes, he moved his hand over Remy's cock, under his balls, and into the crease between his ass cheeks.

He took his time, loving every hitched breath and moan Remy gave. Long strokes of Remy's cock, massaging his balls and inner thighs, and pushing two then three fingers deep inside his ass had Remy writhing in minutes. At the same time, Chase's mouth never left Remy's chest.

Remy groaned and lifted his hips for more. "I'm fucking beyond ready."

So was Chase. He kneeled between Remy's legs then frowned when Remy made a move to turn over.

Remy paused and flicked a look of uncertainty. "You don't want me on my stomach?"

Chase's brows rose, and he wondered if that was what Remy was used to. "No, I wanna see you." At that, Remy looked surprised and...shy? That didn't make sense. "This is exactly what I want." He hovered over Remy and kissed the corner of his mouth. "To see you while you take my cock."

"Damn," Remy breathed out. His hands slid up Chase's biceps, drawing him nearer. "You make me feel shit."

Chase grinned genuinely, a chuckle slipping out. For one second, he felt tons lighter. "As long as it's not *like* shit." Grabbing his cock, he shifted closer and pressed the head against Remy's tight, hot, slick opening. "Hell." He gritted his teeth as he pressed inside.

Remy closed his eyes and moaned, his head tipping back. "Chase—oh fuck, Chase."

"Yeah..." Chase let out a labored breath, pausing when he was all in. He tried to relax his muscles, but it was impossible. Wound tight and throbbing, he wasn't even sure he'd be able to stop once it was over. "Gimme your mouth." Goddamn, he could barely form words.

Chase took Remy's mouth in a long kiss and linked their fingers together on the pillow above Remy's head. Simultaneously, Chase pulled out his cock then pushed back in again and stole Remy's breath.

Remy gasped and squeezed Chase's fingers. "Harder."

Chase fucked him harder. Deeper. Powerless without self-control.

Fresh perspiration dampened their bodies, and they moved together as if they'd done it a thousand times before. When Chase released Remy's hands, they were quick to latch on to Chase's shoulders, arms, chest—wherever they could roam. Each push of Chase's hips was met by Remy's own thrust, and where one mouth went, the other tried to follow.

"Wrap your legs around me." Chase grunted as he slammed in. With a hand between them, he fisted Remy's cock and stroked it until it was hard as steel. "Yeah, fuck—that's it." Remy's heels dug in to Chase's ass, spurring him on, but most of all, making sure more parts of them touched. That was what it came down to for Chase: touch. He'd been sick with loneliness, and now it frustrated him that he couldn't get close enough. He wanted *all* of Remy.

Only Remy, a quiet voice hinted, but the thought scared the life outta him. Too risky to even consider. He silenced that inner voice with a growl, though he couldn't stop the possessiveness flowing through his veins. It seeped into the kiss he gave Remy.

Remy seemed to respond in kind. He kissed his way along Chase's neck and nipped sharply enough for every sting to shoot sparks down Chase's body. Remy's fingers dug in a little deeper, he thrust upward a little rougher, and he sucked on Chase's flesh a little harder.

Chase was getting close, and tasting the bead of sweat trickling down Remy's temple brought him to the edge. His balls drew up, and his muscles ached with tension.

"Come," Remy panted. "I'm…I'm—" He cut off, his eyes closing and a long moan escaping.

Noticing the expression of intense pleasure on Remy's face, Chase looked down between them. Saw his own cock pushing in and out of Remy's perfect ass. Saw his own fist working Remy's perfect cock, slick with pre-come and oil. And saw the first rope of come pulsing out of it.

"Oh, Christ." Chase lost it. His mouth watered at the sight, but he couldn't keep his eyes open. With a low growl, he rammed deep inside Remy and went rigid as the orgasm took over. Buried so tight, he felt his come rushing up his shaft before it filled Remy's ass. He didn't breathe, and the only part of him still moving was the hand stroking Remy.

It was messy, hot, and sticky. Fucking glorious.

Intoxicating.

Spent and drained in the best ways, Chase collapsed on top of Remy and tried to catch his breath. He made a half-assed attempt at easing off to give Remy space, but he was pulled down again. *Thank you.*

"Don't move," Remy whispered. Quick puffs of air hit Chase's shoulder. "Not yet."

Chase didn't need to be asked twice.

FIFTEEN

Remy closed his eyes and could practically see two imaginary roads opening up before him. Which one was he going to take, though? One would take him back to what he'd gotten used to, and he'd die there. The other one... It was the risks he feared, but the outcome could give him everything.

Life.

He fiddled absently with the lighter in the pocket of another pair of basketball shorts.

It was the middle of the night. Chase was asleep in the bed, and Remy stood in the small clearing outside the cabin smoking a cigarette.

The rain had stopped, but the black sky was filled with clouds, the moon only a faint blur behind the gray.

Remy felt...both heavy and light. Well-rested after several hours of uninterrupted sleep without nightmares, sexually sated after the mind-blowing fuck with Chase, refreshed after another icy shower to get rid of the mud that had dried on his legs and feet from earlier, and content in the peaceful night. But torn because of the hope that mingled with the ever-present guilt, exposed because it had been a lot more than just a fuck with Chase, and vulnerable because he couldn't do this alone.

He tilted up his face and blew out some smoke, his stomach clenching in anticipation. The mere thought of doing this, trying one last time, going all in... He knew if he failed, it'd be the end of him. He wouldn't be able to take another person rejecting him or dying. Not when he could barely stand on his own.

OUTCOME

When he'd turned to Clarissa and Fred for support, they'd made it abundantly clear that the only reason Remy was—at that time—invited to Sunday dinners was because he paid for Bill's assisted living. In the late stages of Alzheimer's, dear old Dad didn't remember any of the Stahls; he was always mumbling about a baseball game his grandfather had taken him to when he was a kid.

It had been expensive to make sure he had the best care, but Remy'd done it without hesitation. Until…well, until Clarissa and Fred decided to flee the embarrassment of the kidnapping, move to Milwaukee, and give Bill whatever treatment they could afford there.

Now they were only a blemish on the Bakersfield news archive.

Remy included.

Remy had told his mom he wanted to go back to her last name once. He remembered; it was the first time he'd turned to her after Chase and the others had returned to freedom. Clarissa and Fred had abandoned him, after all those years Remy had spent trying to please them, so he had stupidly held out hope for Mom. *Mom would care.* She'd been sober and clean at the time, strengthening his resolve to trust her.

"Of course you should change your name, kiddo." She'd given him a loud smooch on the forehead, leaving traces of sticky, pink lip gloss behind. *"You wanna be a Coleman like Mommy again, huh?"*

Two weeks later, she'd been too drugged up to form words.

Remy sighed and hung his head, taking another drag from his smoke.

Gullible, that's what he was. Every time Mom had sobered, he'd come crawling back to her. *"I need your help. I can't do this on my own, and I'm not sure therapy's working out."*

"Well, of course it ain't," she'd exclaimed, inspecting her too-long fingernails. He'd given her money for rent and groceries, and she looked like she'd just gotten back from the salon. *"Therapy's for rich folks who need more to spend their money on. I'm telling you, kiddo. This time's gonna be different. I'll help you. To hell with those damn head doctors."*

She'd hugged him and patted his cheek. *"They don't know you. I do. And like you helped me with rehab, I'll help you with this. I swear—it's gonna be different. It's gonna be different."*

Except, it hadn't been different at all, and it had taken a long fucking time before Remy had ventured back. Only to find her dead.

Stubbing out the smoke, Remy rubbed his chest and grimaced at the constriction his nervousness caused. *One last time.* He glanced back at the cabin and imagined Chase's peaceful expression as he slept.

I can trust him.

Remy realized the option of leaving, walking out into the night and disappearing, wasn't even there. No cuffs held him back, but something else did.

Drawn by an invisible force, he returned back inside and soundlessly got undressed before he snuck under the sheets.

He found Chase's warmth.

A few seconds later, Chase pulled Remy closer. "Told you. You wouldn't run away from me."

Remy grinned to himself and released a nervous breath.

*

The day after, they couldn't muster up any real anger to use on the punching bag, so they settled for a walk and some work around the cabin. After they'd cleaned out the shed in the back and washed their sheets down by the campsite, they returned inside to make lunch.

Chase could easily get hooked on this—this feeling, this sense of companionship. It offered a piece of the solid ground he'd been desperate for.

While they hadn't been particularly affectionate since waking up, it had been easy. Comfortable silences, a few touches, a couple jokes.

"An Italian who doesn't know how to cook?" Remy smiled cockily as he poured pasta into a pot on the portable stove. "Can't believe it."

Chase let out a laugh and leaned back against a wall, folding his arms across his chest. "Do I look Italian to you?" He shook his head. "It's so watered down that I think my name is the only thing left. My folks were religious, and my ma had a thing for Italian pet names, but..." He shrugged and scratched his nose.

Remy nodded, eyes trained on the pasta. "They're dead?" He chanced a quick glance at Chase.

"Yeah. I mean, it's been ten years, so..." It wasn't a sore topic, in other words. From Remy's expression, curiosity mingling with some caution, Chase clarified. "Wasn't an accident or anything. Pops died of cancer, and my mother had a heart attack shortly after."

That was the short version, anyway.

"That sucks." Remy focused a little too hard on the pasta. "Any other family?"

"Baby sister. Adriana—she's in college." Chase tilted his head and smiled a little. "I didn't take you as one for small talk."

That earned him a mock-scowl. "I'm only distracting you so you won't interfere with my cooking."

Chase chuckled and showed his palms. "Don't worry. You're safe." He paused, wanting to say something that kept conversation going. "Do you miss working in Andreas's studio?"

Remy straightened at that. His eyes narrowed. "How much have Minna and Andy really told you?"

"A lot." Mostly Minna.

"Figured." Remy's shoulders slumped, and he pulled out a loaf of bread from a cupboard. "I guess I miss it...sometimes...a little." Sounded like an understatement. "Do you like owning a bar?"

"Yeah, definitely." Chase hid a grin he couldn't explain. It was too genuine. "Beats being an employee. I've been a bartender since I was legal, but it's not until now I got my own place." The fact that Remy looked interested in what he was saying made him wanna smile again. Silly shit. "Would, uh...would you be able to visit?" He hadn't thought of that until now. "When you get outta here, I mean. Would visiting a bar be an issue?"

Chase's pulse picked up pace when he realized what he

was implying. Seeing Remy up here was one thing, but what about when they were back in civilization? If they met up every now and then...would it still be only about helping each other move on?

If Chase were smart, he'd draw the line at friends. And friends sure as hell didn't fuck. Being friends was a big step as it was, seeing as it wasn't so long ago Chase had claimed he didn't wanna get to know Remy on a personal level.

He had to draw that line.

"I don't think so," Remy answered hesitantly. "I should probably wait a while, though."

Chase nodded and stared at his feet. "What's hardest to stay away from? You don't gotta answer if you don't want—"

"Alcohol."

Chase looked up in surprise, having thought it would be drugs. Admittedly, he didn't know much about addictions. It had sucked to give up smoking, but he'd found it was more difficult to occupy his fingers than it'd been to stay away from nicotine. It was the whole routine, the habit of holding a cigarette, that had been the hardest to kill. To this day, he could still catch himself holding a pen like a smoke.

Right after he'd quit, he'd been restless and irritated. He'd be in the middle of work or doing some menial task and he'd reach for his smokes, only to remember they weren't there anymore.

At any rate, he figured that was nothing compared with what Remy was going through. No matter if it was drugs or booze.

"I cave easily," Remy admitted. "As long as I'm here in the middle of nowhere, it's sort of like 'out of sight, out of mind' because I've quit so many times. I..." He sighed and turned to distract himself by dicing a couple tomatoes. "I want drugs for what they made me forget, but I haven't done enough to need them. If that makes sense." He furrowed his brows at nothing, and Chase studied him intently, wanting to understand. "I guess I was kind of a weekend warrior?" Chase had heard that term; people who worked during the week and partied—hard—during the weekends. "At least when it comes to drugs. I mixed a lot of shit, thinking I wouldn't get hooked. And maybe it worked to an extent, but—" a humorless chuckle slipped out "—my body took a hit

126

when Minna got to me. I'm used to chemicals in my system, that's for sure." He shifted uncomfortably. "I get mood swings and headaches."

Chase closed the distance and nudged Remy's arm, a wry smirk on his lips. "Mood swings—really?" He wanted to lighten the tension, and it seemed to work.

Remy smirked back and huffed. "Believe it or not, but I've actually held back with you. Andy...? Not so much." His frown returned. "I have a lot of making up to do."

"You getting better will make everything worth it," Chase murmured. "They'll see it as a victory as much as you will."

"Getting better," Remy repeated quietly. "Yeah..."

It looked like he didn't believe it yet—that he could move on from this.

Chase was determined, though. For the both of them. But for now, he got back to the previous topic. "So you crave alcohol more?"

"Huh? Oh. Yeah." Remy nodded once and busied himself with the pasta again. "That's the thing. The drugs were a weekend thing or when I was desperate for a whole night's sleep, and it was only after Mom died. But with the family I have?" Bitterness seeped into his tone. "I've had my fair share of benders since I was fifteen. Alcohol has always helped."

Helped. What a fucked-up word to use. While Chase couldn't fathom what Remy had gone through, the fact he used that word to describe alcohol and getting drunk...that said a lot.

"I think once I get back home..." Pain flitted across Remy's features, though he did his best to hide it. "Temptation is a cunt."

"You're banned from my bar," Chase blurted.

Shit.

Remy's eyebrows rose.

Chase cleared his throat. "I didn't mean it like that, but yeah, you're not allowed to go there." Fuck if he was gonna be responsible for Remy failing. It was nothing Chase wanted on his conscience, but mainly, he wanted Remy to succeed. "I wanna be helpful, not drag you down."

Remy didn't reply; he appeared to be lost in his own little world while he finished preparing their lunch. He worked on autopilot, from what Chase could tell, and Chase got outta the way to give Remy some room.

Chase's thoughts were all over the place. He wanted to help to the point where he was afraid he'd push Remy too far. He also worried that turning Remy into a mission would only force his own shit aside for the moment, not actually eliminate the issues.

Having a purpose in life had to be a positive thing, but he couldn't let it take over.

It wasn't until they sat down to eat—in Remy's bed, much like yesterday—that Remy spoke again.

He stared at his plate, absentmindedly dragging a piece of bread through the tomato sauce. "I'm probably going to fail, you know."

Chase eyed him as he twirled his fork in the pasta. "You settin' yourself up for it?"

"No." Remy glanced up at Chase, a blank expression on his face. "I'm just warning you. I can't promise you I won't—"

"You don't have to promise *me* shit." Chase pointed to himself. "This is about you, and like Minna and Andreas, I plan on sticking around no matter what."

Remy swallowed hard and tested a small smile. "Does that make us friends, Gallardo?" He was going for teasing.

Chase smirked, shoveling some food into his mouth. "Never saw that coming, but yeah, I guess so."

"Did anyone ever tell you that you have horrible taste in friends?"

I never had friends until recently, so no. Chase didn't say that; instead, he observed how similar he and Remy could be. How often did Chase view himself as a less important person than others? The minute he failed at something, he was a champ at beating himself up. Whether it was about helping someone else or himself, and regardless of how high he set the bar, he found a way to blame himself.

It took hearing the same kinda talk from Remy for Chase to realize he had to stop doing that. At the very least, he had to fucking try. He wasn't God; he couldn't do everything—especially not on his own—which…which meant his pops was wrong about yet another thing. The pity Chase had for his old man grew tenfold, and it was starting to get pathetic.

"You really see yourself as a bad guy, don't you?"

Remy shrugged. "I used to think I was decent, but the evidence speaks for itself." Chase didn't know what the hell Remy was talking about, and it must've shown on his face. "Clarissa and Fred always hated me, my mom killed herself, and I obviously did something that made Ben hate me so much he kidnapped innocent people for it."

Halfway through that sentence, Chase was shaking his head, and he thought back to Cam's two cents about therapy. It didn't have to be about healing. Sometimes a person just needed a new perspective.

Remy needed that, too. Clearly.

"And you blame yourself for the whole funding thing, too?" Chase only wanted clarification, which he got when Remy nodded. "Right. Did it ever occur to you that it's not normal to suspect your half brother of being a criminal?"

Remy frowned. "What do you mean?"

Chase was beginning to grow impatient, but it was because he felt they were close to some kind of breakthrough. "You said that if you'd only asked Ben what he was doing with the money… Seriously, Remy, do you think he'd have told you the truth?"

"Of-fucking-course not." Remy rolled his eyes.

"So, you were supposed to *assume* he was doing something shady?" Chase cocked a brow and took a sip of his water. "Seems to me like you'd be a pretty shitty brother if you walked around and judged your family guilty of kidnapping and murder without reason."

The cabin went quiet, and Remy stared at his lap, his face frozen in a frown. Mind spinning, maybe? Chase could only hope.

*

Hours later, Chase was getting antsy.

Andreas would be here any minute, and Chase could count the words Remy had spoken since lunch on two hands. Packed and ready to go, he left his bike and joined Remy in the cabin, finding him tidying up the kitchen table.

"You sure you're okay?" It was the third time Chase had asked something similar since they'd eaten.

He didn't expect to be privy to all of Remy's thoughts, but he needed a gesture—something that said Remy wanted Chase to come back. Soon.

Remy stopped what he was doing and nodded jerkily, then just stared at his feet. "A lot on my mind."

Farther down the mountainside, Chase could hear the rumbling of a vehicle coming closer. Judging by the slight stiffening of Remy's shoulders, he heard it, too.

Chase felt the moment slipping through his fingers and approached without caution, his main priority Remy, not discretion or playing it cool.

"Hey." He lifted Remy's chin and slid his fingers up Remy's jaw. "Whenever you wanna talk, whenever you wanna see me…"

Distress caused a small crease between Remy's brows. "It feels wrong—" He swallowed audibly, seemingly having a hard time speaking, and Chase's hand fell away again. "To unload my issues on you, I mean. Should be the other way around." He puffed out a breath and ran a hand through his hair. "You said you had questions, but—you've barely asked any. Everything's been about my bullshit."

"We have time, don't we? We can focus on my bullshit whenever." Chase tried to make light of it.

Remy managed half a smile, and if Chase wasn't mistaken, there was a pinch of relief in his features. "Can you come back tomorrow?"

It was a joke, but it was also the gesture Chase wanted. This was it. This was the closest Remy would ever get to saying, *"Can you please help me?"*

Once again, Chase was reminded of how similar they could be, how stubbornly they could refuse asking for help.

A plan formed in his head, and he decided to call Minna when he came home. "You're not gonna run back to LA first chance you get?"

"I don't think I'll even be tempted as long as I have more holding me back."

It wasn't a naïve *"No,"* and Chase appreciated the honesty, something tightening in his chest. In an automatic response, he drew closer and tilted his head, only to freeze and hesitate.

Draw the line as friends, for fuck's sake. You don't need to get more involved. You're already in deep shit as it is, man.

As he battled with himself, he searched Remy's eyes, finding them greener than ever and swimming with apprehension and anticipation. The last straw was when Remy wet his bottom lip. Chase closed the distance and kissed him, his hands moving up and into Remy's hair.

Remy hooked his fingers into Chase's belt and tugged their lower bodies together, at which Chase groaned quietly—outta pure lust and something oddly akin to relief. But he didn't read into that. Instead he deepened the kiss and swept the tip of his tongue between Remy's parted lips. One little flick over his piercing, and then Remy was there with his own tongue.

Oh yeah, Chase was in deep shit here. Every desire he'd struggled against for so long had returned with a vengeance, and they were only magnified with Remy.

Only the sound of a car door slamming shut made Chase draw back, and even that... Fuck, he reluctantly took a step back and tried to catch his breath.

Instinct told him to *not* have his back to the new arrival. That had already happened once before, the final nail in the coffin that had turned Chase's life into a cautionary tale.

He forced himself to appear casual; he even managed to land a quick kiss to Remy's forehead. Then he turned for the door as reality snuck up and bit him in the ass.

"We'll talk soon," he promised before making his exit.

Being tucked away in this little corner that God had forgotten was causing Chase to make some fucked-up decisions. Like fucking a man. Sleeping with him and loving it. Kissing him seconds before they wouldn't be alone anymore.

His previous surrender still lingered as he nodded hello to Andreas, who was leaning casually back against his car. But even if Chase had caved with Remy and savored every second of it didn't mean the ghost of his entire upbringing had evaporated.

Would he *ever* be able to share his life with someone without fearing hell and grisly conditions?

"How is he?" Andreas straightened.

Chase looked back toward the cabin and fiddled with his key. He didn't have to talk to Minna, did he? Andreas was standing right here; Chase might as well talk to him.

"Remy is…" *A beautiful fucking mess who wants to get better but is afraid he can't.* And Chase had no business getting emotionally attached. Or fucking him. "Progressing," he settled for, looking back at Andreas. "We've had a few run-ins—" Chase cleared his throat, thinking about the different *kinds* of "run-ins" he'd had with Remy. "He's got one hell of a temper, but…" Andreas's mouth quirked up in a wry smile. "Remy's coming around," Chase said firmly. "He's started to open up, and easing him back into the world of the living wouldn't be wrong."

That seemed to catch Andreas's interest.

SIXTEEN

Cam stepped outside and let the door to the bar close behind him. The sun had finally set, and he lit a smoke and looked up at the sky painted in pink, purple, and orange.

Austin had told Chase again and again that he didn't have to close the bar for a night to have some people over for dinner, but Cam wasn't gonna say no to a bar free of people. And pizza and beer? Only a fool would turn that down.

He sure as hell didn't feel that Chase owed them anything for "everything they'd done," as he'd put it, but it was nice to get outta the house for a night and not have to worry about crowds or drunk motherfuckers who didn't know what personal space was.

Blowing out some smoke, Cam heard the door open, and he looked over his shoulder to see Adriana joining him.

Chase's little sister had apparently arrived today and was gonna spend the weekend in Bakersfield. Majoring in business or whatever, she had a lot in common with Austin—and the two got along well—so Cam was a little confused about her following him now. But the way her blue eyes fell to his smoke gave him a clue.

He let his cigarette dangle between his lips as he searched his pockets for the pack. Then he raised a brow and extended the smokes, to which Adriana bit her lip and widened her eyes, quickly shaking her head.

"I can't—I mean, I don't smoke."

Cam snorted in amusement and pocketed his smokes again. "If you say so."

He took another drag and eyed the curvy brunette. Her

skin tone was a couple shades darker than Chase's, as was her long, curly hair. It was her eyes that gave away the relation. She was pretty—and a shitty fucking liar. "If it's somethin' you're keepin' from Chase, you might wanna work on your acting."

Adriana made a face and looked down. "He'd go ballistic if he knew."

"He used to smoke," Cam pointed out. They'd even shared one when they'd been in the hospital together three years ago.

"Um, yeah. Then I played the guilt card and made him quit." Adriana faced him with a sheepish smile, and Cam chuckled. "In my defense, I thought I'd lost him, you know. Back when you guys were…" She trailed off at the word kidnapped. Or taken. Or whatever-the-fuck.

Cam's shoulders stiffened. He hoped like hell the girl didn't wanna make small talk about that clusterfuck. They didn't even know each other.

"Anyway…" That was better. Adriana changed the topic. "The reason I came out here was because I wanted to ask you how my brother's doing." Her face grew serious. "He's told me about you, and I got the impression you're the one least likely to sugarcoat things."

Cam considered her words and took a drag from the smoke. If she'd asked before today, he would've told her that Chase always struck him as closed off and tired. Austin had mentioned weary and lonely too, but Cam didn't see anything wrong with being around fewer people. Hell, all he needed was Austin and their daughter, and Cam was all set. But, as Austin had pointed out, not everyone was as introverted as Cam was.

Regardless, that was before today.

Something had obviously happened with Chase after spending so much time with the Stahl guy. All throughout dinner, Chase was checking his phone and looking at the clock above the bar. At the same time, he'd also talked more.

"You should ask him about Remy," Cam said eventually.

"Remy Stahl?" Adriana nodded. "Chase told me they've been talking." She seemed to wanna know more, though. From

Cam.

He suppressed a sigh and stubbed out his cigarette. "Sorry, hon. I'm not the right man to ask. Austin can probably tell you more. All I know is it's probably a good thing for Chase and Stahl to talk. Their problems are kinda connected."

Adriana averted her eyes and nodded again, this time more pensively. "I wonder if he's met someone."

"He has." Cam knew that much. "He's called Gale—the therapist we all used back then." He and Austin still went every now and then, but it wasn't often. "Austin told me Chase has his first session after the weekend."

"That's good news—I'm glad." Adriana smiled genuinely before it morphed into a smirk. "But I was talking about a romantic-type of 'met someone.'" Oh. Well, what the fuck did Cam know? "I swear I heard him laughing in his office earlier, and that's definitely new."

"Right." Cam didn't know what else to say, but if Chase was getting better, then great. "We should get back in."

"Oh, of course." Adriana stepped aside as Cam grabbed the door handle. "By the way, Riley asked me if I could paint her nails. Is that all right?"

Cam grimaced, having never liked makeup—and sure as fuck not on thirteen-year-olds—but he knew it was part of the whole growing-up crap.

"Keep it girly," he muttered.

He and Austin were lucky that Riley was mostly a tomboy, but she had her princess moments. And Cam could deal with a little pink and a little glitter. It beat slutty red and black.

It was only a matter of months, maybe a year, before Riley would need to buy her first bra.

Cam wasn't ready for that shit.

Maybe it could happen during one of the rare occasions Jade had time for Riley. Or maybe it was Riley who didn't have time for her mom? Whatever, something always tended to come up whenever the two had plans, and neither seemed upset about it.

Returning to their table, Cam sat down next to Austin, while Adriana headed over to the dart board where Riley was practicing.

The guys were talking about Donna's living situation. A verbally abusive boyfriend was involved, and he'd refused to leave her apartment. Now he had finally left town, but he'd trashed her home.

"Does he still have a key to her place?" Austin asked.

Chase shook his head. "No. I went over there yesterday and changed the locks for her. Installed a chain lock, too."

"That's good." Austin nodded and leaned back, his hand finding Cam's thigh. "Speaking of, have you found a place of your own yet?"

Cam tilted his head, sensing the discomfort Chase was trying to hide. He linked his fingers with Austin's and gave his hand a squeeze. *Enough, baby.*

In general, Austin wasn't the kind of man who had to fix every problem, but he considered Chase a close friend these days, and Austin always took care of his own.

Same could be said for Cam, only on a smaller scale. They complemented each other well in that respect; when Cam closed himself in and only cared for his immediate family, Austin coaxed him out. And now, in this case, Cam drew Austin back just a bit.

They'd concluded that Chase slept in his office, and Cam doubted Chase was a fan of the topic.

"I apologize. Didn't mean to pry—"

Chase cut Austin off with a quick shake of his head. "It's okay, man." He rubbed the back of his neck and managed a faint grin. "My search's been kinda half-assed so far. I'm good where I am for now, and Ade still has her room with the Thompsons over in Seven Oaks."

Cam frowned at that—first time he'd ever heard that name—but Austin seemed to know.

"Ade's foster parents," Chase explained to Cam. "When our folks died, she was still underage, so they placed her in a foster family 'til she turned eighteen. Good people. I don't talk to them much, but they view Ade as a niece or somethin'."

Cam inclined his head in acknowledgment. "Better watch out so Riley doesn't force Adriana to come home with us instead."

He jerked his chin to another table where Adriana was painting Riley's fingernails. Cam scrunched his nose at the smell of nail polish that made its way several feet over.

Chase chuckled and looked away from his sister and Riley, back to Cam and Austin. "Her backup plan was always to work with kids, so I'm not sure Ade would mind."

Cam wouldn't mind, either. Considering how rarely Riley saw her mom, both Cam and Austin encouraged more interaction with good, female role models. Jules, Cam's sister-in-law, adored Riley and often included her in everyday errands to "get away from the boys," which Riley got a kick out of. Additionally, Cam preferred it when Riley painted Jules's nails instead of his.

Purple just wasn't his color.

*

Close to midnight, Cam and Austin had found a babysitter in Adriana, who didn't say no when Riley asked if she wanted a sleepover with movies and girl talk. While Austin helped the ladies set things up in the living room, Cam left the house to walk Bourbon and Nacho.

The neighborhood was silent and bathed in a dim glow from the streetlamps.

It was when Cam headed back he heard something that didn't fit. He squinted in the poor light and saw a guy lurking by the kitchen window of Remy's house, tapping anxiously on the glass.

Nacho was already alert. Though, despite his guard instincts being better than Bourbon's, he was a damn Chihuahua. Nobody took that seriously. Bourbon was the goof, but he was a big Husky and trained to fake better than a woman.

Cam's first thought was that the lurker planned on breaking in, scoring money or whatever for drugs, but he could also be a *friend* of Stahl's.

Cam had heard of Remy's lifestyle choices, and the motherfucker peering into the kitchen window fit the bill of a clichéd addict. Hoodie a couple sizes too large, shoulders bunched up, twitchy mannerisms, and pants that were about to fall down his scrawny frame.

"Can I fucking help you?" Cam asked, slowly and casually crossing the street.

The dude jumped and turned, flashing an image of a greasy forehead, bad skin that belonged to a meth head, and a gaze that flicked all over the place.

"I'm—I'm looking for Remy Stahl." Twitchy sniffled and stumbled out of the front yard. "Do you know him? Trent wants him back in-in LA."

If that was a life Stahl was trying to get away from, Cam kinda wanted to pound in this motherfucker's skull.

Pissed, he tilted his head to Bourbon. "Warn," he commanded quietly. Bourbon stiffened and started growling, his teeth bared. Cam's gaze slid back to Twitchy, and he cocked a brow. "Wanna see what else he can do?"

Twitchy got spooked and showed his palms in surrender. "Look, I'm only a messenger—"

"I don't give a shit," Cam snapped. "Remy doesn't even live in that house." Lie, truth, or a little bit of both, Cam didn't know, but he was glad the woman who did live there wasn't home. "Get the fuck outta here, and if I see you in this neighborhood again…"

Twitchy took another glance at a growling Bourbon before he hightailed it to his rusty truck and drove away.

"Good boy." Cam patted Bourbon on his head and rolled his eyes at Nacho's *"What about me?"* look. "Yeah, you too. Good boy."

SEVENTEEN

"I'm so glad you came to see me, Remy." Gale shook his hand warmly; meanwhile, he couldn't wait to get out of here. She was in her late forties, Remy guessed. Very nice, calm, and she'd actually made him feel comfortable, but one session was more than enough for now. "I'll see you in a few days?"

Remy nodded firmly and then made his way outside where Minna was waiting.

He blew out a heavy breath. He only had to pretend to be chill for another five or ten minutes. Then he'd see Chase again.

It had been over a fucking week, which seemed like forever, but, at the same time, a lot had been accomplished.

As a small hint, a *"something to think about,"* Chase had mentioned Gale and contacting her, and Remy had done more than think about it. A lot more.

He now spent most of his days in various diners on the outskirts of the city. While it was boring and he tended to reek of grease, it was a good beginning. *Easing into the world of the living.* It had been Chase's suggestion, and Remy was relieved. He wasn't ready for too much interaction, but he wouldn't have given it a thought if it weren't for Chase. Remy had simply expected to go from the cabin to home.

This was better, though. The cabin was no longer a prison, but a place of comfort. Peace and quiet. No temptations. A place to process.

After falling into Chase's set pace, Remy had given himself restrictions. He'd bought a second phone with only three people's numbers in it—four now, including his new therapist's—because the last thing he wanted was to hear from the people in LA. He had also relinquished control of all credit cards but one. Andreas and Minna would keep it all for him, keys to his cars too, until he was ready.

Both his cars were parked in a garage in LA, so it wasn't like he could reach them right this minute anyway, but it felt more genuine—like it was his choice—when he'd handed over the keys.

Lastly, he was officially in therapy. Which he hadn't told Chase about, in the event Remy chickened out of going. He didn't want to disappoint Chase, so he'd only told Minna and Andreas.

Minna was in tears when he reached the parking lot, though he already knew nothing was wrong. Last Tuesday when he'd told her he was going to see Gale, she'd been an emotional mess.

"How did it go?" She grasped his arms and then hugged him fiercely. "I'm so, so, so happy, Rem. You have no idea."

He smiled tightly and kissed her temple. "I have an inkling." But it was hard to feel the relief when he wanted to punch a wall, followed by sobbing like a baby.

The session hadn't even been a real one. More of an introduction. Gale had told him a little about herself and how she practiced, and Remy had given her the basics of his fucked-up life. He'd glossed over most things, just mentioning his family, the kidnapping, his mom's suicide, and how his life had looked the past year.

"I want to know everything." Minna unlocked the car, and Remy got in. "What's next?"

Remy checked his watch. Okay, more like ten minutes than five 'til he saw Chase. "Um, I don't know where to start." He slumped back and dragged a hand down his face. "Gale's specialty is in trauma, so she gave me recommendations to others for my addiction." Today had been the first day he'd said that word out loud. Addiction. He was an addict when it came to alcohol. Perhaps not an everyday craving, but it was what he turned to the minute something went wrong. "I'm not ready for some fucking circle jerk—"

Minna giggled and slapped his arm. "Be serious. There's nothing wrong with group sessions."

That may be, but Remy cringed at the thought. No, he'd do this with Gale, first and foremost, and then he'd probably turn to one of the therapists she had recommended. *For solo sessions.*

"Anyway, I'll see her once a week." He looked out the window and scratched his jaw. "I'll rehash all the shit in my life, and we'll go from there."

At this point, he was hopeful but skeptical. He'd go all in and give this a shot, but he doubted talking to Gale would be more therapeutic than talking to Chase.

Remy's head was still spinning from Chase's point of view regarding Remy funding Ben's kidnapping. *I couldn't have known he was going to use the money for crimes.* It was taking a lot to let it settle, and it felt like an undeserved dessert until he reminded himself that maybe he did deserve it. Sort of like waking up on a Saturday morning and thinking it was time for work, only to grin and realize…fuck yeah, it *was* Saturday.

Chase couldn't possibly know how much he'd already saved Remy. Unfortunately, it was difficult expressing gratitude in text messages. Remy was usually attached to either Andy or Minna, so they couldn't speak without an audience. But today Chase could get away from work, so he'd be the babysitter instead.

Texting with Chase was…weird. The two had heavy topics hanging over them like a storm cloud, so cracking jokes and sharing small anecdotes about their days had been awkward at first. It still felt a bit off, but they were getting there. They were finding their little groove.

Remy had especially taken a liking to their good-morning texts. Chase would start off with an *"Okay, I'm up,"* followed by something that was making Remy realize Chase had a sense of humor. Remy's favorite was *"My sister told me to hit ctrl+delete and hold it for a while on my computer if I wanted to change browsers. Now she's on my shit list."* Although, *"Once you hit forty, a discount for backrubs would've been nice"* was solid, too. To which Remy had replied that Chase wasn't forty just yet, and Chase had texted, *"Semantics, KID."*

Remy's mouth twisted.

It was easy to get attached to Chase Gallardo. Too easy.

"Tell me more whenever you want, okay?" Minna patted his hand.

He laced their fingers together and exhaled. "I love you."

Minna started crying again.

*

Remy's fingers nearly shook as he rolled down the window and lit up a smoke. He could see Chase leaning back against his bike—maybe it was new because it was different from the one he'd had last time—that was parked just to the side of the '50s-style diner.

If Remy was going to be honest with himself, he wanted comfort from Chase, but he had a feeling that was a no-go. Chase was, without a doubt, in the closet, judging by his reaction in the cabin when Andy had shown up.

"He's so fucking hot." Minna sighed and killed the engine. "All rugged and…" She pursed her lips and turned to Remy as he stifled a smirk. "He's a cowboy with a bike instead of a horse. You mind checking if he's single?"

Remy tapped his lighter on his knee and blew out some smoke. "Don't you have a date tonight?"

"Yeah…" She scrunched her nose and glanced at Chase. "I'm doing a stupid chick thing. There's this hot math teacher at the elementary school across from where I work, and I want his attention." She shot Remy a sheepish smile. "His friend asked me out, and I said yes."

"Honey, we're *thirty*." Remy's anxiousness dissipated slightly, amusement taking over. "If you like the dude, go up to him and ask him out. Games won't impress him." Not to mention the fact that good guys didn't go after their friends' women. "You're off-limits to him if you go out with his buddy."

"I said it was stupid, didn't I?" Minna huffed. "But you're right. And I guess I can ask more about Chase another time."

"Yeah, you do that." Remy grinned and opened the door. "When's Andy coming to the cabin?"

"After he closes the shop, so around ten. Do you want him to pick you up, or will Chase drive you up there?"

Remy's forehead creased as he got out of the car and looked over to Chase, who was eating a red apple. "I'm not getting on a fucking bike."

Minna's smile was pure glee. "Why, *Remy*. Are you afraid to lose your *life* or something?"

Hardy-fucking-har-har. Okay, so maybe Remy had never really been suicidal. "Eat shit." He kissed two fingers at her then closed the door and made his way toward Chase.

Behind him, he heard Minna's laughter as she started up the truck again. "That's your job, Remykins!"

Remy chuckled, rolled his eyes, and threw his smoke on the ground. Like ominous music growing louder in a horror movie, his discomfort and exhaustion returned slowly but surely.

Chase smirked curiously and tossed what remained of his apple into a trash can. "What's your job, Remykins?"

Hearing that warm voice alight with humor did strange things to Remy. He'd *missed* Chase, but Remy's feelings were easier to control when Chase lived in his cell phone. Standing face-to-face—or almost—with the man now was another matter.

Emotions he'd suppressed surged forward, and the state he'd been left in after therapy weighed him down something fucking awful.

He forced a grin. "To ask on Minna's behalf if you're single or not."

Chase's brows rose in surprise, most likely in response to Remy's answer, before they dipped into a frown. "Somethin's up with you."

Guess playing it cool is out the window. Remy let out a hollow laugh, deflated and beaten, and gestured to the alley between two low buildings.

Chase followed without a word, and Remy side-eyed him cautiously. There was a crease of concern in Chase's forehead, but what made Remy uncomfortable was the way Chase had tensed his shoulders. He was on edge, and Remy's mind came up with countless scenarios in a heartbeat. Was it because Chase thought

Remy was going to kiss him or something—be affectionate in public? Did Chase always assume the worst? Did he think something had happened? Did he have an odd fear of Dumpsters? Maybe he feared alley cats?

Internal eye-roll. Remy came to a stop when they reached the end, and he asked Chase if something was up with *him.*

Chase shrugged, his jaw clenching. "Not very fond of alleys, I guess." He shook his head while Remy narrowed his eyes. "Anyway, what's going on?"

No time like the present, Remy supposed. "You started therapy this week, right?"

"You know I did." Chase tilted his head and showed the barest hint of a smirk. "I texted you—it went fine, and I said I was gonna tell you all about it later."

Remy nodded, nervous as *fuck.* "I started therapy, too. Today—with Gale."

*

Chase was stuck on stupid.

He was surprised and…and *proud,* but he didn't know what to say. It had been a weird week, and Remy had picked the worst place to reveal good news. *"Not very fond of alleys"* was an understatement.

He struggled against the flashback that would take him to an alley in Fresno three-and-a-half years ago. The guy who had just sucked him off had walked away with a satisfied grin, leaving a highly intoxicated and conflicted Chase behind. He'd zipped up his jeans, feeling defeated, and hadn't noticed the headlights until a truck had him cornered. What came next was a pathetic excuse for a fight before Chase had succumbed to the nauseatingly sweet vapors of chloroform. The last thing he remembered was a man cackling, *"How fitting!"* which Chase had never understood. *Fitting?*

He'd woken up in a cage.

"Fuck," he muttered, squeezing his eyes shut. *Get it together, Gallardo.* But fighting dizziness and nausea wasn't that fucking easy. "That's…" *Yeah, go on. Say something to Remy.* "I mean, really?

Therapy? Nice." He managed to open his eyes again and saw disappointment in Remy's features.

Way to show your pride, man.

Chase gave up. Feeling like shit, he acted on instinct and pulled Remy in for a tight hug. "I'm sorry, Remy." He cleared his throat and blinked past the blurriness in his vision. "I can't focus here. I was in an alley when Ben took me, but I'm so glad you've started therapy—"

"Shut up," Remy said quickly. "Damn, I didn't know." He broke the hug and nudged Chase toward the street. "Come on. I'm sorry—I had no idea."

Chase swallowed hard and then drew in a deep breath when they were outta the alley. He felt weak and irritated as hell, and nothing was going as planned.

"Do—do you want to talk about it?" Remy asked apprehensively. "Like, that day, when you were taken? What were you doing?"

Chase shook his head and pressed his lips together, eyes downcast. There was no way he was ready to talk about that. He had never even gotten that far with Gale during the first round of therapy. Everything regarding his sexuality had remained secret for so long, and opening up wasn't gonna be easy.

"Another time." He coughed and looked up. "Let's get something to eat, okay? I wanna know about your session."

Remy didn't look all too pleased, but he nodded and headed inside the diner.

Chase followed, and they found a booth and ordered before they addressed each other again, though not without awkwardness.

Was this what first dates were like? In that case, Chase was glad he'd never been on one. While Remy was fidgeting with his lip ring and the toothpick dispenser, Chase kept shifting in his seat and running a hand through his hair.

"You go first," Remy blurted. "Your session was earlier in the week, so…"

Right. Some kind of logic. "Uh…" Chase scratched his scruffy chin and tried to relax. "Sure. I guess. All right." He took a sip of his water then sat back and gathered his thoughts. *Therapy. Gale. Talk.* Since Chase had seen Gale before, he'd been somewhat relieved when she'd told him he didn't have to recap everything about the kidnapping. Instead she'd encouraged him to start from the beginning. The beginning-beginning. Chase's upbringing and how he grew up.

He still didn't really know to what end, but it was a fairly safe topic, so the first session hadn't been all that dreadful.

"We talked about my childhood." He shrugged with one shoulder. "I told you I've had Gale as my therapist before." Remy nodded. "Right, so she already knows pretty much everything about what went down with Ben. And she remembered that I mentioned guilt and hopelessness back then, so now…I think she wants to get a clear picture or somethin'." That was the only way it could make sense to Chase, anyway. "I mean, I ain't stupid. I know some of the shit my pops said and believed in has fucked with my head, but…" Really, his childhood had been decent. "You'll notice that with Gale, by the way. She won't give you all the answers you want. She prefers to nudge you in the right direction and let you come to the conclusions on your own."

Which frustrated Chase, but at the same time he acknowledged she knew what she was doing. Because the one person you usually believed more than others was yourself. Or it should be, and it was like that for Chase, too. For the past twenty years, he'd known all about the flaws in his father's beliefs; it was just doing something about it that was the issue.

"That's good, I suppose…" Remy pondered that for a beat, then hesitated and moved on. "What about your dad, though? Were there problems with him?"

Chase considered his answer before telling Remy about Pops's lectures and strict beliefs on how to be a *real* man. Hard work, standing on your own two feet, never accepting help from the outside—which included a son who'd just happened to move a few blocks away.

"To him, I was no longer *in the family*," he explained, only pausing when the waitress brought them their food. "I was his son, of course, but I didn't live at home any longer. That made me a guest when I visited."

And if Pops had alienated Chase so easily, simply for moving out, how shunned would he have been if he'd even thought about admitting he was gay?

Remy frowned and picked absently at his food. "So…this is connected to the helplessness? You wanted to be able to help, but he didn't let you?"

Chase offered half a nod, half a shrug. "Yeah. I was left out." He didn't know why, but he was embarrassed. "It killed me when I wasn't allowed to help them. They needed it." He stared at his burger, not feeling an ounce of the hunger he'd felt when he'd arrived earlier. "Thing is, I started resenting my dad. And started to pity him."

That seemed to pique Remy's curiosity. "Pity him?"

"Yup." Chase forced a sense of casual and took a bite of his burger. "He failed at most things, when you think about it. Bad health—" At Remy's raised brow, Chase elaborated. "Diabetes, smoker's cough, and bad kidneys. Then lung cancer that killed him. But aside from that, he couldn't support his family for shit, and he preached about pride and dignity until I wanted to punch him in the throat." He set down his burger again, agitated by the memories of his attempts at pitching in. Dammit, his dad had barely even let *Mom* work. Her place was at home, he'd said firmly. Only every now and then had he let her sell beauty products and Tupperware between friends and whatever. "He was one of those guys in high school—the jock who goes through his best days in school and then watches all his friends succeed later in life." And his mom had looked up to Pops as if he was a god. Chase shook his head. "He was a patriarch without any reason whatsoever— nothing backing him up."

Remy appeared to understand now. "And so every time he told you how important it was for a man to make it on his own, all you saw was his inability to practice what he preached."

Exactly. But Chase didn't *want* to pity his own flesh and blood; he wanted to remember his pops like the man he'd looked up to once—a *long* time ago—much like his ma had done. Back when Chase didn't know better and soaked up every word Pops said.

This had been another reason for Chase to hide his sexuality. Because if he piled together all of Pops's mistakes and failures, and then added a gay son, to boot? Come on. What son wanted to be another mistake?

Ma's final words about making Pops proud had buried Chase in a way. He'd said goodbye to ever finding that kind of freedom and started a ridiculous quest of giving Pops a legacy.

Laughable.

"Anyway…" He coughed lightly into his fist and reached for his water. "I hate feeling helpless. Five months in that basement didn't make things better, and Gale's gonna help me sort shit out, I guess."

Remy looked away with a pained expression. "I don't think I'll ever stop feeling guilty about what Ben put you through."

Chase stared at Remy intently, and one of the reasons this week had been weird popped into his mind again.

Not a lot had actually *happened* since he'd seen Remy last time—apart from seeing his little sister, which had been nice, and beginning therapy again—but there was this fucked-up question that had snuck up on him.

What if they could make it all worth it?

Austin and Cam had done it.

EIGHTEEN

Remy felt the need to speak—say something, anything—before his depression pulled him under. "My turn?" He rushed out the words and pretended to be fascinated by the fries on his plate. "The session with Gale, I mean. My turn to talk?"

"Huh?" Chase looked like he'd zoned out for a while, but he refocused and nodded. "Right. Yeah, your turn." The dazed look in his eyes cleared, and a small but genuine grin appeared. "I'm seriously fucking stoked about this, Remy. I didn't think you'd be ready yet."

Warmth spread in Remy's chest, and he was hit by another case of the Undeserved Dessert syndrome. Or did he deserve it? He could never be sure.

Rather than read into all that and overanalyze until he got grays, he told Chase about the introduction of sorts he'd had with Gale. In a timeline-fashion, he'd filled Gale in on the mere basics of his life, starting when he was nine and left his mom's trailer in Oildale to live with the Stahls—

"Wait," Chase interrupted, "I didn't know that. When you mentioned Oildale, I figured the Stahls were from there."

"Oh. Yeah, no." Remy shook his head. "I was a secret at first. My mom didn't give a shit about Clarissa and having an affair with a married man, but apparently she drew the line at involving kids in family drama." He paused, remembering the first time Bill Stahl had come over and Mom introduced him as "Dad." She'd looked nervous, hopeful, and skeptical all at once. "Maybe she needed money and contacted him or he found out on his own

149

somehow, but sometime after I turned five, Dad became a regular."

"Huh. So, then what? You moved and changed your name just like that?"

Sure, if one didn't care about the details. "Not *just like that*," Remy replied, stalling a bit. He wasn't proud of his family history, nor did it exactly leave him warm and fuzzy. "Mom was dirt poor and struggled with pills and alcohol. Dad offered me a brighter future if I became part of his family. So yeah, I moved and had to change my name when I was nine."

Chase's jaw clenched as he looked out the window, his thoughts obviously running wild. "This…fuck, I don't know, but it doesn't make sense." His gaze slid back to Remy. "How can he have had such good intentions—and even been a good man—if he also raised the son of a bitch who turned out to be a raving lunatic?"

Remy noticed that Chase spoke of Bill Stahl as if he were already dead, instead of in a home for Alzheimer's. Then again, they'd never get any answers from Bill—about Ben or anyone else. It would be Clarissa and Fred who'd be able to shed some light, but it'd be like talking to a brick wall. A brick wall that hated your guts. Clarissa, in particular. She was pure poison. Fred had been quieter—clear with his hatred toward Remy but not often spewing insults. Fred had been fonder of shooting glares or pretending Remy didn't exist.

As for Chase's question…? "Seems like something for a psychologist to answer," Remy responded, dragging a fry through some ketchup. But he didn't eat it. "That said, my dad has never been an angel. He was good to me as long as I did well in school and became successful. Money mattered." When he'd come out, Bill hadn't even batted an eyelash. He'd *ignored* it, pretended the admission had never been voiced, because Remy's perfect grades and the zeroes in his bank account meant everything. "To be perfectly honest, I despised when he put me on a pedestal because it ostracized me further from the rest of the Stahls. They hated me enough already. Dad bragging about me only made it worse."

Chase nodded pensively and sat back with a sigh. "So, Ben

and Fred were jealous of the so-called affection Bill gave you."

Pretty much. "When I came out to them, I almost *hoped* Dad would lash out at me," Remy confessed, averting his eyes. "I wanted it to level the playing field. Or battleground—whatever."

"Now, *that* makes sense."

Remy looked up to find Chase smirking. "How so?"

Chase chuckled and went on. "Up in the cabin—Christ, kid. I couldn't figure out why you kept pushing me about you being gay. It was like you wanted me to hate you for that specific reason."

Oh. Well...yeah, maybe. "I'm one of a kind like that," Remy quipped. He ignored how his ears heated up in embarrassment. "So anyway." It was probably best to move the fuck along now. "I filled Gale in about the major events. Moving in with the Stahls, going off to college, starting my business, and then how it all went to shit. Ben kidnapping you guys, trying to get help, and lastly, Mom killing herself and how I reacted." He cleared his throat and forced himself to eat.

His knee bounced, and he couldn't shake the tightness building up in his chest. It felt like he was going to cry, and he hated it.

"Hey." Chase locked his feet with Remy's under the table, causing Remy to freeze. "I'm not even gonna ask if you're all right. I can see you're not."

Remy gulped down some Coke but failed to form a response.

"Wanna get outta here?" Chase asked.

Yes, but that felt like quitting. Remy wanted to be strong for once. "Just tell me something," he managed to say. "Anything. Something random. How was your week—or tell me about your damn bikes; I don't care."

Chase stared at him long and hard, debating. In return, Remy pressed their feet together a little more and sent him a brief, pleading look.

"Fine." Chase conceded with a sigh. "Nothin' much to say about my week, otherwise. I saw my sister for a few days, had dinner with Austin and Cam, worked..."

That little tidbit about Austin and Cam had Remy's attention. "Are you close to them? Huntley and Nash, I mean."

A flash of contentment flitted over Chase's features. "Sorta, yeah. We meet up every now and then for dinner, poker, beer—that kinda thing."

Remy hid his envy. He wanted that, but he'd thrown it all away. Hopefully he'd get another chance, and hopefully...hopefully, Chase would be part of it.

Suddenly he ached for it—a semblance of normalcy. "Come to think of it, I want to get out of here after all." He didn't have a poker table at his house, but there was a pool and good music.

*

Chase grinned when he pushed down the kickstand and removed his helmet. "I think you can let go of me." Not that it hadn't been nice to have Remy plastered to his back during the ride, but they were here now. "Remy?"

"Yeah," Remy muttered, slowly releasing Chase's midsection.

Chase had planned ahead earlier, having brought an extra helmet in case he'd drive Remy to the cabin later. But now, as they made their way into Remy's house, Chase was told that'd never happen. Ever.

"Andy will pick me up," Remy finished. "A longer ride on that death machine and I'll probably piss my pants."

Chase chuckled and shrugged outta his leather jacket. "They're perfectly safe, kid."

"Perfectly—!" Remy spun to face him, incredulous. "Fuck you. Now, there's all things non-alcoholic in the fridge, and the pool is in the back. I'm gonna go change my diaper and then I'll join you."

Chase's shoulders shook with silent laughter, which felt...so fucking good. Making his way to the kitchen, he smiled to himself and thought what a complete 180 the day had taken. For the better.

OUTCOME

After draping his jacket over a kitchen chair, he opened the fridge, and Remy hadn't been kidding. Chase didn't think Remy spent a whole lot of time here right now—if any—but Minna was definitely preparing for Remy's return. Juice, soda, iced tea, milk, root beer, water, lemonade; if it didn't have alcohol, it was here.

He was grabbing a bottle of water when classic rock started playing in the living room, and Remy joined him shortly after. He was on the phone, and he was only wearing a pair of board shorts.

Fuck.

"I'll be here until Andy's off tonight," Remy told whomever. He smiled at Chase and mouthed Minna's name. "Yeah, he's here now." He grabbed a Coke from the fridge. "All right. Enjoy your conference—and the date, *unless you cancel*—and thanks again for taking time off for me earlier." There was a slight pause. "You, too. Bye."

Chase leaned back against the kitchen island and did his best to not picture Remy outta those shorts, but it wasn't going very well.

"Let's go to the back." Remy took the lead, his mind clearly not in the gutter alongside Chase's. "I'd let you borrow a pair of trunks or something, but I don't think I have anything that fits." He threw a smirk over his shoulder. "We can call it my excuse to see you in nothing but underwear."

You don't need an excuse for that.

Remy opened the patio door, and Chase thought for a second he'd been transported to Austin and Cam's backyard. But instead of a ground made of flat stone and a pool that was kidney-shaped, Remy's pool was rectangular and surrounded by freshly cut grass. Flowerbeds, a lemon tree, and grapevines that crept along the six-foot tall wooden fence added to the oasis. There was also a slightly elevated patio and a barbecue area. Rounding out the space were lounge chairs, a low table, and pots with various vegetables.

The canvas roof over the patio shielded them from the afternoon sun, and Chase had probably never been to a place this inviting before.

"Nice, huh?" Remy seemed to love it, too. "You should've

seen it before Minna moved in."

"She did all this?" Chase asked.

Remy nodded. "A few weeks after Mom died, I'd just signed the final papers to sell my company, and I came back here and completely trashed the place. Andy was here, and when I started packing to get the fuck out, he made me promise to meet him a week later. That was all he wanted; otherwise he wouldn't let me leave." He looked down and opened his soda can. "I kept my promise and met him in LA. Other than signing over the house to Minna, Andy told me he wanted to control my biggest bank account." Remy shrugged. "I didn't give a shit, so I signed everything. Then I went off the grid, only resurfacing the few times Andy and Minna tracked me down to see if I was still alive."

Having met Minna and Andreas, Chase knew what Andy had been up to. "They wanted to save it for you. The money and the house—make sure there was something left when you got back."

"Yeah. If only I had realized back then that *they* were my family." Remy blew out a breath. "I'm not satisfied with 'better late than never,' but I'm going to make it up to them." He looked determined at that, for which Chase felt proud and more hopeful than ever. "Come on, I want to get in the water. Strip off those threads, Gallardo."

In a carefree manner that Chase had never seen him display, Remy jumped into the pool cannonball style and resurfaced, shaking his head like a dog.

Chase grinned and set down his water, then pulled his shirt over his head and unbuckled his belt. His clothes ended up strewn over a chair before he dove into the pool at the deep end and let the water cool his overheated skin.

When he broke the surface, he found Remy sitting on the other edge of the pool smiling at him. With the sun behind him, Remy was more of a silhouette—all shadows, water droplets, pale skin, ink, and steel.

"What'cha doin'?" Chase pushed back his hair and swam closer, drawn like a magnet.

Surrendering to Remy once hadn't taken much.

Surrendering a second time would take no effort at all. Chase couldn't get the man outta his head, and he constantly found himself wanting more.

He feared he was pretty much done for. Feelings had snuck up on Chase, which both terrified and excited him.

"Enjoying the view." Remy flashed a brief grin, but it was smothered by something intense. At that point, Chase reached him and stood up, his hips coming in contact with Remy's knees. "You make me believe there's something worth fighting for," he murmured, parting his legs a little.

Remy's admission sent a shiver down Chase's spine, and goose bumps appeared along his arms, neck, and chest.

"Ditto." Chase's voice was quiet and gravelly as he stepped in between Remy's legs. He knew his response had been inadequate, but at the moment he would either say too little or *too much*, so he'd opted for the former.

Chase stared as he trailed his hands up Remy's thighs, afraid the "too much" would be visible in his eyes—truths Chase wasn't ready to share and feelings he couldn't bring himself to acknowledge. Or...or one look at Remy would draw it all out, and Chase couldn't afford to lose that control.

Too much was at stake.

"Chase..." Remy leaned forward and skimmed his nose along Chase's cheek. "Do you want me to stop?"

God, no.

In answer, Chase tilted his head and claimed Remy's mouth with his. Heat surged through them, igniting their bodies. In a matter of a second, they went from a firm kiss to hands everywhere, tongues tasting, and movements that brought them closer.

Remy scooted forward and snaked his legs up the backside of Chase's thighs. Chase cupped Remy's neck and deepened the kiss, then pressed his hardening cock against Remy's. *Oh, fuck.* Would he ever get enough?

"Switch places with me," Remy groaned into the kiss. "I want you in my mouth."

Chase wasn't gonna deny him. He broke the kiss, panting,

and pushed himself up to sit on the edge of the pool. His wet boxer briefs were plastered to his skin, but Remy made quick work of them, tugging them down past Chase's knees, then off completely. They landed with a splat somewhere behind Remy.

"Fucking perfect." Remy licked his bottom lip and stroked Chase's rock-hard cock. "Can—" He hesitated and looked up. "Can I ask you something?"

Chase could barely think straight, but he managed a nod as he pulled Remy closer and kissed his neck.

Remy shivered. "Why are you in the closet?"

Chase stiffened, a long line of curses and fears rushing through his head, but then he forced himself to relax. This was Remy; he could be trusted, and it didn't take a genius to figure out that Chase was a closet case, even though he'd never actually said anything.

He let out a breath and moved his hands up Remy's sides.

"I don't even know anymore." Chase dropped his forehead to Remy's shoulder, his confession at least partly true. He didn't know—*at the moment*. Or rather, he doubted he could go on with the hiding. After being with Remy, the whole thing seemed more and more ridiculous for every day that passed.

Once upon a time, Chase had wanted nothing more than to be Pops's good deed in the world. A pride and joy, a purpose, a legacy. *One thing*…that didn't make Chase feel so damn sorry for his father, who had failed in all other aspects of his life.

But Pops didn't fucking deserve better, did he? Only a fool would be proud of a straight son and not a gay one.

Chase could still imagine his dad's voice if he'd been alive when the kidnapping took place. He could picture Pops's shame, another failure. *"This wouldn't have happened if you weren't queer."* Maybe the words would've been shouted. Or said quietly, with disgust.

Well, fuck that, Dad.

Though, if Chase was gonna be completely honest, his embarrassment over what had happened in that alley three-and-a-half years ago was probably holding him back more than his promise to restore some of his dad's pride. And he wasn't sure he could talk about that with Remy because the kid would find a way to blame himself.

Lifting his head, Chase kissed the corner of Remy's mouth. He felt nervous at the prospect of letting go of his past; it was something he ached for, but old habits died hard.

"I'm not sure I *can* hide any longer," he whispered. It was the closest he'd get to telling Remy he was the main reason Chase questioned everything.

Remy palmed Chase's cheeks and kissed him. "Come on. I want you under the covers for a while. The outside world can go fuck itself, all right?"

Chase liked the sound of that.

NINETEEN

Over the next several weeks, Remy and Chase created a new routine. Diners along the edges of Bakersfield were replaced with Remy's house, and they closed themselves in whenever they had the opportunity.

There were several matters Remy wanted to push Chase on, but he never did, telling himself Chase would talk when he was ready. But yeah...fuck...Remy was itching to know more about Chase's issues with his sexuality, the reasons behind hiding—if it really was only because of his dead parents—and if Chase had brought it up with Gale yet.

Remy also wanted to know how honest he could be about all this with Minna and Andy. As it was now, nobody knew anything. They didn't know that Remy and Chase occupied the backyard or the guest room several days of the week while the rest of Bakersfield was at work. They didn't know about any kind of relationship—or whatever one could call what Remy had with Chase.

It was making Remy uncomfortable to hide so much, but he couldn't bring himself to voice his concerns when he was busy reveling in Chase's company. Whether they were fucking each other's brains out, arguing over music, using the punching bag that now hung in the backyard, laughing at Chase's failed attempts at cooking, or taking naps together, Remy was hooked. He didn't want to lose any of that by asking too much.

Time with Chase had made Remy greedy. He couldn't deny that he wanted more—a lot more—and that his heart and mind were already there. It had happened effortlessly, without Remy's consent, and there was nothing he could do about it. Not that he wanted to, but…

He was lucky Chase was here at all.

Here, right this minute, was the bed. They'd cranked up the air conditioning after a long morning of soaking in the sun and swimming laps in the pool. They'd even showered cold, only so they'd enjoy taking refuge under the covers more.

Remy breathed in their scent and nudged his knee between Chase's legs.

For the first time in his life, Remy felt so at peace in another man's arms that he couldn't imagine wanting anything more than this. Cuddling wasn't a necessary evil anymore, a kiss didn't have to lead to groping, and a naked body pressed against him didn't mean he had to bend over.

He felt thoroughly desired and cherished by Chase, which was a new experience.

Remy had never fucked slow, either. Now it was high up on his list, along with the raw and rough sex that left his body sore and aching for hours.

He could go for either option right now. They both needed it. Remy wanted the connection, and he knew Chase had a session with Gale soon—one he'd said he was dreading—so perhaps Remy could take his mind off things.

*

Chase was dozing on and off when he felt Remy's hand trail down his torso.

"I want you." Remy shifted so he was on top of Chase, his mouth dropping openmouthed kisses on Chase's chest. "I know you're awake."

Chase cracked a sleepy smile and pulled Remy in for a quick but hard kiss.

"What time is it?" Chase murmured drowsily. He lifted his head and glanced at the alarm clock on the nightstand. *Damn.* "I gotta go in an hour." He had that *fucking* session with Gale, and how he was gonna work afterward was beyond him.

So far, therapy had been relatively easy—even helpful and useful. He was slowly but surely working on being more optimistic, not shouldering everyone's troubles, and not feeling guilty for shit that didn't have anything to do with him.

"There will always be people who are worse off than you, Chase," Gale had told him. *"And better off, of course. But neither means you don't deserve the good things you create for yourself."* She'd paused and scribbled something in her notepad. *"Next time you feel the need to make comparisons between you and others, take a minute and consider if what you're doing is fair. For instance, would you be as demanding toward your sister as you would to yourself?"*

Chase needed to cut himself some fucking slack, in other words. And he'd been trying, mainly by indulging in every moment with Remy and not feeling guilty about it. Because it was there, the guilt, as fucked-up as it may be. But was that so weird? He'd promised to *help* Remy, not screw him six ways to Sunday and practically move into his house during the day.

There was more, too. The attraction Chase had for him had spiraled outta control, and as he searched Remy's eyes, all the right and wrong words were at the tip of his tongue.

I think I love you.

Remy smirked down at him and reached for the lube on the nightstand. "I can work with an hour."

Chase grinned, content to let Remy run the show. While he prepared Chase's ass with magic fingers and kissed him sensually, Chase focused on just feeling. He ran his hands down Remy's back, stroked his cock, and squeezed his sexy ass.

The kiss grew hungrier as Remy fucked him a little harder and moved his fingers a little faster. Chase cursed, his mind swimming with images of the two of them from the past few weeks. Sometimes they were both dominant, fighting until one submitted. Sometimes they tripped on their way to bed and ended up laughing during foreplay. Sometimes it was a sleepy fuck, where closeness mattered more than coming. Sometimes they both wanted to bottom, so they took turns until they were exhausted to the point where they fell asleep in a pile.

"Now," Chase moaned.

"Fuck, yes." Remy slicked up his cock and pushed in, filling Chase in one deep thrust. "I love—this. I love this." He let out a stuttered breath against Chase's neck and stayed still for a few beats.

Chase closed his eyes, the overwhelming pleasure mingling with a bite of pain. It was fucking addictive, almost as good as the damn orgasm that would follow.

Was there anything better than being with Remy?

Chase didn't wanna deny this part of himself anymore.

He reached up and kissed Remy's neck. "I want more, baby." How true those words were, although he knew Remy would interpret them differently.

Chase was right.

Remy grabbed Chase's jaw, kissed him hard, and picked up the pace. "I want your come on me, so tell me when you're close," he said, grunting as he hooked an arm under Chase's knee and slammed in. "*Fuck.*"

Chase gritted out a curse and fisted his cock, but Remy batted away his hand and took over. With each thrust Remy delivered, Chase clenched his ass and got rougher when he touched Remy.

The rhythm and the continuous sounds of skin slapping, heavy breaths, and the bed creaking wrapped Chase in a fog of lust he couldn't see past. When Remy went harder, it spurred Chase on like nothing else. He met each push and pull by lifting his hips and tugging Remy closer, but no matter how much he gave back, it wasn't enough.

In the end, he let out a growl and took Remy by surprise when he flipped them over. He had his cock coated in lube before he knew it, and then he got in between Remy's legs and forced himself deep inside.

Oh, fuck, fuck, fuck.

"Okay, that works—fuuuck!" Remy moaned breathlessly and dug his blunt fingernails into Chase's shoulders. "*Jesus*, Chase."

Chase froze. "Christ, I'm sorry—"

"No!" Remy laughed through a groan. "Fuck—no. I'm

good. Just caught me off-guard. Keep going." He hissed and shivered when Chase shifted inside him. "Take whatever you want." But Chase couldn't. Not yet. He felt like shit. Remy seemed to notice, and something in his eyes softened. "Sweetheart, look at my dick. It's rock-fucking-hard. You didn't hurt me. Please continue."

Chase didn't need to look; he could feel it pressed between them. Instead he closed his eyes, his body taking over. He couldn't fucking help it.

"That's it." Remy palmed Chase's cheeks and tilted their foreheads together. "Take it."

"All of it," Chase heard himself mumble. Drawing back, he rammed forward again and kissed Remy so hard his jaw ached.

"Take it," Remy repeated in a gasp.

So Chase took. Driven by his need to possess and love, Chase took all he could in that moment, and he took it savagely. He touched and manipulated every spot he'd learned excited Remy, and he gave all of himself back in return. Until there was nothing left but erratic heartbeats, silence, consuming orgasms, and stunning clarity.

There was no "think" about it. Chase loved Remy and would do anything for him.

*

A while after Chase had left, Remy wandered around aimlessly, lost in his thoughts. Things were changing; he could feel it. The house had become *home* again. Touches, smiles, and kisses with Chase lingered more. Remy could envision pictures on the walls in his living room—pictures of the only family that mattered. Laughter was returning to his life. And maybe—just maybe—he could imagine walking into Andy's studio, hearing the buzzing of a tattoo gun, and feeling his fingers itching to hold it.

Remy's gut tightened at the realization of how much he had to *lose*.

He was so hopeful for a bright future, but it absolutely terrified him at the same time.

OUTCOME

Minna believed in him, and letting her down would crush Remy. Chase...fuck, Chase. Remy could suddenly see everything with Chase. Like a freshly paved road that hadn't been there before. But the on-ramp was still unstable—a little too shaky to walk on—and he needed Chase to take that turn first.

He needed Chase to want the same things.

It *was* a possibility, though. The way Chase had left things today had only sparked more hope in Remy. The tight hug, the whispered *"I'll call you later, baby,"* and the long kiss by the door couldn't have been more relationship-like.

In the same breath, Remy had to be careful about moving too fast. He had to put a leash on the part of him that was ready to move back home and give Chase a new address. Because the truth was, on the days Remy had therapy, he couldn't be more thankful for the solitude the cabin brought him.

"That fucking Gale," he muttered to himself, walking into the kitchen.

Gale was like a sadist for the mind. She grabbed ahold of memories he shared about his childhood, put proverbial nipple clamps on them, and twisted whenever Remy came to conclusions that put him at fault.

Worse was when she caned his ego with facts and observations.

"Let me just see if I understand this," she'd interrupted him patiently. *"Are you saying that if you'd known more about Ben's intentions, you would have been able to stop him?"* Sort of? Remy had nodded hesitantly, instinct telling him he was about to get his ass handed to him. And Gale hadn't disappointed. *"I see. Well, allow me to put it this way, then. If your best friend had only predicted your reaction to your mother's suicide by hiding all the alcohol in the state of California, you wouldn't have been able to drink."*

Remy had felt so fucking stupid when she'd put it that way, and so had Chase, apparently. They'd discussed how similar they could be and were baffled as to how completely blind they'd been.

A new perspective, Cam had evidently told Chase once. But wasn't it ridiculous? So much pain; Remy and Chase had both been so snowed in, thinking they knew best. Believing they knew *themselves* best.

Gale had struck her cane with, *"Some might call it arrogant to think a person has the power to change someone else."* She was right, of course. *"You can very well open up a person's mind to new possibilities, but change comes from within. Regardless of what is right and wrong, only you can decide to change your behavior or rethink something you have planned to do."*

Mind. Fucked.

They'd touched the subject again when Remy had mentioned the therapist he'd seen the one time he'd tried to get help. Remy had asked why shit hadn't worked out then.

"Because that therapist didn't tell you what you wanted to hear, Remy. At that point in your life, you wanted the blame. You weren't open to other possibilities." She'd smiled softly, a reminder of their previous talk about open minds and changes. *"It's different now. You're not here to tell me how it is. You're not pretending to know the solution. Perhaps you've even understood that I can't magically fix you. But I can do my best to guide you and help you gain understanding."*

Remy slumped down in a kitchen chair, exhausted just *thinking* about his sessions with Gale. He still had a few days before his next one, but... Chase was there now, and despite having focused on the deeper connection that was developing between them, Remy had to have been blind to miss the extra weight Chase carried on his shoulders when he'd walked out the door.

Considering he still didn't have a car, Remy swiped the cordless from next to the microwave and dialed Andy's cell. Minna was working, but he didn't know about Andreas.

Remy had told himself to research AA today before he called the guy Gale had suggested, so maybe he couldn't physically be there for Chase, but he could at least help out a little. If the session was a bad one, Remy didn't like the idea of Chase getting on his bike afterward.

There was something else Remy wanted to do for Chase too, but it was a task Remy planned to do on impulse. Because thinking about it made him sick.

"You've reached Andy. Leave a message or try later..."

Damn it. Remy needed the number to the studio, and he'd

never fucking learned it.

He ended the call and blew out a breath as he looked toward the cabinet where he knew Minna had hidden his old phone. He'd found it the other day when he was looking for a notepad.

For one second, he made a face at the fridge—or at the thought of Minna—because back when Remy's house was a nondescript bachelor pad, there were business cards decorating the fridge. *With certain phone numbers.*

"Let's get it over with," he grumbled. The last thing he wanted right now was any kind of contact with the people from LA, and he hoped that guy...fuck, what was his name, again? Travis...no...Trent. Yeah. Remy hoped Trent wasn't blowing up his inbox with messages.

Remy opened the cabinet and grabbed his phone—charger, too—and plugged it in. He waited anxiously as the phone flashed with life, and then how text after text popped up on the screen.

They were all from Trent, or "Malibu Hustler" as Remy had labeled the guy the night they'd met, been high off their asses, and thought they'd been funny.

Remy scrolled down, his body tensing up more for each message.

> *Party in Vegas, u in?*
> *Got new shipment, lemme know what u need, bruh.*
> *Haven't seen u around lately. Whatchu up 2?*
> *Need a favor, call back.*
> *Can u front me three k? Big money in it 4 u.*
> *WTF Stahl. Call me.*
> *Sending a friend 2 check in on u. Need ur help.*

Remy swallowed past the tightness in his throat and deleted the entire text conversation. Then he pushed the phone away from him and just stared at it as he willed his heartbeat to slow the fuck down. It wasn't like Trent was right here in the kitchen with a bottle of vodka and two lines of blow. He was in LA, where he belonged, doing the same old shit.

Trent was all bark and no bite. The fact that nobody had

"checked in" on Remy proved as much. Fuck it, Trent just wanted a rich kid who could lend him money whenever he wanted to expand his business.

Steeling himself, Remy went for the phone again and located the number to Andy's studio.

Andy himself answered after the third ring, and Remy stomped down the longing he felt when he heard the music and bitching between Dan and Martinez in the background.

"It's Remy." Remy leaned back against a counter and looked down at the floor.

"Shut the fuck up, guys!" Andy yelled, holding away the phone. "And Martinez, clean your goddamn station or have Newbie do it, but it gets done before your next client comes in."

Remy grinned to himself, remembering now that Dan and Martinez were always at each other like a couple two-year-olds.

"Sorry 'bout that," Andy chuckled. "What's up, Rem?"

Jesus Christ, Remy missed it. "No worries. You've taken on a new apprentice?"

"Yeah. Nine months now. He's not you, but I had to find a new one, you know?" Oh, twist the knife, Eriksson. "He has the same specialty as Dan though, so we'll see if I can give him a position later." Dan was the master of anything Japanese, but the demand for that wasn't crazy high in Bakersfield. "If you're calling to say you wanna come back, I'll smack you upside the head and thank you. I'll ride your ass too, but not the way you like it."

Remy couldn't help but laugh. It was shaky, genuine, and full of both fear and relief. He *wanted* to come back—more than he could say—but he was afraid to have even more to lose. The stakes were suddenly so high, and Remy felt the pressure to succeed.

He put that pressure on himself, but he couldn't help it.

"Hopefully one day soon," he settled for saying. It was the best he could come up with that wasn't a promise he could fuck up by breaking. "I called to ask if you have any clients within the next hour. If not, I have a favor to ask you. And shit—" A memory hit him, for which he felt like hitting *himself* for not remembering sooner. "How did the doctor's appointment go?"

Andreas's fiancée was seven months pregnant, expecting a

boy. Apparently the little fella had been shy, so the doc hadn't been able to see the gender until recently.

"It went well." There was a grin in Andy's voice. "Don't worry, I won't ask you to be godfather."

Remy laughed again, this time amused. "Dude, I was seventeen when I told you kids freaked me out."

"Have things changed?" Andy shot back.

"Well." Remy smirked and scratched his chin. "Maybe not. Projectile vomiting isn't my thing, and they're so fucking dependent on you. Aren't you afraid you're gonna screw up?"

"Uh…" Andy let out a chuckle. "First of all, thank you— for *that*. Second of all…Remy, of-fucking-course I'm gonna screw up. It's sort of part of the parenting thing. At least that's what the books say."

Remy smiled and shook his head in wonder. His friends had a way of making things sound so natural. *Of-fucking-course I'm gonna screw up.* Because it was okay to do that sometimes?

It hadn't been for Remy when he grew up.

"Anyway, what's the favor?" Andreas asked. "I'm off for another few hours. Just came down here 'cause my girl was sick of my overprotective ass. And, let's face it, sometimes I'm afraid Dan and Martinez are gonna burn down the place."

Right. The favor. Remy didn't like to ask because Andy and Minna had already helped him so much, but this was for Chase. Was there anything Remy wouldn't do for that man?

Shit. That was kind of an aha moment he hadn't seen coming. Caring for someone, even loving them, was…entirely different. Making sacrifices for someone mattered more because it *showed* just how much that love meant.

"It's Chase," Remy said, slightly dazed from his realization that Chase was his top priority in life. "He's in therapy now, and I'm not sure he should get on a bike when he's done. I think they're going to talk about something he's not comfortable with."

Andreas hummed. "Interesting. Well, I can pick him up. He goes to Gale too, right?"

"Yeah, and I think he'll be done in like half an hour." Remy's brows furrowed. "But what's so interesting?"

Andy just laughed. "It's nice to have you back, man. I'll pick him up." With that, he ended the call.

"What the hell," Remy said flatly and stared at his phone. "Fucknut."

He shook that off and pondered for a second what he'd do next. Minna wasn't due home yet, so Remy had a while before he even had to think about going back to the cabin. And then it hit him, that other thing he wanted to do for Chase.

Remy cursed, knowing if he thought about it for too long, he'd never go through with it. Chase had questions about the kidnapping, and Remy felt compelled to help. And since he didn't have all the answers—futile as it was—there was only one thing to do.

Remy had to contact Fred and Clarissa.

TWENTY

Chase had forced himself to be truthful with Gale, but he hadn't expected to share *this* much. In fact, the talk he'd had in his head before entering Gale's office only included being truthful about the hows and whys he'd been kidnapped. He'd gone as far as to tell her he'd been with a man prior to the kidnapping, and how it had to have been Ben's reason for choosing *him*.

But it'd gotten worse. Once Chase had started talking, the words had kept tumbling outta his mouth. Which included his fear of telling Remy everything, or rather, Chase being afraid of Remy blaming himself.

"I don't want this to be a setback for him," he'd explained. *"We've got a good thing goin' on, you know?"*

"I actually don't, Chase. I have a pretty good idea, but I would like some clarification." Gale had tilted her head and studied him closely. Never any judgment. Only interest and curiosity. *"Are you romantically involved with Remy?"*

Well, Chase hadn't exactly been lucid enough to lie, nor would he want to lie. Dizzy with memories, triggers of flashbacks lurking dangerously close, he'd nodded and admitted that, yeah, they'd started seeing each other in secret.

After that, Gale had paused the session, urging Chase to take a minute alone to gather his thoughts, and now he was waiting for her to return.

Rubbing his temples, Chase squeezed his eyes shut but almost found that worse. He needed to *see* reality; he was in his therapist's office, not in that motherfucking basement or in an

169

alley.

His exhaustion ran bone deep, but it was more than the session that had taken its toll on Chase. It was the front he'd put up for decades, the hiding, the bullshit excuses, and the denial.

For each second that ticked by, he grew more and more pissed with himself. All this time, he could've been open and honest with who he was. Instead he was now stuck with regrets.

You know that's not true.

It kinda was, though. Yeah sure, Gale was right; parents had a big impact on their children, and Chase's dad had definitely fucked with his head. But after all that…? After Pops had died, Chase had continued like he was still alive—like his dad's word was still law.

That ended now.

Chase wasn't gonna wreck his own life anymore just because Pops had wrecked his. And hell, Adriana could be the fucking legacy.

It was time for Chase to have some peace in his life. If Remy was willing, Chase wanted to take baby steps and overcome his irrational fears—because there would always be kidnappers nearby waiting to strike, right?—with Remy at his side.

Christ. Remy. Chase had to tell him how he'd been taken by Ben.

And when Gale returned with two glasses of water, Chase didn't beat around the bush. He asked bluntly how he could be honest with Remy without sending him running for the nearest bottle.

Gale seemed momentarily surprised, perhaps because Chase rarely spoke willingly or asked many questions, but she caught on quickly. "Well. First of all, I want to revisit the fact that you're involved with Remy. Is it all right if we do that next session?"

"Uh, yeah. Sure." Chase wasn't sure what that could be about, but he officially no longer had any secrets, so he was game.

"Excellent. Aside from the events that led up to Ben taking you, have you been honest with Remy?" Gale asked. "As you know, he's my patient too, so I'll have to tread carefully regarding what we talk about—unless you choose to come here together."

"Austin and Cam do that." Chase nodded, and he didn't mind coming with Remy.

"They do, yes." Gale smiled. "So. Honesty. Of course it's always important, and I'm glad you want to be up-front with Remy. And since you mentioned 'running for the nearest bottle,' I assume you know of Remy's addiction." Chase nodded with a dip of his chin. "My advice is to sit him down where he's comfortable in his surroundings—and seclusion certainly won't hurt."

Chase could only agree. "He's told me he caves easily."

"Exactly. Perhaps you can go up to his cabin," Gale suggested. "If he gets upset—"

"Oh, he'll get upset," Chase muttered.

That was the whole point—why he'd been so reluctant to tell Remy.

Gale grinned wryly. "Keep him away from car keys and escapes, okay?"

Chase huffed a small chuckle 'cause it was probably the first time Gale had been so blunt. "Copy that."

For the next twenty minutes, Gale gave Chase advice on how he could approach this with Remy, and he was thankful. Anything to cushion the blow. And eventually, they returned to the reason Chase was there today.

"Start small, Chase," she told him gently. "That you're getting ready to accept this part of you and move on is wonderful, and you don't want to move too fast. Whether you choose to come out, so to speak, with or without Remy, I advise you take baby steps."

"I'm not gonna plan my own Pride parade," Chase deadpanned.

Gale's mouth quirked up. "You know my thoughts on sarcasm in therapy, Mr. Gallardo."

Oh yeah, she called it *sugarcoated hostility*. Chase couldn't help but grin. "Gotcha. Baby steps." He sobered as the funny moment was over. This was real. They were talking about his being gay, for fuck's sake. Something not even his sister knew about him.

Christ. "It's easier to have a goal than taking the first step," he admitted.

"Of course it is. But keep in mind that the people closest to you aren't waiting for a reason to judge you," Gale reminded him, leaning forward. "It won't be easy, I know. The way you were taken, months of degradation for Remy's sexual orientation, and your childhood… I cannot stress this enough, Chase: do not rush things." She leaned back again. "So far, we've discussed your father, a so-called victim of his generation. It was nothing but fear and ignorance on his part."

Uh-huh, but that didn't make it easier. Chase would always remember the snide remarks Pops made the few times homosexuality popped up in conversation. Whether it was the anniversary of a gay politician's murder in San Francisco Pops had heard about on the radio or another case of the "gay plague" in the '80s…he'd never run out of spiteful things to say, and Chase had always been close enough to hear it.

Chase grew uncomfortable in his chair and starting bouncing his knee. "It won't be easy to tell Ade."

"Perhaps she'll surprise you." Gale raised a brow and smiled. "From what you've told me about her, she looks up to you very much."

Chase didn't know what to say to that.

*

After the session, Chase was too overwhelmed and tired to analyze the shit that had just happened. His plan was to chuck it all into the back of his head for now 'cause he had to get his ass to work. God, *work*. He needed a dozen pain-killers for his headache, and a few drinks wouldn't hurt.

The late-afternoon sun was punishing, so he slid on his shades and started making his way toward his bike—

"Chase!"

Chase cursed, caught off guard, and turned to see…Andreas?

Andreas jerked his chin in hello and opened the door to

his car. "Rem was right. You shouldn't drive, man." Another chin jerk, this time toward the passenger's seat. "Get in. We can always come back for your bike later."

Chase ran a hand through his hair and looked between Andreas and his bike. Warmth seeped into his chest at Remy's thoughtfulness, and it made Chase miss him incredibly. He couldn't describe how much he wanted to say *fuck it* and skip work. But the bar would fill up nice and slow over the next few hours, and Donna couldn't work alone.

He got into Andreas's car and tried to come up with something polite to say, but Andreas beat him to start the conversation.

"How you feelin'?" he asked as he backed outta the parking lot.

"Uh…" How *did* Chase feel? Overwhelmed. Yeah. Still overwhelmed. "A bit slow on the uptake. Too much to process."

Andreas side-eyed him. "Yeah, so this is where you tell me to drive you home and not to your work. Remy's told me you work too much."

Chase let out a low laugh and shook his head. Then he gave Andreas the address—to his work that was also his home— and asked, "What else has Remy gossiped about?"

Andreas smirked. "Surprisingly little, which says a lot."

There was no way to misinterpret that. This was one of Remy's best friends. Chase wasn't even gonna try to play it off. "You know about us," he stated quietly and looked out of his window. In his periphery, he saw Andreas's nod. He tensed up in reflex, but his heartbeat stayed steady and calm. "And Minna?"

For some reason, that made Andreas laugh. "My sister can be very unobservant. She tends to see what she wants."

"Which is?"

Another smirk from Andreas. "You—single and straight. Don't worry, it's just a crush, but I'm still grateful you're neither."

"I'm…I'm not sure if I'm offended or flattered." Chase scratched his eyebrow.

"Go with flattered." Andreas shrugged. "Considering I haven't bitched at you about being with Remy, you're safe. But for

Minna…? Dude," he chuckled, "she needs a guy who can put a leash on her. I don't think you're him."

Right. Add *that* to the pile of crap that already had Chase walking around in a daze.

He got it, though. Andreas was not only a big brother to Minna, but sorta to Remy, too. And Chase would always admire people who took care of their own.

In an attempt to put the therapy session behind him, Chase let a blanket of numbness cover his mind, which would hopefully allow him to work through the night without losing his shit.

"So…" Andreas tapped his fingers along the wheel. "You and Rem. Is it serious?"

I hope so. "I don't know." Chase absently watched an old pickup roll up next to them. It was a beauty that Cam would probably love to work on. By focusing on cars and bikes, it was easier to relax, but it also meant he had less control of his verbal filter. "We have some stuff to figure out. He has to stop blaming himself for every little thing, which…" He chuckled humorlessly. "I'm exactly the same, but I'm doing my best to quit."

"Did he cause a hurricane somewhere?" Andreas sounded like he was used to Remy taking blame. In this case, it was nothing yet, but it would be once Chase had spoken to him. "What's his fault this time?"

Heh. "No hurricane." Chase pinched the bridge of his nose. "It's about how Ben targeted me. For the others, he obviously only cared about the fact that they had shitty jobs. But for the guy who was gonna be Remy in captivity, Ben wanted a gay man." *Maybe you should shut the fuck up, Gallardo.*

"Ah." Andreas cringed. "So what, you'd been with your partner or something? I mean, how did Ben know?"

Chase swallowed bile. The numbness was gone, and he was in disbelief as to why he was spilling his guts to Andreas. Yet, the words kept pouring out. "Little less romance than that. Random hookup in an alley."

Andreas nodded once, quiet for a beat. "Sorry, man."

The rest of the ride was quiet, and when Andreas dropped

Chase off at the bar, he only smirked and rolled his eyes—since Chase was obviously gonna work and not rest.

Chase thanked Andreas for the ride and then did his best yet again to forget about the session and focus on drinks, guests, and paying bills.

*

At the fifth time Remy's old phone buzzed with a text from Trent, he wanted to throw the damn thing against a wall.

Really, Remy should've known better. It was iMessage. Trent had clearly been alerted to Remy having read the messages.

He didn't want to see Trent—at all—but after contacting Fred and Clarissa in Milwaukee, Remy was painfully close to leaving the house and going to track down a bottle of vodka. His stomach churned, either in approval or nausea. Maybe a bit of both.

Minna was home, though. That kept Remy in his room.

She was thoroughly distracted too, otherwise she would've noticed something was wrong with Remy. But as it was, Minna was busy looking through the listings for houses and condos Remy had printed out for her.

The day she'd told him she'd remodeled the whole house solely for his sake, to give him a real home to come back to, he'd decided to give Minna her dream home in return.

Every now and then, he heard her squealing and throwing out "Oh my Gods" in the kitchen. They were usually followed by a, *"Remy! Are you suuuure?"*

"Yeah," he'd reply.

"Oh my God!"

He was going to do the same for Andreas.

Rolling over on the bed, Remy muttered a curse into the pillow. He was waiting for the anxiety to recede, the cravings to disappear, and for the image of Chase to pop up and be enough for Remy to relax. But nothing worked. Over and over, Clarissa's voice pierced his fucking skull.

"How dare you call here?" she'd spat out. *"Haven't you ruined*

my family enough?"

Remy had struggled with his temper, no longer hurt by their bullshit, but downright furious for what a cunt Clarissa was.

"Look," Remy had gritted out, *"I'm not calling for my sake. A friend of mine has questions about Ben—about the kidnapping—and if you could* please *just answer them—"* Clarissa had scoffed, but Remy was adamant about getting his words out. *"I sent the questions to Fred's email. I'm begging you, Clarissa. It's not for me. It's for one of the guys Ben took—"*

He'd been cut off there. Clarissa had called out to Fred. *"Oh, thank God! You're back. Remy's on the phone; you deal with it. My heart can't take it."*

Rolling his eyes, Remy had been forced to rehash it all to a fuming Fred, telling him about Chase's questions concerning the case, or rather, the puzzle pieces needed for confirmation of their theory.

Fred hadn't been pleased. *"Listen to me, Remy. You do not call us here again. You fucking got that? I don't care about you or your...your faggot friend. Wanna know what I do care about? Huh? I care about picking up the pieces of the family you destroyed. Ben lost his mind after you barged into our lives, my father is in a home, my mother can't even live on her own anymore, and I—"*

It had been Remy's turn to fume because at that point he'd lost every bit of composure. *"Yeah, what about you, Fred?"* he'd seethed into the phone. *"Tell me how you mourn the loss of your perfect fucking brother. Or better yet—since I'm sick and tired of all those stories and have heard them too many times—how about you explain to me why he didn't see you as perfect!"* He'd shouted the last few words, so goddamn heated he could barely function. *"Or have you forgotten that he kidnapped an innocent man to play the part of you, too?"*

Back to the present, Remy turned again and stared up at the ceiling, remembering the silence that had followed. He could've heard a pin drop.

He didn't know how many seconds had passed, only that his heart had continued pounding until Fred had disconnected the call.

That was that.

Remy hadn't accomplished shit, other than throwing a fit and being nauseated by the memory of how his biggest goal in life had once been to please the Stahls.

On his nightstand, the phone buzzed again.

Then it started ringing, and Remy's eyes widened before he realized it was his new phone and not his old. Therefore, it couldn't be Trent. Thank fuck.

Feeling heavier than a ten-ton truck, Remy dragged himself up into a sitting position and saw it was Andy calling. He answered with a hoarse "What's up?" and was met with music in the background.

"Hold on, Rem." Andy walked closer to where Remy knew the speakers were and then disappeared into his office. At least Remy guessed so, since the music stopped. "Jesus Christ, finally a break."

Remy checked the clock on the wall and saw it was pretty late. Minna had to be totally immersed in her house hunt because they were usually at the cabin by this hour.

"I got your text earlier," Remy said. Andy had sent a quick message to let Remy know he'd picked up Chase and that everything had gone well, for which Remy was grateful, but he was hoping to hear from Chase himself soon.

"Yeah." Andy yawned. "So...saddest part of being a tattoo artist?"

Remy knew that one. "Tramp stamps."

Andy grunted in agreement. "Four fucking butterflies, man. Starting a beautiful back piece tomorrow, though. But that's not why I called. I wanna talk about Chase."

Remy was a little taken aback by how fast it became serious. "Why? You said everything went fine when you picked him up. Did something happen?" He wouldn't be able to take another thing going wrong today. It was already too much.

"Nothing *you* can't fix," Andreas replied. "I get that it must've been tough to hear about Chase getting kidnapped for being gay, but you gotta stop putting that on yourself. It's not your fault Ben took Chase, regardless of the fucking circumstances behind Ben's reasons for targeting him."

Remy shook his head, confused as hell, and a cold chill ran down his spine. "Wait...what?"

Andy grew impatient. "What do you mean, 'what?' It's pretty damn obvious what I'm talking about, isn't it? I'm just sayin', Rem. Talk to Chase—solve that shit. I mean, it's not like *you* made him gay. Yeah, Ben went for him because of that, but Ben's the— *was* the—fucking psycho."

Just like that, the world slowed down. Dizziness and nausea took over, and Remy was sent straight back to hell.

Remy had hoped for some backlash when he'd come out to his dad, simply because maybe it would've made Ben and Fred hate him less. It could've meant that Remy was suddenly not so perfect. But no...Remy had continued to receive praise from Dad since he was rolling in the big bucks. And Fred's resentment had grown. Ben's hatred had spiraled out of control.

To the point where he'd evidently needed his victim to be gay.

Chase had been the one who had paid for everything.

"I...I gotta go," Remy mumbled, swaying in place. "I'll c-call you back."

He hung up the phone and let his arm fall, and with it went all his strength. He broke out in a cold sweat and swallowed dryly. *Oh, God. Chase.* Why...how...fuck. Remy couldn't think.

The walls closed in on him.

His phone buzzed, and he checked it automatically.

TWENTY-ONE

"Feel free to take your time with those beers," Cam told Chase, resting his elbows on the bar.

Chase grinned tiredly, and Donna swished past to grab something from the bottle rack. Last call had just been announced by playing Semisonic's "Closing Time" on the jukebox, so they were both busy getting everyone's final orders.

"What're you guys talking about now?" Chase asked.

"Golf." Cam rolled his eyes. He was here with his brother, Austin, and their fathers because apparently they weren't allowed at home. Riley and her grandmothers, aunt, and cousins had taken over. "Only Austin has the patience to pretend he's interested."

Chase looked over to their table and caught Landon yawning.

The dads were enjoying themselves, though.

"Rematch tomorrow, old man?" a guest slurred, clapping a hand down on Old Tuck's back. "I gotta win back my ex-wife's alimony."

Tuck took his regular place at the end of the bar and shrugged, a lazy smile on his face. "I'm sure the dart board will still be here."

Chase smirked and turned back to Cam with a tray of five beers. "Damn, I need this night to be over."

Cam huffed. "How you can even be a bartender, man..." He gave the establishment a disgruntled look. "Goddamn people."

It was those *goddamn people*, or rather the false sense of not being alone, that had contributed to Chase never getting outta this

179

business. But ever since getting closer to Austin and Cam, not to mention Remy, Chase found himself not needing that fakeness. Though, he still very much enjoyed his job.

Just not today. It was a miracle he'd worked his way through the entire night without either falling asleep or having a meltdown. Though, that said, there was also a small sense of relief. Even if it was only to Gale and Andreas, Chase was, in a way, *out*.

Now he only had to be more open with Remy, and part of him actually looked forward to it. It was exciting, terrifying, and meaningful all at once.

Still, it had been a long fucking day, and he was more than ready to call it a night.

"Isn't that...?" Cam nodded at the door. "Whatsherface. Stahl's friend."

Chase followed Cam's gaze and saw Minna awkwardly making her way through the crowd of six or seven beefy bikers who were leaving.

When Chase saw she'd been crying, he hurried toward the end of the bar and called her name.

"Oh, there you are!" She blew out a breath, her eyes welling up at the same time. "Please tell me Remy's here."

Obviously he fucking wasn't, and Chase could see Minna didn't really think he'd be here, anyway. And now Chase was worried. "He's not. What happened?" He leaned over the bar slightly to hear her better.

"I..." Minna gestured with her arm, but helplessness seemed to pull it down again. "Something's wrong. I can feel it." She did her best to keep her emotions in check. "A couple hours ago, he asked to borrow my car. He said he was only going out for smokes, but—" Her bottom lip trembled.

Chase pressed his lips together in a grim line. It would be easy to get pissed and throw his fists down on the bartop, but it would only delay the answers he needed.

"Tell me everything," he told her, pointing toward the door that led to his office. When he passed Tuck and Donna, all he needed to do was give them a look and they nodded in understanding. They'd cover for him.

OUTCOME

Once he had Minna in his office, she broke down and stuttered through words about Andy having misunderstood something. "He thought Remy knew," she rambled tearfully. "We've been looking all over, and I said we should call you, but Andy felt bad—said he wanted to fix it and not worry you. Then, like, twenty minutes ago, we got back to the house, and I found this in Remy's room." She sniffled and pulled out a phone. "We need your help, Chase."

Rigid, overwhelmed, and bewildered, Chase accepted the phone. "Andreas thought Remy knew *what?*" There was no password on the phone, so as soon as the screen lit up, Chase saw several texts from…someone.

"Party in Santa Barbara," one read, followed by an address. And the text after read, *"I know ure reading this. Come on, man."*

"'Malibu Hustler'?" Chase muttered.

Oh, fuck.

"I don't know!" Minna's cry of frustration made him look up momentarily. "He wouldn't tell me! Andy just said he'd talked to you about something, and then he'd spoken to Remy about the same thing, thinking you'd already told Remy, or…" She was confusing herself. "Fuck if I know!"

Chase knew.

Chase knew exactly, and *this* freaked him out. Now he needed that bartop to bang his fists onto, but the wall worked, too. Anger, fear, and worry exploded inside of him as he cursed and punched the nearest wall.

You weren't supposed to find out that way, baby.

Minna gasped and took a startled step backward. "Look—" She swallowed. "He didn't respond to Trent's texts. Remy might not've gone there. I'm going to borrow a friend's car and drive up to the cabin—"

"Let's be realistic here, Minna." Chase didn't mean to snap at her, but he couldn't worry about that now. "He—*fuck.*" He pinched the bridge of his nose and took a few deep breaths. "I gotta find him."

He didn't dare think about in what state he'd find Remy 'cause if he allowed himself to go down that path, he'd lose his

181

goddamn mind.

"Andy's already on his way to Santa Barbara," Minna whispered.

Chase nodded curtly. "So am I."

*

Chase hadn't expected company, though maybe he should have known better by now. Once he had barged into the bar again, his mood hadn't gone unnoticed by anyone who knew him.

Landon had been quick to offer his truck—and a baseball bat—and Cam had, oddly enough, been the first to volunteer to tag along. While muttering about a guy named Twitchy. Or whatever. After that, Landon had insisted on going too, and Austin had stayed behind to make sure Minna didn't do anything reckless when she was that upset.

Chase was thankful; he hadn't meant to lash out at her, but apologies would have to wait. Hell, he wasn't even mad at Andreas—at all. Chase knew a misunderstanding when he saw one.

He was also thankful that Landon didn't give a shit about speed limits. And that was saying a lot in a city like Bakersfield, where the cops loved to pull you over for speeding.

"I'm not gonna lie," Landon said as they drove outta town, "I'm feeling pumped. Austin told me about Stahl's former *friends*, and getting into a fight might make me feel less old."

Chase said nothing, busy staring out at the black night, and Cam was muttering again in the back seat.

"Why do you feel old, Landon?" Landon started talking to himself. "Well, because I'm in my mid-forties, and my twin daughters can almost outrun me. They're three."

"I should've told you this sooner, Chase," Cam stated randomly. "A while back, there was a motherfucker lurkin' outside of Remy's house. I didn't think too much about it, other than he needed to get his meth-head ass away from Stahl. He was sent by a dude named Trent, who wanted Stahl back in LA." Chase sighed heavily and massaged his forehead. When it rained, it fucking poured. "I didn't realize it was serious. I'm sorry."

OUTCOME

Wasn't much Chase could say. He didn't care about circumstances, as long as he could get his ass to Santa Barbara and find Remy. But first Chase had two more hours in the car with the Nash brothers.

*

About half an hour before they got off the interstate, they'd caught up with Andreas. Nods were exchanged, and everyone's expression had tightened with determination.

Chase hadn't talked much during the ride, but he'd answered the few questions Landon had asked about Remy's past and addiction. Cam had been quiet, only breaking his stoic façade to give Chase an odd look when Chase had mentioned how worried he was about Remy to Landon.

"Worried" didn't come close. Chase was sick to his stomach, and his mind battled against his heart. He wanted to believe in Remy—he *did* believe in Remy—but he also knew there were gonna be downs to accompany the ups. It wasn't realistic to think Remy had risen above his depressed state and suddenly turned around and driven home. But Chase couldn't help but *hope*.

I don't wanna find him drunk.

Or high.

Or with someone else.

Chase's gut churned at the possibility. Because it was one. He'd heard about Remy's party ways, but...no. Chase couldn't go there. He had to have some fucking faith in Remy, whose priority was gonna be booze. Forgetting reality by drinking. Maybe drugs, too.

Unless he's changed his mind and—

"Looks like we're getting close." Landon made a turn after Andreas's car, and they ended up on a street lined with lavish beach houses. "Yeah, there's a party up there."

Chase saw a dozen cars parked near the house at the end of the street, all the lights on, loud music pouring out, and people everywhere. It reminded him of a stupid frat-house party from the movies.

When he spotted Minna's truck that Remy had borrowed parked among the others, Chase's spine chilled with ice. At the same time, fury blazed through him so hot that he could've ignited. And he knew if he saw that motherfucking Trent, Chase wouldn't be able to hold back from beating his goddamn face in.

As Landon pulled over, Cam lit up a smoke and stepped out, looking tenser than Chase had ever seen. Landon wasn't his usual carefree self, either. And Andreas looked ready to kill.

He'd obviously seen Minna's truck, too.

"You've met Trent before?" Chase asked.

"Once." Andreas's voice was steely as he closed the door to his car and pulled on a hoodie. "He's mine. I'll make sure he'll never call Rem again. Trent's no real threat, just a fuckin' pest, but he likes to keep a couple guys with him."

"I'll go with you," Landon said. It wasn't the time for introductions. "Bro?" He looked to Cam.

Cam nodded once. "I'm in."

Chase nodded, too. "I'll find Remy." He wasn't exactly waiting for approval, so he made his way toward the big house, all the people fading into nothingness. He didn't see them unless they shared features with a certain green-eyed man.

What Chase did see were flashes of time he'd spent with Remy. He pushed past obstacles as he entered the house, images of the two of them floating around in his head—them screaming at each other in the pouring rain, them observing one another during quiet moments, them kissing and rolling around on a bed... Chase's skin prickled with awareness, his every sense on high alert.

He'd created memories with Remy, and he was dead set on creating more—for the rest of his damn life.

The heavy music pounded into his skull, but it wasn't louder than the sound of his pulse. It carried its own beat, and as it quickened, the world seemed to slow down. Himself included. His frustration and desperation grew tenfold, as did his anger.

"Watch it, man!" A college kid who was drunk off his ass ended up with his drink spilled over his chest when Chase pushed through to the crowded kitchen.

Remy wasn't there, so Chase continued toward the living

room, or wherever the music seemed loudest.

Behind him, he could hear Andreas demanding to know where Trent was, and Chase was pretty sure he had the answer when his eyes fell on a group of older people in the living room. Occupying a set of couches and chairs, half a dozen men, long past college age, were busy drinking, laughing, and snorting lines of what Chase could only assume was coke.

He couldn't control himself; his feet brought him closer of their own volition, his hands balling into fists along his sides. He'd bet his life that the lanky fucker laughing the hardest was Trent. Dirty blond hair, shadows under his eyes, a sinister grin, a nose that looked like it'd been broken a couple times, and clothes a few sizes too large.

Andreas had spotted him, too. "Chase, lemme at him." He flew forward and caused three of Trent's buddies to rise to attention. "Where the fuck is he, motherfucker?" Two guys blocked Andreas from moving farther, so Chase acted on instinct and punched the guy closest to him.

It was only the first of many blows.

"Whoa, whoa!" Trent laughed uneasily and stood up. He was confident because he still had protection, but he had to see that Chase and the others weren't gonna go down.

"Tell me where he is, Trent." Chase growled and then shoulder-checked a fidgety creep who had a broken beer bottle for weapon. "I don't fucking think so." He grabbed a fistful of the guy's greasy hair and pushed him down to knee him in the face. The beer bottle hit the floor at the same time as a few girls screamed in the background.

Cam took over there. "If it ain't Twitchy!" A dark chuckle. "I was hoping I'd find you here."

Chase didn't see what Cam did, but he heard the sickening crunch of bones breaking when there were a couple seconds of silence between two songs. Then Chase's attention was stolen when he was clocked in the ribcage. He grunted as pain radiated throughout him, but his rage made him undefeatable, and he threw himself at the motherfucker, who ended up shattering a china cabinet.

"Call the police!" some kid yelled.

"Oh my God!" More girls screaming. "My parents are gonna kill me!"

"For Christ's sake, dude!" Trent wasn't laughing anymore. Instead he was backing into a corner as Chase and Andreas advanced. "All this for Remy?"

Landon took down the last guy standing in the way, and then Andreas had his hands around Trent's throat, a murderous look in his eyes.

Trent choked and spluttered. "Up-upstairs, I think."

Chase didn't stick around. With his heart pounding furiously and his body throbbing from the punches he'd taken, he ran up the stairs and started yanking on doors.

Two kids getting laid in there. A goth chick on the phone in another room. A couple arguing in the hallway. "I saw the way you were looking at her!" Redhead shouted at her boyfriend. Chase passed them and tried another door, but that room was empty. Which left him with the bathrooms.

The first one was locked, and he could hear two girls' moans coming from the other side. Second bathroom was empty. And the third...

Locked. Chase knocked impatiently and peered down the opposite hall with just as many rooms. Rich fuckin' folks had too much space.

"Go away," someone groaned. No, not someone; it was Remy. Chase's heart froze. "Oh, fuck..." A retching sound followed, which sent Chase into action. He pushed at the door, and when it didn't budge, he took a step back and kicked at it with all his strength.

It took him three tries before the hinges had loosened enough, and then he was met by the sight of Remy hugging the toilet.

He's alive, at least. The relief was so immense that Chase could cry. *He's in one piece.* Chase closed the distance between them after filling a glass with water.

Remy stuck two fingers into his mouth and gagged, throwing up again. He hadn't even seen it was Chase yet, and he shoved weakly at Chase as he kneeled down behind Remy.

"No," Remy croaked, slumping down with his forehead touching the toilet seat. "F-fuck off."

"It's me, baby." Chase carefully cupped the back of Remy's neck and rubbed his clammy skin. In response, Remy froze for a beat, but then tremors racked his body and he began crying. "Shhh, I've got you."

"I'm sorry!" Remy's entire body shook as Chase gathered him close. "I'm s-so fucking sorry, Chase..."

Chase didn't want any apologies. Now that he had Remy in his arms, the fierce protector in him wanted Remy as far away from this place as possible.

TWENTY-TWO

Chase moved on autopilot. Remy had been frantic at first, apologizing and begging Chase not to leave him, but he'd calmed down now. Maybe after hearing, *"I'll never leave you, Remy."* He'd slumped, defeated, against Chase and accepted water, mouthwash, pain-killers, and a damp towel.

"Let's get outta here," Chase murmured. He pocketed the bottle of pain-killers he'd found in a cabinet and led Remy out of the bathroom and down the stairs. A lot of people lingered, but it was clear that the party was breaking up.

Everything was a blur. Trent's "security" guys had bailed, and Andreas was standing over Trent's injured body, shouting at him, but Chase couldn't hear a word. He did see the blood on Trent's face, though. He also saw Cam with a menacing look in his eyes, a forearm pressed tightly over the lanky addict's sternum, and a finger pointed in his face. Didn't take a genius to figure out it was threats spilling out of Cam, not pillow talk.

Chase's ears rang with the chaos going on around him.

The girl who was obviously regretting hosting this party in her parents' house was crying in the arms of a guy. Said guy smirked over her shoulder, nodded at a buddy, and gave a thumbs-up.

Landon was showing a few drunk chicks pictures of his daughters.

"Oh, God…" Remy groaned at the sight of a jock throwing up in a plant.

Chase pressed a brief kiss to Remy's temple, a pinch of

amusement tugging at his lips. "Yeah, time to get you out." He glanced over at Andreas and Cam again, only to find them both focusing on him and Remy. Chase couldn't be bothered to care about Cam's wry smirk. "We're leavin'."

Andreas nodded. It was clear he wanted to approach Remy, but he stayed put. "We're out of here, too." He hesitated, his eyes flicking between Cam and Chase, then spoke again. "I'm guessing you're heading to the cabin?"

Chase hadn't given that a single thought, but it suddenly seemed like the best fuckin' idea ever. Seclusion, privacy—God, yes.

"You have the keys to Minna's truck?" he asked Remy.

Remy rubbed the towel over his forehead and pulled a set of keys from his baggy chinos with a shaking hand.

*

Remy was so crushed by guilt and shame that his brain sort of shut down the second Chase started up Minna's truck. Nausea rolled in his gut, and the ocean air that came in through the open window wasn't doing its job in helping.

I failed. It was all he could think about. *I failed and let everyone down.* It had been so fucking easy, too. The two hours it had taken him to drive from Bakersfield to Santa Barbara hadn't swayed him one bit. If anything, each mile had made him sink lower and lower.

He'd barely even greeted Trent. His focus had been singular—downing shot after shot. Which he'd done. He'd sat there in that fucking living room surrounded by strangers, and he'd downed half a bottle of vodka in record time. The sweetest buzz had taken over quickly, providing a thin veneer between him and everything that hurt.

It had been glorious.

Until he'd envisioned Chase's reaction…

The last shot hadn't been as easy to swallow. It had burned as he'd thought about how Chase would react. Disappointment? Hurt? Anger? Disbelief? Shock? Resignation? There were too many options, and each one had caused Remy's insides to churn with self-loathing. He'd looked around himself, at all those strange faces and shitheads, and realized the only reason he'd been there—at that level—was because he'd driven there. Nobody had forced him to hang out with scum. It was all on him, and Chase—not to mention Minna and Andy since Remy had actually started listening to them—had made him believe he might be a lot more than this…this low-life piece of shit.

All that had brought him to the bathroom upstairs, where he'd tried to get rid of the poison his body loved.

He'd been through this too many times already, but this was worse. Even if his slip hadn't lasted long—nor had he consumed that much alcohol—he was throwing away more now. While he didn't know exactly where he stood with Chase, there was certainly something there, and Remy had finally come to terms with who his real family was: Minna and Andy. And hopefully Chase, if he didn't run away after tonight.

Remy lolled his head along the headrest and watched Chase drive in silence. It was dark, but it wouldn't be long before the sun rose. *He went looking for me. He found me.* Combined with Chase's promise of never leaving him, Remy felt hopeful; maybe he wouldn't run away, after all. But at the same time, the guilt weighed down heavier and he wouldn't blame anyone for bailing.

Not only had Chase and Andreas tracked him down, but they'd brought friends. Cam Nash and…Remy wasn't sure about the other man. It wasn't Austin, anyway.

"Is there anything we need to pick up for the cabin?" Chase checked the rearview as he stopped at an intersection. They'd be on their way into the desert soon enough. "Food, water, sodas, smokes…?"

"No," Remy whispered, facing forward. "It's all there." He closed his eyes but found it made him dizzier. *Fuck.* He thought of Gale and her encouraging him to seek help for his addiction, and he knew he had to do that—stat. He also thought of how the fuck he was going to tell her about his failure.

That last word went on a loop in his head.

Otherwise it was only silence, and it stretched out much as the dark road did.

In his periphery, he saw Chase tightening his grip on the wheel several times, and Remy didn't dare ask what he was thinking. It couldn't be positive.

"I was so goddamn worried, Remy."

So much for not knowing. Remy gnashed his teeth together, tears blurring his vision. "I'm sorry—"

"Don't." Chase's voice was quiet but firm, warm but no-nonsense. "We'll take a step back to regroup. Don't worry about it."

Remy did worry, though. "When you say *we…*"

Chase reached over and grabbed Remy's hand, threaded their fingers together, and kissed Remy's inked knuckles. "I mean we, baby. I'm not going anywhere."

If it sounded too good to be true, it probably was.

Right?

Chase couldn't possibly mean what he was saying.

"I just want you to know I'd get it." Remy forced out the words. "I wouldn't hold it against you if you decide it's too much."

"Would you stop that shit?" Chase snapped. Next he pulled over to the side of the deserted road, evidently not caring about any violations, and killed the engine. "Look, it's been a long damn night, and right now I'm just thankful you're still breathing, so can we save the talking 'til tomorrow?"

"Why are you thankful?" Remy asked desperately. He needed to *understand.* "You've basically saved me, and what the hell have I done for you, huh?" Chase threw him a lethal glare at that, but Remy wasn't done. "Tell me that. Tell me why you haven't cut your losses—"

Chase exploded. "Because I fucking love you, Remy!"

Remy blinked, shocked and startled. Time stopped and restarted. A single breath was released, but he didn't know from whom. *Because I fucking love you…* Oh, Christ. Oh, Jesus Christ. Remy's breathing picked up, his skin prickling and his head pounding.

Having sensed their connection was one thing, but to find out this…? Whole other matter.

"I didn't—" Chase groaned and scrubbed his hands over

191

his face. "I didn't mean for it to come out like that, but *Jesus*, you frustrate me. I thought I was bad when it comes to putting yourself down, but you take the fucking cake."

Remy barely paid attention to those words. Too busy letting the previous words sink in.

He wanted to cry with relief. In fact, he couldn't hold back. Emotions welled up so fast that he couldn't contain the first whimpered breath. Which probably alerted Chase to his imminent breakdown. *For Christ's sake, hold it together.* Remy scolded himself over and over, but nothing worked.

"Come here." Chase shifted in his seat and pulled Remy close, his arms enveloping and providing warmth. Comfort. Love... Chase pressed his lips to Remy's head and shushed him every time Remy choked out an apology.

*

Chase had no idea how much time passed, only that the horizon was morphing into purple and orange. It reminded him so much of the morning he and his fellow survivors watched the traitorous sun rise higher and higher after they'd escaped that burning building and months of darkness.

A lot had changed. A lot had happened.

All of which led to this exact moment. Just him and Remy—together. Three years of freedom, yet nothing compared to everything he'd been through these past three months with Remy. Even the bad times; hell, sometimes especially those 'cause they were the ones that tended to lead to progress.

Chase was running on fumes, but the exhaustion couldn't touch him. His tears had dried, and Remy was down to tremors and sniffles.

Despite the struggles and ups and downs they had to look forward to, Chase realized he was happy. Genuinely and incredibly *happy*. His fears were fading rapidly.

It...it had been worth it. All of it.

God, he'd been waiting for this moment.

He drew in a deep breath and let his lips linger at the top

of Remy's head. And he knew without a shadow of doubt that this was it—him and Remy. They hadn't talked about it, but it suddenly didn't matter because Chase already knew. It was too fucking obvious.

"Remy," he murmured.

Remy hummed and shuddered, appearing to be caught between sleep and awareness.

"Let's head to the cabin." Chase brushed his knuckles over Remy's cheek. "We both need some serious sleep."

And tomorrow we'll talk.

*

Remy woke to the sound of rain falling outside the cabin. He didn't move. His eyes opened, but he remained still, his head on Chase's chest.

Remy had slept fitfully the first few hours, and after one particularly gruesome nightmare where he was surrounded by bodies, drugs, alcohol, and no air, he'd escaped to take a cold shower, brush his teeth for half an eternity, have a smoke, and just sit outside for a bit. Then back to Chase and sleep. More restful this time. Maybe because his last thought before he'd succumbed to sleep had been about Chase's confession last night.

I didn't say it back. I have to tell him I love him, too.

It was colder than usual for October, but Remy reveled in it. With the open window, the breeze poured into the cabin and raised goose bumps along his arms. The air seemed fresher.

He felt stronger.

Noticing that the rise and fall of Chase's chest had changed patterns, Remy lifted his head to find his man awake.

"Mornin'," Chase rumbled in a sleepy voice.

Remy smiled briefly. "It's three in the afternoon."

Chase merely hummed and rolled on top of Remy. He dropped soft kisses along Remy's collarbone and chest, to which Remy sighed in contentment and let his inner demons go quiet.

It would be easy to say something along the lines of *"You're still here—I can't believe it,"* but he had to stop doing that. He had to believe there was good in him and that he could contribute in a relationship.

"I love that you're here," he murmured instead.

Chase smiled into the kiss he placed on Remy's chin. "Get used to it. Now…can I have you?"

Remy grinned and parted his legs farther. "Have at it."

Was this really happening? Could Chase be this forgiving—light and carefree right after Remy had fucked up so royally?

It was amazing.

"You little shit. That's not what I meant." Chase chuckled and raised himself off the bed. "But hey…" He reached for the lube on the nightstand.

"What *did* you mean?" Remy sat up and slid his hands up Chase's thighs. He closed the distance and sucked Chase's semi-hard cock into his mouth.

"I—fuck." Chase shivered and weaved his fingers into Remy's hair, guiding him. "I was talkin' about you, period." That made Remy shiver, too. Chase grasped Remy's chin and made him look up. "This is real. Be mine."

God, yes.

*

"God, yes."

Chase smiled widely, not sure Remy was even aware he'd said that out loud, and nudged him back on the bed. He kissed Remy hard while he slowly pushed inside, savoring every goddamn second.

"All yours," Remy mumbled into the kiss. "And I…I love you."

"Fuck." Chase had to stop before he lost it too soon. Then he grabbed Remy's jaw and kissed him painfully hard. The utter fucking joy that washed over him was unlike anything else. "I love you, too." So this was what belonging felt like. "You have no idea how much."

"Tell me." Remy spurred him on by pushing back, giving

Chase no choice but to give up on his attempt at keeping it together.

He went deep, withdrew, and thrust forward again. Fluid movements set the bed in motion, and their moans echoed one another's.

"You're…" Chase released a breath and rested their foreheads together. "You're so worth it, Remy." He closed his eyes to savor that truth, and he'd never been this at peace. "Everything…I'd go through it again if it meant you were waiting for me."

Remy's hitched breath slowed everything down, and Chase opened his eyes to see Remy's green eyes swimming with emotion. All his insecurities were visible; Remy wanted to believe but was afraid to.

"I mean it." Chase kissed him deeply. "Not just when life sucks. Every day."

"Even when I fail and fuck up?"

Chase growled at Remy's choice of words and slammed inside as hard as he could. Remy groaned loudly and screwed his eyes shut. There was some cursing, too.

"Yeah. Even then," Chase muttered, outta breath. "Even when you don't give me enough credit." He smirked a little to show he was half teasing.

Remy didn't smirk. He pulled Chase down for a bruising kiss, and he mumbled apologies, murmured words of affection, promised to fight, and told Chase how much he loved him.

"That's better." Chase let out a low laugh. Dizzy with desire, happiness, and love. Getting close, he grasped Remy's cock and stroked him firmly.

It wasn't long before their orgasms took over.

TWENTY-THREE

The day after, Chase was busy catching up on paperwork in his office. He checked the time and saw Remy was gonna call soon. If he felt up to it, he was even gonna swing by the bar. Since it hadn't opened yet, Chase wasn't too worried about that. He was more concerned about Remy's meeting at AA.

Chase and Remy had spent all of yesterday talking things out, setting up a semblance of structure in their lives, rolling around in the sheets, and making plans. They'd also laid all cards on the table, which was how Chase had found out about all the things that had triggered Remy's relapse.

It was unfathomable that Remy had contacted Clarissa and Fred for Chase's sake. Shedding some light on Ben's life would've quenched Chase's curiosity and given him some comprehension, but it wouldn't change anything. Yet, Remy had called the two people who had treated him horribly...

"Honey, I'm home!" Donna called from the bar, announcing her arrival. "Chase, you here?"

Chase stood up, figuring he could use a break anyway, and left the office.

Donna was beaming when he reached the bar. "Hi!"

"How are ya?" Chase quirked a brow and smiled just because she was.

"I'm having a girl!" she burst out.

"Well, damn." Chase's smile widened and he rounded the bar to pull her in for a tight hug. "Congratulations, honey. I'm so happy for you." Understatement. Donna was a fighter, and Chase couldn't be prouder. "Who took you to the doc?" He ended the hug and grasped her shoulders.

She shrugged and smiled innocently.

To which Chase frowned. "I told you I could take you. You don't have to do everything alone, you know."

Jesus fucking Christ. His words settled, and he couldn't believe the irony. Something that had always been so easy for him, helping others, had only recently been embraced in the other direction. He now knew he didn't have to do everything alone, either.

"That's our mascot cookin' in there." He grinned and brushed his palm over her little baby bump.

"You were busy getting your bike and working." She shrugged again. "It's really okay." She looked it too, but Chase wasn't satisfied.

"I don't give a shit." He looped an arm around her shoulders to guide her behind the bar. "Family comes first, and that means you, too." He opened the fridge and grabbed two sodas. "I wanna know all your appointments. All right?"

Donna was beaming again. Also, she appeared to be close to tears, so Chase thrust the soda into her hands and changed the topic to work. He didn't deal with emotional women very well. Every time Ade was down in the dumps, he made a fool of himself.

"Hold up!" Donna laughed. "You can't do a 180 like that—"

"I can and I will," Chase argued petulantly. "Now, unless you have other news to share—"

It was Donna's turn to cut him off. "I do, actually. I got a part-time position at a security company, but it won't interfere with this job. It's just in the mornings—I'll be taking calls and stuff."

Hmm. That was no good. Chase had been thinking about this today; he needed to hire another bartender. Mainly 'cause Remy was putting his foot down, stating that Chase worked too much, but also because every time Chase had to bail, it was Donna—not to mention Austin—who had to pick up the slack. Additionally, Donna wasn't gonna be able to keep it up forever. She was good now, but in another couple months she'd be waddling all over the place when all she'd really need was rest.

That said, he knew she had no benefits. He couldn't afford that, although he was gonna do his best to help her.

"Don't overdo it," he told her, making a mental note to talk to Remy about it.

One of the many things they'd discussed yesterday was Chase moving in with Remy. Remy had insisted, despite the fact that he wasn't himself ready to move back home. But he wanted Chase in that house. And Minna was moving out soon…

Chase couldn't say the thought of waking up in the middle of the night to a screaming baby held any appeal, but he was protective of Donna. If he could help, he was going to. Besides, if—when—Chase moved in with Remy, he didn't have to do his paperwork in the office.

"You're thinking hard about something." Donna narrowed her eyes.

Chase grinned faintly. "Maybe." Off the top of his head, he could come up with a studio solution for Donna. It would take some money he didn't have yet, but if he and Donna pitched in together, they could have a wall removed in the office, which would open up one of the two supply closets. It would add some much-needed space but be a decent-sized, temporary studio. If Donna couldn't afford her place. "Anyway, don't make any rash decisions before asking for help. Deal?"

Donna scrunched her nose. "Who are you, and what have you done to my boss?" Humor seeped into every word. "Someone might think you've met someone."

Chase smirked and opened his soda, all while taking a few steps backward toward the office again. "Someone might."

"Oh, don't be so vague." Donna clearly wanted gossip. "Who is she? You haven't brought anyone around." Chase chuckled and turned around, closing in on the door. "Or is it a he? Don't think I haven't considered that option, boss!"

Chase laughed a little harder and disappeared down the hall.

*

OUTCOME

Remy was comfortable with his decision. The therapist Gale had suggested was nice as hell, but Remy hadn't been able to shake the whole being a patient thing. And the sponsor he'd just had coffee with through a contact at AA had taken care of that issue. Because Harvey, the fifty-something-year-old who was now officially Remy's sponsor, didn't have a degree to preach about addiction. He had experience, and he'd been on the road to recovery for the past twenty years.

It made Remy feel more equal.

Harvey seemed like a nice guy, too. Funny, open-minded, blunt, and caring. Completely pussy-whipped, but whatever. His wife had brought them some cake that tasted like charcoal, but Harvey had gone for seconds and thirds.

Regardless, Remy was at peace. Everything was out in the open, no problem was being ignored, and he had a great support system. *Family.* He had a family.

One of his family members pounced the minute he got back to the house. Andreas was treating his girl to a day in LA, while also picking up one of Remy's cars—two birds, one stone— so it was evidently Minna's job to handle the inquisition.

"Do you like AA?"

"What happened to not wanting group sessions—oops, my bad, circle jerks."

"Is your sponsor nice?"

"Do they really give out those chips?"

Remy was slightly overwhelmed but answered every question as best he could. Then it was time to get something out of the way before he headed over to Chase's bar.

"I have something to tell you," he said, sitting down at the kitchen table. It was full of lists and samples for Minna's move. She'd narrowed it down to two places, one house nearby and one condo, and she already knew exactly what colors to paint her new home.

"That sounds ominous." Minna sat down carefully, trepidation in her eyes. "You better not make me cry. I have a date tonight, and I can't go all puffy."

Remy snorted in amusement. "Don't worry, you'll look

perfect." He was a little nervous, but not for himself. It was all Chase and how he'd handle this. "I'll just cut right to the…" He couldn't help it; he laughed. "Chase."

"Okay, you're being weird." Minna chuckled and gave him a strange look. "What's so funny about cutting to the chase?"

"*Chase*," Remy emphasized, smiling. "He and I…we're together."

Minna's mouth popped open.

Remy waited.

Five…

Four…

Three…

"You ruined my fucking fantasy, Stahl!" she suddenly cried out. Remy's eyebrows shot up, and Minna huffed and scowled and huffed again. "*God.* Out of all the guys, you had to fucking steal that one! He was like the perfect book boyfriend!"

The perfect *what*? Remy shook his head, trying to clear it and catch up with Minna's thoughts, but that wasn't always easy. "I…I got nothin'."

Minna wasn't listening, too busy muttering crap Remy barely understood. "I'm down to three fantasy guys now…" She started stacking papers together on the table. "…and I don't fucking get why the hottest ones are gay—"

"Minna!" Remy snapped his fingers in front of her face. She looked up and blinked. "Focus, you little nymph."

She huffed, because she was good at that. "Fine. Okay." She pinned him with a serious look. "Like, really? You're together?"

"Yes." He smiled.

Her look softened immediately. "You're not joking," she murmured. "That's why you've been so tranquil lately—other than…" Yeah, other than when Remy took off. "You're in love." Remy nodded with a dip of his chin. It felt…new…and too intimate to talk about it with Minna. For now, anyway. "And Chase feels the same?"

Another nod from Remy. *For some unknown reason, he loves me, yeah.*

Minna's face broke into a beautiful smile. "Okay, I can see it now. You're each others' strengths. You support and guide each other and—"

"All right." It was getting a bit too sappy. Remy rose from his seat and rounded the table to kiss the top of Minna's hair. "I love you like crazy, Min, but you should lay off the romance novels."

"Never!" Minna mock-scowled up at him. "Don't speak such filth. Now, tell me everything. How it started, how you exchanged 'I love yous,' who initiated it—"

"I'm already late," Remy blurted out. Jeesh, there was no stopping this chick. "If you want the dirt, you'll just have to come with me to the bar. I'm going over there now."

Minna glanced at the clock, probably determining if she had time. Date, dirt, date, dirt—what was more important?

"Okay, give me five minutes."

Dirt, apparently.

TWENTY-FOUR

It was only half an hour before the bar opened that Chase saw Remy walking through the door. Donna was in the back, Tuck never showed up until they opened, and…Remy wasn't alone. Minna walked in, too.

Chase drew in a deep breath, nervous and excited and determined and scared all at once. He was *out*. Nobody was lurking in the shadows, ready to kidnap him for being gay. His pops wasn't alive to haul out homophobic insults.

Chase was free from the ghosts of his past. Now he only needed to get used to it.

"Hello, Chase." Minna was being way too polite. The glint in her eye told Chase everything he needed to know. Remy had spoken to her. "How are you today?"

"I'm fine, sweetheart. You?" Chase's mouth twisted up.

"Stop being weird." Remy chuckled and gave her an odd look before going around the bar, meeting Chase halfway. "Hey."

"Hey." Chase grinned.

Remy grinned.

They were both just kinda staring at each other, matching expressions of happiness.

Despite the struggles they had ahead, Chase wasn't worried. They were strong enough to handle it. They'd *grown* stronger by being together. Shadows were fading, creases were smoothing out, and colors were brightening.

"Come here." Chase cupped the back of Remy's neck and pulled him close, then dipped down and kissed him. Slowly. Taking his time to taste, nip, and savor. "I missed you today."

Remy hummed and inched closer. "Me too." He let out a shaky laugh and pecked Chase a few times. "Yeah, fuck, me too."

"Should I get popcorn?" And that was Donna. "Hey, you're the naked guy!"

While Chase cracked up, Remy groaned and planted his forehead to Chase's collarbone.

"No, no, let's be social now, baby." Chase turned Remy around but kept Remy's back to his chest. "Naked Guy—or Remy—this is Donna, my cheeky brat of an employee."

Donna smirked and walked forward to shake Remy's hand. "Nice to meet you, Naked Guy."

Chase was having a field day with this, relieved it was going so well. In the meantime, it was suddenly Remy who appeared too nervous to function.

"You too," Remy replied, stumbling over his words. "You're pregnant—" He stopped himself there and cursed.

Minna giggled.

Chase hid his grin in Remy's hair.

Donna looked down. "Oh shit, you're right. I am."

"No—fuck. What I mean is…oh, what the hell am I doing," Remy muttered. Then he took a breath and pointed to Minna. "Her brother's also having a kid. Baby boom in Bakersfield."

Minna saved Remy from his rambling and greeted Donna.

*

A week later, Chase was riding a high he was afraid was about to end. Everything had gone too well. He and Remy were spending their days at the house—which was slowly morphing into Chase's home, too—or they were in therapy together, or they went on drives and spent hours talking about everything and nothing while lying in the bed of Remy's truck.

They spent their nights apart, which was good for both of them at this time. Chase doubted he'd ever stop craving more of Remy, but the cabin was a good barrier. It ensured they didn't rush everything and that Remy got the space he needed at the end of the day to process and reflect. Chase was doing the same, but in his and Remy's bed at the house.

Even their groups of friends were getting along and spending time together. Austin and Cam had been busy with work lately, but Landon and Andreas had stopped by the bar for a beer a couple times, and Minna and Donna had exchanged numbers to go shopping for baby clothes.

"Is there somethin' in the water around here?" Landon had asked when he'd learned about Chase and Remy. *"Perhaps I should warn Jules I might be into dudes soon."* He'd had a teasing glint in his eye, and then he'd only slapped Chase's shoulder, given it a squeeze, and returned to his beer.

No judgment.

"You're acting as if I'm going to curse you out," Austin had chuckled over the phone. *"I'm happy for you, my friend."*

It was surreal.

When's the other shoe gonna drop?

Maybe tonight? Ade was on her way.

Chase had closed the bar for the evening so they could all have dinner there. Chase and Remy, Austin and Cam and Riley, Adriana, Landon and his family, Minna with a date, Andreas with his fiancée, Donna, Old Tuck… But, thankfully, Chase would have some alone time with Ade before everyone showed up.

"I'm off to my meeting soon." Remy wiped some sweat off his forehead with the sleeve of his shirt. They'd cleaned the entire establishment together and prepared for tonight. "I'll pick up the barbecue on my way back. Was there anything else?"

Chase pursed his lips and stared pensively at the tables they'd pushed together to form a long one. "Gale advised you to pick a seat." She'd declined the invitation to come, flattered but careful not to form friendships with patients, and she'd told Remy to stay away from temptation by sitting with those he was most comfortable with.

Chase wasn't gonna drink, no matter how many times Remy had told him it was okay.

"I don't know, a corner spot?" Remy shrugged and

scratched his eyebrow.

"She also told you not to alienate yourself," Chase reminded him.

"Then you pick my damn seat, baby." Remy laughed and passed him with a kiss to his bicep. "Did you talk to the landlord about permits?" He walked over to the bar and got a glass of water.

Chase nodded. They were waiting for the okay to hire contractors to tear down a wall in the office. Donna wouldn't technically be allowed to live there, but the landlord, who seemed fond of Donna, had promised to overlook it for a while.

Chase had tossed around ideas about it with Remy, who'd said there was no reason to wait until they'd "saved up." Remy had money, he'd stated, followed by a long rant of wanting to help out, even if it was only materialistic stuff so far—it was the least he could do, he'd said. To which Chase had rolled his eyes 'cause if Remy didn't see all the other things he did for people, he was fucking nuts.

Donna was beside herself with relief and gratitude. She'd always come off as a carefree young woman, but since Chase broke the news to her about turning the office into a studio for her, it was clear that a huge weight had been lifted off her shoulders.

"Materialistic stuff" or not, it was Remy who'd made it possible this soon.

"Have you thought about the other thing I suggested?" Remy asked. "You need to talk to the landlord about that, too. If you want to go for it."

Uh-huh. Chase was learning that Remy had a good eye for business. Which shouldn't come as such a surprise since Remy had owned a multimillion-dollar company himself. But turning a biker hangout into a coffee shop during the daytime hours? Chase wasn't so sure.

He slid Remy a dubious look.

Remy grinned. "Quit thinking about coffee shops. It's what you're hung up on, isn't it?" Well, yeah. "I also mentioned *diner*. Some bikers pass through just to get food, and we're close enough to the outskirts." He shrugged one shoulder and leaned back against the bar. "I need a project, something to occupy my mind, before I think about getting back to work full-time."

Yeah, Andreas was itching for that day to arrive, but Chase was glad Remy refused to rush.

"You wanna be my partner or somethin'?" Chase winked.

"How punny of you," Remy shot back, laughing. "But no, this is your baby. I just want to help and get my hands dirty." He smiled.

That could certainly be arranged.

*

Chase's nerves returned with a vengeance the minute Ade walked in the door and hugged the shit outta him.

"God, I missed you!"

Chase managed a smile and tightened his hold on her. "Right back at'cha, kiddo. You're a busy girl." He backed off and kissed her on the forehead. "How's the big city treatin' ya?"

Ade sighed heavily and threw her bag down on the bartop. "It's exhausting. I miss home."

That was definitely new, but Chase was thrilled. "So move home. Finish your studies and come back." He tilted his head at Ade's scowl, which she directed at the floor. "Hey." He lifted her chin and raised a brow. "Did somethin' happen?"

She waved it off. "Nothin' I can't handle, big brother." She hopped up on the bartop and slid over to the other side and jumped down. "Just some guy trouble." At Chase's instant glare and the way he tensed up, she was quick to elaborate. "I swear it's nothing. I was sorta dating this one dude, and I made it clear I'm focusing on school and work. He agreed, but now he's being a douche. Says I don't give him enough attention, and his way of getting back at me—like this is some game—is to flirt with my friends." She rolled her eyes and grabbed a Coke from the fridge.

Chase huffed and folded his arms across his chest. Of course he was relieved it was nothing worse, but... "You know, there *is* a way to avoid this kind of trouble."

"By avoiding guys altogether?" Ade replied wryly.

"Damn right."

She giggled. "Soon you'll tell me I'm too young, too."

Well, you fucking are. "I'm serious," he argued. "I should know—I'm a man. We're shitheads."

"Uh-huh." She grinned and leaned her elbows on the counter. "So tell me, shithead. What's new with *you*? Last we talked on the phone, I counted seven times you either laughed, chuckled, or snickered. It can't all be therapy."

Chase snorted then sighed and rubbed the back of his neck. Guess there was no use in beating around the bush. "I suppose I do have some news." He dragged his ass over to one of the barstools and sat down.

"I knew it. You've met someone." Ade was faking seriousness. She threw a rag over her shoulder and poured two shots of *soda*. "Lemme hear it, cowboy." Okay, this wasn't a saloon in the Wild West, but whatever.

"You were always a clown, honey." Chase shook his head, amused, and followed suit when Adriana downed the first shot of Coke. She pretended it burned and shuddered visibly. "All right..." He took a breath and gathered his thoughts. *Please don't fucking judge me, sis.* "Yeah, I've met someone. It's serious, too." Jesus Christ, his gut tightened to the point where it hurt. "I've told you about—about him. It's Remy."

Adriana's expression gave away *nothing*. She stared at him blankly, which sure as shit didn't make it easier for Chase.

Then, cool as a cucumber, she set down the Coke bottle and turned around to grab one of the bottom-shelf tequilas. "I see," she said as she poured.

She threw back two shots right away.

Chase could almost hear the clock on the wall. *Ticktock, ticktock.* The silence stretched on, driving him fuckin' bonkers.

She didn't have to endure much of Pops's bullshit growing up because she was the little princess. It was Ma's job to raise her. And she was only ten when they died. That said, the last ten years of their father's life were also the worst ones. He was bitter and almost everything was wrong. Nothing was his fault. Always others'. The government, hippies, yuppies, queers, punk rockers, anarchists, atheists...he always found someone to blame.

"So you're gay…" Ade stared down at her empty glasses. "Why didn't you tell me?" She lifted her gaze at that, but she didn't give Chase enough time to answer. "I mean, I'm not blind. I've thought about it. I've even considered why you'd hide something like that. The way we grew up…?" She puffed out a breath. "I get it. But why not tell *me*?"

Chase felt like he was underwater, a rushing sound in his ears. Disembodied, far away. He felt *small*.

"I was ashamed," he answered numbly, quietly. "I was scared shitless." He let out a low, humorless laugh. "I couldn't take any more judgment." There were more reasons, but Chase chose not to get into the whole clusterfuck of why Ben had targeted him. "I was just tired, Ade. It was easier to hide." Like a coward.

Adriana shook her head and smiled sadly. "It's cost you a lot, though. Hasn't it?"

Yes, it had. But what mattered now was whether or not honesty was gonna cost him even more. "Up until recently, I only had you in my life," he pointed out. "The thought of losing you now is fuckin' devastating, but before, when I was alone? Christ, it woulda slayed me."

"Oh, Chase." Ade's eyes welled up, and she hurried to join Chase on his side of the bar. He held out an arm as she flew into him. "You'd never lose me." She sniffled. "And not over something so damn trivial." She slapped his arm then hugged him again.

Trivial.

It was *supposed* to be trivial, but reality was different.

All Chase could do was thank his lucky stars Adriana was more open-minded and accepting.

"I love you." He kissed the side of her head and gave her another squeeze.

She looked up and pecked his cheek. "Love you too, Chase."

He sighed contentedly and breathed in the familiar scent of Ade's apple-scented shampoo. The brand changed over the years but never the scent. It was the same their mom had used. But…hold on.

OUTCOME

Chase took another sniff before he eased away and cocked a brow at his sister. "Why the fuck do you smell like cigarettes?"

TWENTY-FIVE

After dinner, Remy headed outside to have a smoke with Andy and Cam. For some reason, Chase's sister was sulking. *Odd.* She'd been happy and friendly all night.

"Dad!" Riley slipped out right before the door closed, and Cam looked to her as he lit up a cigarette. "Can I have money so I can make a bet with Uncle Landon and Chase?"

Remy and Andreas smirked.

"Depends what the bet is, baby," Cam said thoughtfully. "Gallardo has you beat in pool, and Landon's decent at dart—"

"We're gonna play Go Fish," Riley said frankly. "Me and Aunt Julie and the boys. I'd ask Daddy, but he's busy talking intern…something…with Adriana now."

"Oh." He pulled out his wallet and slapped a ten-dollar bill in her outstretched hand. "Go nuts."

She thanked Cam and grinned in triumph as she disappeared inside the bar again.

"Well, parenting seems easy enough." Andy grinned wryly. "All I gotta do is give it money."

"And stop calling it *it*," Remy advised.

Cam nodded. "That'd be a good start, yeah." He faced Andreas. "What're you havin'?"

"A boy." Andy was getting more nervous the closer they got to the due date. "I hear they piss on you when you change their diapers."

"I…uh. Right." Cam huffed a laugh. "I don't know what to say about that. Maybe I should call my mom and apologize?"

"He sends me texts sometimes," Remy said, jerking his chin at Andy. "The most random shit about what babies do."

"Suck it up, Stahl." Andreas chuckled. "You're lucky I don't send you pictures."

"There are pictures? Never mind, don't answer." He shook his head. "I had a hamster or a gerbil or something when I was a kid. Then I forgot about it." He waited for the familiar pang that usually came with childhood memories, but it wasn't there. Interesting. "I think my mom released it." Still no pang.

"My mom sometimes forgets my dad at the store." Cam shrugged.

Remy cracked up. "Does she ever release him into the wild?"

"I'm sure she wishes sometimes," Cam replied, grinning. Then he stubbed out his smoke and declared he was done socializing for the night. "I'll steal one of Chase's car magazines and find an empty corner," he added.

Then they were two.

Andy took a sip from his beer and nodded. "They're good people, Chase's friends."

Remy agreed, having been nervous to officially meet Austin and Cam, but yeah, they were nice. The Cam he'd spoken to today was a lot different from the one he'd given a letter to three years ago to pass on to Chase.

"My friends are pretty fucking stellar, too." Remy nudged his shoulder to Andy's.

His eyes lit up with humor. "Are we about to have a moment?"

"Bastard, you just ruined it," Remy laughed. "No, but seriously." He sobered a little, and he'd wanted to have this conversation for a while now. With Andy. He'd already had the talk with Minna. "I wouldn't be alive if it weren't for you, Minna, and Chase."

"I'd do it again, little brother." Andy threw an arm around Remy's shoulders. "Possibly sooner too, if I knew I'd get a spankin' new house out of it."

"I'm feeling the love, Eriksson," Remy deadpanned,

joking. He sighed and smiled. "It's nice, being happy."

Andy hummed and let his arm drop. "And we're not only here for the good days. You know that, right?"

For once in Remy's life, he actually did.

*

Chase was losing.

To a thirteen-year-old.

Go Fucking Fish.

"This ain't right," Landon muttered, who was also losing.

Chase blamed the little ankle biter on his lap for being distracting and unable to sit still. Landon and Julie's three-year-olds had deemed him and Landon worthy of being chairs for the moment. Chase had no idea which twin he was holding; they looked the same.

He asked Julie if she had any aces, which she hadn't, and soon enough it was Riley's turn.

"Chase," she said sweetly, "fork over your aces, please."

"I second that," Chase told Landon. "This ain't right." He gave away his aces.

"Suh-weet!" Riley lay down her four aces to add in her collection. "I'm getting rich here. That's good 'cause I make less than a kid in China on my allowance."

"I heard that, brat," Austin said dryly from the next table. Then he turned to Cam, who'd found a new spot near the bar. "Cam, what do you say we introduce Riley to yard work?"

Cam was clearly on board with that idea.

Riley wasn't.

A few minutes later, she pocketed enough money to get her smiling again, and Remy sat down in the spot she left, announcing it was time to shoot some pool with Tuck.

"You have a child in your lap." Remy patted the girl's head.

"Very observant of you." Chase looked at the munchkin. "I've named her Drooler." Were three-year-olds supposed to drool? She was cute, though.

"She takes after her daddy," Julie teased. Landon only looked proud. "Anna, how about we get some ice cream, huh?"

"Yes!" The kid on Chase's lap jumped down, as did the other one from Landon's lap, yelling, "Me too, Mommy! Me too!"

"What about me?" Landon was insulted.

Left somewhat alone, Chase turned to Remy and draped an arm along the back of his chair. "Hey, you."

"Hey." Remy leaned closer and rested his cheek on Chase's shoulder. "Is that a banana or are you just happy to see me?"

"Huh?" Chase looked down and groaned a laugh when he saw that Anna had left bits of her after-dinner snack on his jeans. "This is why I'm uncle material."

"No kids for us," Remy agreed. "I'm kind of looking forward to Andy having one, though. We can spoil him, teach him all the wrong things, and send him back to his folks."

"You're cruel," Chase chuckled. But he loved the idea of all the things he and Remy could do as an official "us." After everything they'd been through, they deserved to be selfish. They deserved to enjoy their outcome and focus on each other. "What else are we gonna do?"

Remy tilted his head up and kissed Chase's chin. "You've told me about the long drives you used to go on years ago."

Chase hadn't expected to hear that. "On my bike, you mean? But you're scared of it."

"It's a death machine," Remy stated flatly. "But I like the thought of seeing the country with you. Just drive and see where the road takes us."

That was one of Chase's favorite things about having motorcycles. Few experiences felt more liberating than road trips. So…he decided to not tell Remy how sore his ass was gonna be—for all the wrong reasons. 'Cause sitting on a bike for days took some getting used to. Plus, it'd be fun to see Remy bitching.

"I think that sounds great," Chase murmured. "We could use a break." He pictured all the landscapes, the roads, sunrises, sunsets, motels, and having Remy behind him on his bike. "Shit, can we leave yesterday?" Unable to help himself, he closed the distance and kissed Remy.

He was acutely aware of his surroundings and the people they were with, but Chase was growing comfortable in his new shoes. He knew he'd be wary around strangers; however, this was family. Real family. Blood didn't matter. It was all about loyalty and being nonjudgmental.

"Sure—" Remy smiled into the kiss "—you just have to let me help you with the bar. Hire a few bartenders and we're off."

Oh, this again. "Begin another talk about investing and I won't use lube next time."

Remy hissed. "Motherfucker. You call *me* cruel?"

Chase laughed and deepened the kiss. "I love you."

"Love you too," Remy snickered, "even without lube."

*

Remy spent that night with Chase—at home. It had been a great evening, and this was the perfect ending to it. Remy couldn't get the perfect ending in the cabin. He needed some downtime soon enough, but he needed this first. This…this with Chase. Getting twisted in the sheets, kissing, tasting, fucking fast, fucking slow, cracking jokes, getting up for midnight snacks, getting back in bed, falling asleep spent and sated.

And the next morning, Remy made breakfast with an audience.

"Okay, I think I can do that." Chase observed as Remy cracked a few eggs into a skillet. "Maybe mine would come with some shell, though."

"I prefer mine without."

"So picky."

It was the perfect beginning of a day, much like the ending of last night had been. Lazy and all about them. Something to look forward to while Remy took baby steps toward more. Until he was ready for it all.

They ate breakfast on the terrace, Remy mentioning that Minna must've gotten lucky last night. A text waiting in his phone confirmed it. Then they made loose plans about where they wanted to go on their road trip, places they wanted to see, places one had been and wanted to show the other.

"I'm just going to get the mail," he said a while later.

He left Chase with some paperwork on the patio and walked through the house. The pavement was warm under his bare feet, but nowhere near the blistering heat he vaguely remembered from the time he'd stumbled home from the first time in Chase's bar.

Crazy how it all started, huh?

"Hi, Remy!"

Remy looked up, having just reached the mailbox, and saw Riley and Austin walking their dogs.

"Hey, guys." He grinned back at them and collected his and Minna's mail.

"Thanks for last night." Austin smiled. "Tell Chase you'll both hear from Julie soon. She and Landon are in charge of Thanksgiving this year."

"Oh. Oh, okay." Remy was kind of dumbfounded because he'd never had this before. "I'll tell him."

He made his way back inside again, dividing the mail into three piles that he put on the kitchen counter. *Minna's, mine, mine, Minna's, friggin' coupons...* He stopped at an envelope addressed to him in a handwriting he'd seen before.

Posted in Milwaukee.

"Shit." Shit, shit, shit. Remy barely even registered his feet carrying him out to the back. He did notice that his hand was shaking, though. "I, uh..." He glanced up at Chase, who was watching him with a frown. Unable to say anything else, Remy simply dropped the envelope on the table and sat down next to Chase.

Had Fred really replied?

Or maybe something had happened to Bill...but then, wouldn't the nurses or whatever contact Remy? Fred and Clarissa wouldn't give a crap.

"Want me to open it?" Chase asked quietly. His jaw was clenched.

Remy nodded jerkily and sat forward. He felt nausea

creeping up, but he was determined not to do anything stupid this time. It wasn't worth it. And, he found Fred and Clarissa didn't have the same effect on him as they'd once had.

Chase slid the pointy end of a key into the envelope and ripped it open, splaying the single sheet of paper on the table before them. Remy's hand found Chase's, and he read.

TWENTY-SIX

Remy,

The theory you shared in your email is correct—for the most part. You've heard how I failed in school but succeeded later in life, and you know Ben was the complete opposite. He had it all in high school when we grew up, and he loved to bully me and make sure I knew he was Dad's favorite. At the time, he was. I was pushed down by Dad because I couldn't make it. He praised Ben. But I got my act together eventually, and it was around the same time Ben lost his first job. It went downhill after that; he got fired because he didn't show his superiors any respect. He acted as if he was still in high school.

Remy's heartbeat slowed down infinitesimally. So far, so good. Chase seemed less tense, too.

Dad was losing his respect for Ben, and I was still bitter from the years they'd both treated me like dirt. I admit, it was my revenge to let Ben know he was a failure. In the meantime, he got the worst beating from Dad. Ben had to move home again, so he never escaped Dad's hatred.

I resented my father like nothing else, but in many ways I was still a kid. When he gave me the attention he'd once only reserved for Ben, I couldn't help but soak it up. I sought it out, grew addicted to it, and constantly struggled to improve myself.

Over time, Dad probably got bored. Ben remained the black sheep of the family, and I was simply not interesting anymore. Mom and Dad argued a lot, which I assume led to his having an affair with your mother.

When you entered the picture as the nine-year-old child who Dad had already declared as smart, innovative, and promising, Ben lost it. He couldn't handle another person coming before him in his own family.

I owned up to my mistakes and took care of him best I could. When he called and rambled about all the good things Dad was saying about you, I was the one who calmed him down.

Fear was instilled in us from an early age, Remy. Success equaled power, and powerful people were never to be touched. So yes, I placed the blame on you for destroying Ben. Because despite your achievements in school, no one was more powerful than our father. He could not be wrong. It wasn't possible because that would mean everything we knew was a sham.

Ben loathed you and feared you, hence your theory being mostly correct. That was why he went after ten innocent men. And as for me, he remembered the years I bullied him, not the rest. Not what he had put me through first. That's why he took someone to portray me. And I have no real answer as to why I defended him after Chase and the others were released. I suppose grief played a big part. Bitterness and sadness. Guilt.

Here's what not many know: Ben's victims weren't as randomly picked as one would think.

Remy's head snapped up, and a second later, Chase's followed.

"Not random?" Remy asked in disbelief.

They read on.

Since his twenties, Ben carried journals of people who let him down, insulted him, and wronged him somehow. As the years passed, the reasons for people to end up in these books got more and more ridiculous, but I didn't know about the journals at the time. If I had, I would've stopped him and gotten him help.

I found the journals in his room after he'd died, and once I had connected the dots, I burned them. For this, I am not sorry. He was deranged; there was plenty of proof to come to this conclusion. More wasn't necessary. But for your peace of mind—or your friend's—I can share the following.

I wrote down ten entries from two of Ben's journals. You'll find them on the back of this letter. That is all I have to say. These are all the reasons we can find, unless there's a way to bring back the dead.

Fred

Chase was quick to flip the letter, and there they saw ten scribbled paragraphs in quotation marks.

"'*Despite my assurances that I can be an accountant, my application got rejected before I could even get an interview,*'" Chase read out loud. "This was dated four years before the kidnapping, and it lists the firm Austin works for." What the hell? Chase read the next line. "'*I got the name of the company director. Subject found: Austin Huntley.*' Shit. And get this: '*Subject update, Huntley is presumed to have lost his status. He works for a local construction company now, and he's mine.*'"

"Holy fuck," Remy whispered. Ben must've updated his journal *after* he'd already kidnapped Austin, who happened to be the last victim to be taken. "So Austin rejected a work application from someone who didn't even have a degree in that, and…"

"It means Austin ticked off both of Ben's boxes of demands," Chase went on.

Remy nodded. "Austin was supposedly not successful anymore, and he had *wronged* Ben."

"It's all about us, Remy…" Chase was scanning the letter again. "Victor, James, Pete… Tim's on the list for not delivering mail on time. Lance is here because he'd cut in line at the fucking grocery store. *Jesus.*"

Dread filled Remy when Chase closed his eyes and accidentally crumpled the paper in anger.

"You're on the list too, aren't you?" Remy already knew he was. "What does it say?"

Chase shook his head and handed over the letter to Remy, who smoothed it out and searched for the right entry.

There.

"*Went to Grapes & Malt for a beer. Both bartenders ignored me completely. Subjects found: Chase Gallardo and Sandra Kim.*"

"You used to work there?" Remy asked, knowing it was a stupid question. This entry had been written seven fucking years prior to the kidnapping. Ben could hold a grudge. Once he'd decided to move forward with this kidnapping, he'd picked out these ten men from his journal. They all fit the bill.

"Yeah," Chase muttered. "High-end place, mostly suits. They came in after work, and it was always packed." He sighed tiredly and leaned back in his seat, running a hand through his hair. "Guess I got my answers, huh?"

"You don't—um." Remy hesitated. "You don't blame yourself for this, right?"

"No," Chase said quickly, then chuckled humorlessly and brought Remy's hand to his mouth. A brief kiss to his knuckles. "I'm not *that* masochistic."

Good. Good. Remy was relieved.

Then Chase stiffened. "Christ." And he sat up straight in a beat, his gaze finding Remy. "It makes sense now. When Ben took me, I was in fuckin' Fresno. He'd obviously followed me there, and he didn't take me 'cause I'm gay." He pointed to the letter. "That's why he came after me. Remember what I told you in the cabin after Santa Barbara?"

Remy's brow furrowed. "You gave me the details on how Ben took you."

Chase nodded. "And what was the last thing I remembered before I passed out from the chloroform?"

Remy remembered now. "He'd laughed and said it was *fitting*."

"Exactly. It was fitting that I was gay, since I'd be playing you. My being gay was a coincidence. His only real demands were that I had a shitty job and that I'd offended him somehow in the past."

A heavy breath escaped Remy as he slumped back.

*

An hour later, they were on another patio. Austin and Cam's.

Chase wondered if their reactions would match his.

Austin appeared pensive after having read the letter, and Cam was currently pacing, smoking a cigarette, and checking the journal entries for the reason he'd been taken.

"As much as I hate it, I sort of agree with Fred," Austin mused. "About burning the journals, I mean. Well," he backtracked, "it would've shed light on something that was current three years ago, but now…? It doesn't really matter to me. I'm sure as hell not going to feel guilty about rejecting a man who wasn't qualified for a job." He rolled his eyes.

Chase was almost on the same page. This new revelation had shocked him at first, but now, only an hour later, he was calmer. Ben had been fucking insane, for several reasons; however, Chase was finally beginning to put it all behind him. It was over and done with. The past was a part of him; it had shaped him in more than one way, but it wasn't his future. His future sat right next to him.

Nevertheless, Chase was happy to have gotten his answers.

He was also glad it hadn't set them back.

"What the fuck," Cam said flatly. He turned to the three men at the table and pointed angrily at the letter. "I'm on the list 'cause I called his car a piece of junk six years ago? That's not even funny."

Austin pursed his lips to hide a grin and held out a hand, a silent request to read the entry. Cam sat down with a scoff and handed over the letter.

Austin read out loud. "*Took my car to Nash's Auto Service. Subject Cameron Nash said he was too busy to give my "dented pile of rust" a*

221

paint job." While Chase and Remy chuckled, Austin smirked wryly at his husband. "Always so polite, aren't you? Landon's lucky to have you."

"Whatever." Cam stubbed out his smoke. "This is why I never gave a shit about finding answers. You can't find anything rational when all you have is Psycho. That's like looking for dick in a lesbian bar."

In retrospect, Chase would agree. But he'd always itched for answers. He needed to understand.

Now he did.

"Anyway…" Austin snorted in amusement and faced Chase and Remy. "We were going to order pizza for dinner. You guys in?"

Hell yeah, Chase and Remy were in. All in.

EPILOGUE

Two years later…

"Remy!" Andreas bitched from his station. "What have I said about running in the studio? Christ, you're just like Dan and Martinez sometimes."

"Someone needs to get laid," Remy laughed, hurrying to clean up. Ink everywhere, dammit. "When's the six-week checkup?" Andy became a father for the second time a few weeks ago, this time to a little baby girl.

"Tomorrow, fucking finally!" Andy exclaimed. Then he apologized for his outburst to the dude whose calf he was currently working on.

"Okay, well…*sayonara*, bitches." Remy shouldered his messenger bag. "Don't miss me too much while I'm gone."

"Have fun, *Stahl*." Dan winked.

Remy smirked and flipped him the bird as he left.

Stahl would soon only be a nickname.

The name "Gallardo" was inked across his left ring finger, in place of an engagement ring.

He made his way to the parking lot and jumped into his car, eager to get home. For the next three weeks, it would just be him, Chase, and the open roads. *I can't wait.* In fact, they'd both loved their first road trip together so much that they'd turned it into an annual tradition. Three weeks, three states.

This year, they were planning on exploring Arizona, New Mexico, and Colorado. Well, the first night would be spent in

223

Vegas since they were leaving pretty late. Remy had suggested they leave earlier, but Chase had insisted on Vegas for some reason.

On his way home, he picked up Chinese and texted a little with Minna, who was visiting family in Duluth. He also called his sponsor, just to check in and say they were leaving in a few hours. He promised to give Harvey weekly reports and to never hesitate to call.

Remy had slipped around this time last year, so they'd been careful lately. It was because Bill had died, and…Remy didn't like to think about it. It had simply stirred up too much shit, so he'd bought a bottle of vodka and driven up to the cabin. But he'd only had one drink before guilt had taken over, and he'd come clean to Chase.

Otherwise, it had gotten a lot easier to deal with backlashes, which Remy allowed himself to be a little proud of. He was doing his best—always.

He may be doing the fighting, but he wouldn't have been able to without his family, especially the man he'd proposed to a few months ago.

Now we just have to set a date.

Remy turned onto their street and eased into the driveway before he honked the horn. Chase's favorite bike was already out of the garage, gleaming in the sun.

Grabbing his stuff, he left the car and walked inside. "You here, sweetheart?" he called.

"Kitchen!"

Remy found him studying the maps laid out on the kitchen table. Two saddlebags sat packed on the counter, too.

"Hey." Chase turned and grinned at him. "Fuck yes, dinner. I'm starving." He drew Remy close and kissed him hard. "*Mmm.* I packed your sketchpad."

"Thanks." Remy was looking forward to working on Chase's first tattoo during the trip. By the time they got back home, he'd have the stencil ready for a Joshua tree with a bike parked underneath it. Then he'd have Chase in his chair in the studio, which…frankly, it got his cock hard just thinking about it. "Damn," he muttered, taking a step back. "Do we have time before we go?"

Chase could no doubt guess what Remy needed time for. "We'll make time."

*

Chase felt the squeeze Remy gave his midsection as he drove under the signature, blue and yellow Bakersfield sign. *Yeah, we're on our way, baby.* He grabbed Remy's hand and kissed it—before he dutifully returned his hand to the handlebar. 'Cause Remy had a tendency of freaking out when Chase let go. Even for a second.

They hit the interstate with the sun sinking lower and lower over the horizon.

It turned the desert landscape red and gold, and the liquid heat along the road darker.

For every mile they put behind them, thoughts about everyday tasks faded away. It was all covered. Donna ran the bar and the other employees like a boss. His sister, who had finally returned to Bakersfield, would check in on the house. As would their friends across the street. No paperwork for three weeks. A break in therapy.

Chase smiled to himself, no longer expecting disaster at every turn. He'd learned it was no way to live. And for the days he got stuck in the past, Remy was there to pull him out if it.

Another thing he'd learned was to stop chasing the end results.

That wasn't what life was about.

They wouldn't know the outcome until they took their final breaths, and they had way too much living to do before that.

He grinned and sped up, Vegas being the first stop on their journey.

Tomorrow he'd be a married man.
Carpe fuckin' diem.

More from Cara Dee can be found at www.caradeewrites.com

34226524R00138

Made in the USA
Middletown, DE
13 August 2016